New beginnings . . .

A few snowflakes floated down, soft and lazily spinning in the wind, and through them Jax cocked his head, watching her as if something about her didn't quite add up for him.

She could have told him not to bother trying to figure her out. No one had managed yet, not even herself.

"You okay?"

"Working on it," she said and gave him a small smile. It was hard not to—he just had that kind of face.

He returned the smile and stepped a little closer to her, which was when she discovered several things.

He smelled good. *Guy* good. As in, she wanted to inhale him. Her body tingled, suddenly brought to a hyper-awareness that felt almost foreign.

Desire. Bone-melting desire.

When she opened her eyes again, he was even closer, and his eyes weren't the solid warm caramel she'd thought but had flecks of gold dancing in them, as well. She could have happily, willingly, drowned in all that deliciousness. Death by deliciousness.

Not a bad way to go.

"Jill Shalvis is a total original! It doesn't get any better."
—SUZANNE FORSTER,
New York Times bestselling author

Please turn this page for
more praise for Jill Shalvis . . .

Praise for
Jill Shalvis
and Her Novels

"Shalvis thoroughly engages readers."
—*Publishers Weekly*

"Jill Shalvis has the incredible talent of creating characters who are intelligent, quick-witted, and gorgeously sexy, all the while giving them just the right amount of weakness to keep them from being unrealistically perfect."
—RomanceJunkies.com

"Ms. Shalvis's characters leap off the page."
—*RT Book Reviews*

"Shalvis's writing is a perfect trifecta of win: hilarious dialogue, evocative and real characters, and settings that are as much a part of the story as the hero and heroine. I've never been disappointed by a Shalvis book."
—SmartBitchesTrashyBooks.com

Simply
Irresistible

Also by Jill Shalvis

The Lucky Harbor Series

Simply Irresistible
The Sweetest Thing
Heating Up the Kitchen (cookbook)
Christmas in Lucky Harbor (omnibus)
Small Town Christmas (anthology)
Head Over Heels
Lucky in Love
At Last
Forever and a Day
"Under the Mistletoe" (short story)
It Had to Be You
Always on My Mind
A Christmas to Remember (anthology)
Once in a Lifetime
It's in His Kiss
He's So Fine
One in a Million
"Merry Christmas, Baby" (short story)

The Cedar Ridge Series

My Kind of Wonderful
Second Chance Summer
Nobody but You

Simply
Irresistible

♥

Jill Shalvis

FOREVER

NEW YORK   BOSTON

Copyright © 2010 by Jill Shalvis
Excerpt from *The Sweetest Thing* copyright © 2010 by Jill Shalvis
Recipes from *Heating Up the Kitchen* copyright © 2011 by Jill Shalvis

Cover design by Melody Cassen. Cover photo © Jamie Kingham/Cultura/Corbis. Cover copyright © 2010 by Hachette Book Group, Inc.

Forever
Hachette Book Group
1290 Avenue of the Americas, New York, NY 10104
forever-romance.com
twitter.com/foreverromance

Originally published as mass market and ebook by Forever in October 2010
Reissued Edition: December 2017

Forever is an imprint of Grand Central Publishing. The Forever name and logo are trademarks of Hachette Book Group, Inc.

The publisher is not responsible for websites (or their content) that are not owned by the publisher.

The Hachette Speakers Bureau provides a wide range of authors for speaking events. To find out more, go to www.hachettespeakersbureau.com or call (866) 376-6591.

ISBNs: 978-1-5387-4448-2 (reissue mass market); 978-1-4555-3635-1 (orig. mass market), 978-1-4555-3636-8 (ebook)

Printed in the United States of America

OPM

10 9 8 7 6 5 4 3 2 1

*To another middle child, the middle sister,
the middle everything. To Megan, the peacemaker,
the warrior princess, the fierce, loyal protector
of our hearts.*

Simply
Irresistible

Chapter 1

*"I chose the path less traveled,
but only because I was lost. Carry a map."*
PHOEBE TRAEGER

Maddie drove the narrow, curvy highway with her past *still* nipping at her heels after fourteen hundred miles. Not even her dependable Honda had been able to outrun her demons.

Or her own failings.

Good thing, then, that she was done with failing. *Please be done with failing,* she thought.

"Come on, listeners," the disc jockey said jovially on the radio. "Call in with your Christmas hopes and dreams. We'll be picking a random winner and making a wish come true."

"You're kidding me." Maddie briefly took her eyes off the mountainous road and flicked a glance at the dash. "It's *one* day after Thanksgiving. It's not time for Christmas."

"Any wish," the DJ said. "Name it, and it could be yours."

As if. But she let out a breath and tried for whimsy. Once upon a time, she'd been good at such things. *Maddie Moore, you were raised on movie sets—fake the damn whimsy.* "Fine. I'll wish for..." What? That she could've had a do-over with her mother before Phoebe Traeger had gone to the ultimate Grateful Dead concert in the sky? That Maddie had dumped her ex far sooner than she had? That her boss—may he choke on his leftover turkey—had waited until *after* year-end bonuses to fire her?

"The lines are lit up," the DJ announced. "Best of luck to all of you out there waiting."

Hey, maybe *that's* what she'd wish for—luck. She'd wish for better luck than she'd had: with family, with a job, with men—

Well, maybe not men. Men she was giving up entirely. Pausing from that thought, she squinted through the fog to read the first road sign she'd seen in a while.

WELCOME TO LUCKY HARBOR!
Home to 2,100 lucky people
And 10,100 shellfish

About time. Exercising muscles she hadn't utilized in too long, she smiled, and in celebration of arriving at her designated destination, she dug into the bag of salt and vinegar potato chips at her side. Chips cured just about everything, from the I-lost-my-job blues, to the my-boyfriend-was-a-jerk regrets, to the tentatively hopeful celebration of a new beginning.

"A new beginning done right," she said out loud, because everyone knew that saying it out loud made it true. "You hear that, karma?" She glanced upward through her slightly leaky sunroof into a dark sky, where storm clouds tumbled together like a dryer full of gray wool blankets. "This time, I'm going to be strong." Like Katharine Hepburn. Like Ingrid Bergman. "So go torture someone else and leave me alone."

A bolt of lightning blinded her, followed by a boom of thunder that nearly had her jerking out of her skin. "Okay, so I meant *pretty please* leave me alone."

The highway in front of her wound its way alongside a cliff on her right, which probably hid more wildlife than this affirmed city girl wanted to think about. Far below the road on her left, the Pacific Ocean pitched and rolled, fog lingering in long, silvery fingers on the frothy water.

Gorgeous, all of it, but what registered more than anything was the silence. No horns blaring while jockeying for position in the clogged fast lane, no tension-filled offices where producers and directors shouted at each other. No ex-boyfriends who yelled to release steam. Or worse.

No anger at all, in fact.

Just the sound of the radio and her own breathing. Delicious, *glorious* silence.

As unbelievable as it seemed, she'd never driven through the mountains before. She was here now only because, shockingly, her mother's will had listed property in Washington State. More shockingly, Maddie had been left one-third of that property, a place called Lucky Harbor Resort.

Raised by her set-designer dad in Los Angeles, Maddie hadn't seen her mother more than a handful of times since he'd taken custody of her at age five, so the will had been a huge surprise. Her dad had been just as shocked

as she, and so had her two half-sisters, Tara and Chloe.
Since there hadn't been a memorial service—Phoebe had
specifically not wanted one—the three sisters had agreed
to meet at the resort.

It would be the first time they'd seen each other in
five years.

Defying probability, the road narrowed yet again.
Maddie steered into the sharp left curve and then immediately whipped the wheel the other way for the unexpected
right. A sign warned her to keep a lookout for river otters,
osprey—what the heck were *osprey?*—and bald eagles.
Autumn had come extremely late this year for the entire
West Coast, and the fallen leaves were strewn across the
roads like gold coins. It was beautiful, and taking it all
in might have caused her to slide a little bit into the next
hairpin, where she—oh, crap—

Barely missed a guy on a motorcycle.

"Oh, my God." Heart in her throat, she craned her
neck, watching as the bike ran off the road and skidded
to a stop. With a horrified grimace, she started to drive
past, then hesitated.

But hurrying past a cringe-worthy moment, hoping to
avoid a scene, was the old Maddie. The new Maddie
stopped the car, though she did allow herself a beat to
draw a quick, shuddery breath. What was she supposed
to say—*Sorry I almost killed you, here's my license,
insurance, and last twenty-seven dollars?* No, that was
too pathetic. *Motorcycles are death machines, you idiot,
you nearly got yourself killed!* Hmm, probably a tad too
defensive. Which meant that a simple, heartfelt apology
would have to do.

Bolstering her courage, she got out of the car clutching

her Blackberry, ready to call 911 if it got ugly. Shivering in the unexpectedly damp ocean air, she moved toward him, her arms wrapped around herself as she faced the music.

Please don't be a raging asshole...

He was still straddling the motorcycle, one long leg stretched out, balancing on a battered work boot, and if he was pissed, she couldn't tell yet past his reflective sunglasses. He was leanly muscled and broad shouldered, and his jeans and leather jacket were made for a hard body just like his. It was a safe bet that *he* hadn't just inhaled an entire bag of salt-and-vinegar chips. "Are you okay?" she asked, annoyed that she sounded breathless and nervous.

Pulling off his helmet, he revealed wavy, dark brown hair and a day's worth of stubble on a strong jaw. "I'm good. You?" His voice was low and calm, his hair whipping around in the wind.

Irritated, most definitely. But not pissed.

Relieved, she dragged in some air. "I'm fine, but I'm not the one who nearly got run off the road by the crazy LA driver. I'm sorry, I was driving too fast."

"You probably shouldn't admit that."

True. But she was thrown by his gravelly voice, by the fact that he was big and, for all she knew, bad, to boot, and that she was alone with him on a deserted, foggy highway.

It had all the makings of a horror flick.

"Are you lost?" he asked.

Was she? Probably she was a little lost mentally, and quite possibly emotionally, as well. Not that she'd admit either. "I'm heading to Lucky Harbor Resort."

He pushed his sunglasses to the top of his head, and

be still her heart, he had eyes the *exact* color of the caramel in the candy bar she'd consumed for lunch. "Lucky Harbor Resort," he repeated.

"Yes." But before she could ask why he was baffled about that, his gaze dipped down and he took in her favorite long-sleeved tee. Reaching out, he picked something off her sleeve.

Half a chip.

He took another off her collarbone, and she broke out in goose bumps—and not the scared kind.

"Plain?"

"Salt and vinegar," she said and shook off the crumbs. She'd muster up some mortification—but she'd used up her entire quota when she'd nearly flattened him like a pancake. Not that she cared what he—or any man, for that matter—thought. Because she'd given up men.

Even tall, built, really good-looking, tousled-haired guys with gravelly voices and piercing eyes.

Especially them.

What she needed now was an exit plan. So she put her phone to her ear, pretending it was vibrating. "Hello," she said to no one. "Yes, I'll be right there." She smiled, like *look at me, so busy, I really have to go,* and, turning away, she lifted a hand in a wave, still talking into the phone to avoid an awkward good-bye, except—

Her phone rang. And not the pretend kind. Risking a peek at Hot Biker Guy over her shoulder, she found him brows up, looking amused.

"I think you have a *real* call," he said, something new in his voice. Possibly more humor, but most likely sheer disbelief that he'd nearly been killed by a socially handicapped LA chick.

Face hot, Maddie answered her phone. And then wished she hadn't, since it was the HR department of the production office from which she'd been fired, asking where she'd like her final check mailed. "I have automatic deposit," she murmured, and listened to the end-of-employment spiel and questions, agreeing out loud that yes, she realized being terminated means no references. With a sigh, she hung up.

He was watching her. "Fired, huh?"

"I don't want to talk about it."

He accepted that but didn't move. He just remained still, straddling that bike, sheer testosterone coming off him in waves. She realized he was waiting for her to leave first. Either he was being a gentleman, or he didn't want to risk his life and limbs. "Again, sorry. And I'm really glad I didn't kill you—" She walked backward, right into her own car. Good going. Keeping her face averted, she leapt into the driver's seat. "Really glad I didn't kill you?" she repeated to herself. *Seriously?* Well, whatever, it was done. *Just don't look back. Don't—*

She looked.

He was watching her go, and though she couldn't be certain, she thought maybe he was looking a little bemused.

She got that a lot.

A minute later, she drove through Lucky Harbor. It was everything Google Earth had promised, a picturesque little Washington State beach town nestled in a rocky cove with a quirky, eclectic mix of the old and new. The main drag was lined with Victorian buildings painted in bright colors, housing the requisite grocery store, post office, gas station, and hardware store. Then a turnoff to the beach itself, where a long pier jutted out into the water, lined with more shops and outdoor cafés.

And a Ferris wheel.

The sight of it brought an odd yearning. She wanted to buy a ticket and ride it, if only to pretend for four minutes that she wasn't twenty-nine, broke every which way to Sunday, and homeless.

Oh, and scared of heights.

She kept driving. Two minutes later, she came to a fork in the road and had no idea which way to turn. Pulling over, she grabbed her map, watching as Hot Biker Guy rode past her in those faded jeans that fit perfectly across his equally perfect butt.

When the very nice view was gone, she went back to studying her map. Lucky Harbor Resort was supposedly on the water, which was still hard to believe, because as far as Maddie knew, the only thing her mother had ever owned was a 1971 wood-paneled station wagon and every single Deadhead album ever recorded.

According to the lawyer's papers, the resort was made up of a small marina, an inn, and an owner's cottage. Filled with anticipation, Maddie hit the gas and steered right…only to come to the end of the asphalt.

Huh.

She eyed the last building on the left. It was an art gallery. A woman stood in the doorway wearing a bright pink velour sweat suit with white piping, white athletic shoes, and a terry-cloth sweatband that held back her equally white hair. She could have been fifty or eighty, it was hard to tell, and in direct contrast to the athletic outfit, she had a cigarette dangling out the corner of her mouth and skin that looked as if she'd been standing in the sun for decades. "Hello, darling," she said in a craggy voice when Maddie got out of her car. "You're either lost, or you want to buy a painting."

"A little lost," Maddie admitted.

"That happens a lot out here. We have all these roads that lead nowhere."

Great. She was on the road to nowhere. Story of her life. "I'm looking for Lucky Harbor Resort."

The woman's white eyebrows jerked upright, vanishing into her hair. "Oh! Oh, finally!" Eyes crinkling when she smiled, she clapped her hands in delight. "Which one are you, honey? The Wild Child, the Steel Magnolia, or the Mouse?"

Maddie blinked. "Uh…"

"Oh, your momma *loved* to talk about her girls! Always said how she'd screwed you all up but good, but that someday she'd get you all back here to run the inn together as a real family, the three of you."

"You mean the four of us."

"Nope. Somehow she always knew it'd be just you three girls." She puffed on her cigarette, then nearly hacked up a lung. "She wanted to get the inn renovated first, but that didn't happen. The pneumonia caught her fast, and then she was gone." Her smile faded some. "Probably God couldn't resist Pheeb's company. Christ, she was such a kick." She cocked her head and studied Maddie's appearance.

Self-conscious, Maddie once again brushed at herself, hoping the crumbs were long gone and that maybe her hair wasn't as bad as it felt.

The woman smiled. "The Mouse."

Well, hell. Maddie blew out a breath, telling herself it was silly to be insulted at the truth. "Yes."

"That'd make you the smart one, then. The one who ran the big, fancy production company in Los Angeles."

"Oh." Maddie vehemently shook her head. "No, I was just an assistant." To an assistant. Who sometimes had to buy her boss's underwear and fetch his girlfriend's presents, as well as actually produce movies and TV shows.

"Your momma said you'd say that, but she knew better. Knew your worth ethic. She said you worked very hard."

Maddie *had* worked hard. And dammit, she had also pretty much run that company. May it rot in hell. "How do you know all this?"

"I'm Lucille." When this produced no recognition from Maddie, she cackled in laughter. "I actually work for you. You know, at the inn? Whenever there's guests, I come in and clean."

"By yourself?"

"Well, business hasn't exactly been hopping, has it? Oh! Wait here a second, I have something to show you—"

"Actually, I'm sort of in a hurry…" But Lucille was gone. "Okay, then."

Two minutes later, Lucile reappeared from the gallery carrying a small carved wooden box that said RECIPES, the kind that held 3x5 index cards. "This is for you girls."

Maddie didn't cook, but it seemed rude not to take it. "Did Phoebe cook?"

"Oh, hell, no," Lucille said with a cackle. "She could burn water like no other."

Maddie accepted the box with a baffled "Thanks."

"Now, you just continue down this road about a mile

to the clearing. You can't miss it. Call me if you need anything. Cleaning, organizing...spider relocation."

This caught Maddie's attention. "Spider relocation?"

"Your momma wasn't big on spiders."

Uh-huh, something they had in common. "Are there a lot of them?"

"Well, that depends on what you consider a lot."

Oh, God. Any more than one was an infestation. Maddie managed a smile that might have been more a baring of her teeth, gave a wave of thanks, and got back into her car, following the dirt road. *"The Mouse,"* she said with a sigh.

That was going to change.

Chapter 2

*"Don't take life too seriously. After all, none of us
are getting out alive anyway."*
PHOEBE TRAEGER

Turned out Lucille was right, and in exactly one mile,
the road opened up to a clearing. The Pacific Ocean was
a deep, choppy sea of black, dusted with whitecaps that
went out as far as Maddie could see. It connected with
a metallic gray sky, framed by rocky bluffs, misty and
breathtaking.

She had found the "resort," and Lucille had gotten
something else right, too. The place wasn't exactly hopping.

Dead was more like it.

Clearly, the inn had seen better days. A woman sat on
the front porch steps, a Vespa parked nearby. At the sight
of Maddie, she stood. She wore cute little hip-hugging
army cargoes, a snug, bright red Henley, and matching
high-tops. Her glossy dark red hair cascaded down her
back in an artful disarray that would have taken an entire

beauty salon staff to accomplish on Maddie's uncontrollable curls.

Chloe, the twenty-four-year-old Wild Child.

Maddie attempted to pat down her own dark blond hair that had a mind of its own, but it was a waste of time on a good day, which this most definitely wasn't. Before she could say a word, a cab pulled up next to Maddie's car and a tall, lean, beautiful woman got out. Her short brunette hair was layered and effortlessly sexy. She wore an elegant business suit that emphasized her fit body and a cool smile.

Tara, the Steel Magnolia.

As the cabbie set Tara's various bags on the porch, the three of them just stared at one another, five years of estrangement floating awkwardly between them. The last time they'd all been in one place, Tara and Maddie had met in Montana to bail Chloe out of jail for illegally bungee jumping off a bridge. Chloe had thanked them, promised to pay them back, and they'd all gone their separate ways.

It was just the way it was. They had three different fathers and three very different personalities, and the only thing they had in common was a sweet, ditzy, wanderlusting hippie of a mother.

"So," Maddie said, forcing a smile through the uncomfortable silence. "How's things?"

"Ask me again after we sort out this latest mess," Tara murmured and eyed their baby sister.

Chloe tossed up her hands. "Hey, I had nothing to do with this one."

"Which would be a first." Tara spoke with the very slight southern accent that she denied having, the one she'd gotten from growing up on her paternal grand-parents' horse ranch in Texas.

Chloe rolled her eyes and pulled her always-present asthma inhaler from her pocket, looking around without much interest. "So this is it? The big reveal?"

"I guess so," Maddie said, also taking in the clearly deserted inn. "There don't appear to be any guests at the moment."

"Not good for resale value," Tara noted.

"Resale?" Maddie asked.

"Selling is the simplest way to get out of here as fast as possible."

Maddie's stomach clenched. She didn't want to get out of here. She wanted a place to stay—to breathe, to lick her wounds, to regroup. "What's the hurry?"

"Just being realistic. The place came with a huge mortgage and no liquid assets."

Chloe shook her head. "Sounds like Mom."

"There was a large trust fund from her parents," Maddie said. "The will separated it out from the estate, so I have no idea who it went to. I assumed it was one of you."

Chloe shook her head.

They both looked at Tara.

"Sugar, I don't know any more than y'all. What I *do* know is that we'd be smart to sell, pay off the loan on the property, and divide what's left three ways and get back to our lives. I'm thinking we can list the place and be out of here in a few days if we play our cards right."

This time Maddie's stomach plummeted. "So fast?"

"Do you really want to stay in Lucky Harbor a moment longer than necessary?" Tara asked. "Even Mom, bless her heart, didn't stick around."

Chloe shook her inhaler and took a second puff from it. "Selling works for me. I'm due at a friend's day spa in New Mexico next week."

"You have enough money to book yourself at a spa in New Mexico, but not enough to pay me back what you've borrowed?" Tara asked.

"I'm going there to work. I've been creating a natural skin care line, and I'm giving a class on it, hoping to sell the line to the spa." Chloe eyed the road. "Think there's a bar in town? I could use a drink."

"It's four in the afternoon," Tara said.

"But it's five o'clock somewhere."

Chloe's eyes narrowed. "What?" she said to Tara's sound of disappointment.

"I think you know."

"Why don't you tell me anyway."

And here we go, Maddie thought, anxiety tightening like a knot in her throat. "Um, maybe we could all just sit down and—"

"No, I want her to say what's on her mind," Chloe said.

The static electricity rose in the air until it crackled with violence from both impending storms—Mother Nature's *and* the sisters' fight.

"It's not important what I think," Tara said coolly.

"Oh, come on, Dixie," Chloe said. "Lay it on us. You know you want to."

Maddie stepped between them. She couldn't help it. It was the middle sister in her, the approval seeker, the office manager deep inside. "Look!" she said in desperation. "A puppy!"

Chloe swiveled her head to Maddie, amused. "Seriously?"

She shrugged. "Worth a shot."

"Next time say it with more conviction and less panic. You might get somewhere."

"Well, I don't give a hoot if there are puppies *and* rainbows," Tara said. "As unpleasant as this is, we have to settle it."

Maddie was watching Chloe shake her inhaler again, looking pale. "You okay?"

"Peachy."

She tried not to take the sarcasm personally. Chloe, a free spirit as Phoebe had been, suffered debilitating asthma and resented the hell out of the disability because it hampered her quest for adventure.

And for arguing.

Together all three sisters walked across the creaky porch and into the inn. Like most of the other buildings in Lucky Harbor, it was Victorian. The blue and white paint had long ago faded, and the window shutters were mostly gone or falling off, but Maddie could picture how it'd once looked: new and clean, radiating character and charm.

They'd each been mailed a set of keys. Tara used hers to unlock and open the front door, and she let out a long-suffering sigh.

The front room was a shrine to a country-style house circa 1980. Just about everything was blue and white, from the checkered window coverings to the duck-and-cow accent wallpaper peeling off the walls. The paint was chipped and the furniture not old enough to be antique and yet at least thirty years on the wrong side of new.

"Holy asphyxiation," Chloe said with her nose

wrinkled at the dust. "I won't be able to stay here. I'll suffocate."

Tara shook her head, half horrified, half amused. "It looks like Laura Ingalls Wilder threw up in here."

"You know, your accent gets thicker and thicker," Chloe said.

"I don't have an accent."

"Okay. Except you do."

"It's not that bad," Maddie said quickly when Tara opened her mouth.

"Oh, it's bad," Chloe said. "You sounds like Susan Sarandon in *Bull Durham*."

"The *inn*," Maddie clarified. "I meant the *inn* isn't so bad."

"I've stayed in hostels in Bolivia that looked like the Ritz compared to this," Chloe said.

"Mom's mom and her third husband ran this place." Tara ran a finger along the banister, then eyed the dust on the pad of her finger. "Years and years ago."

"So Grandma ran through men, too?" Chloe asked. "Jeez, it's like we're destined to be man-eaters."

"Speak for yourself," Tara murmured, indeed sounding like Susan Sarandon.

Chloe grinned. "Admit it, our gene pool could use some chlorine."

"As I was saying," Tara said when Maddie laughed. "Grandma worked here, and when she died, Mom attempted to take over but got overwhelmed."

Maddie was mesmerized by this piece of her past. She'd never even heard of this place. As far as she knew, none of them had kept in regular contact with Phoebe. This was mostly because their mother had spent much of her life out of contact with anything other than her own whimsy.

Not that she'd been a bad person. By all accounts, she'd been a sweet, free-loving flower child. But she hadn't been the greatest at taking care of things like cars, bank accounts... her daughters. "I wasn't even aware that Mom had been close to her parents."

"They died a long time ago." Tara turned back, watching Chloe climb the stairs. "Don't go up there, sugar. It's far too dusty; you'll aggravate your asthma."

"I'm already aggravated, and not by my asthma." But Chloe pulled the neckline of her shirt over her mouth. She also kept going up the stairs, and Tara just shook her head.

"Why do I bother?" Tara moved into the kitchen and went still at the condition of it. "Formica countertops," she said as if she'd discovered asbestos.

Okay, true, the Formica countertops weren't pretty, but the country blue and white tile floor was cute in a retro sort of way. And yes, the appliances were old, but there was something innately homey and warm about the setup, including the rooster wallpaper trim. Maddie could see guests in here at the big wooden block table against the large picture window, which had a lovely view of... the dilapidated marina.

So fine, they could call it a blast from the past. Certainly there were people out there looking for an escape to a quaint, homey inn and willing to pay for it.

"We need elbow grease, and lots of it," Chloe said, walking into the kitchen, her shirt still over her nose and mouth.

Maddie wasn't afraid of hard work. It was all she

knew. And envisioning this place all fixed up with a roaring fire in the woodstove and a hot, delicious meal on the stovetop, with cuteness spilling from every nook and cranny, made her smile. Without thinking, she pulled out the Blackberry she could no longer afford and started a list, her thumbs a blur of action. "New paint, new countertops, new appliances..." Hmm, what else? She hit the light switch for a better look, and nothing happened.

Tara sighed.

Maddie added that to the list. "Faulty wiring—"

"And leaky roof." Tara pointed upward.

"There's a bathroom above this," Chloe told them. "It's got a plumbing issue. Roof's probably leaking, too."

Tara came closer and peered over Maddie's shoulder at her list. "Are you a compulsive organizer?"

At the production studios, she'd had to be. There'd been five producers—and her. They'd gotten the glory, and she'd done the work.

All of it.

And until last week, she'd thrived on it. "Yes. Hi, my name is Maddie, and I am addicted to my Blackberry, office supplies, and organization." She waited for a smart-ass comment.

But Tara merely shrugged. "You'll come in handy." She was halfway out of the room before Maddie found her voice.

"Did you know Mom didn't want to sell?" she asked Tara's back. "That she planned on us running the place as a family?"

Tara turned around. "She knew better than that."

"No, really. She wanted to use the inn to bring us together."

"I loved Mom," Chloe said. "But she didn't do '*together*.'"

"She didn't," Maddie agreed. "But we could. If we wanted."

Both sisters gaped at her.

"You've lost your ever-lovin' marbles," Tara finally said. "We're selling."

No longer a mouse, Maddie told herself. Going from mouse to tough girl, like...Rachel from *Friends*. Without the wishy-washyness. And without Ross. She didn't like Ross. "What if I don't want to sell?"

"I don't give a coon's ass whether you want to or not. It doesn't matter," Tara said. "We *have* to sell."

"A coon's ass?" Chloe repeated with a laugh. "Is that farm ghetto slang or something? And what does that even mean?"

Tara ignored her and ticked reasons off on her fingers. "There's no money. We have a payment due to the note holder in two weeks. Not to mention, I have a life to get back to in Dallas. I took a week off, that's it."

Maddie knew Tara had a sexy NASCAR husband named Logan and a high-profile managerial job. Maddie could understand wanting to get back to both.

"And maybe I have a date with an Arabian prince," Chloe said. "We *all* have lives to get back to, Tara."

Well, not all *of us,* Maddie thought.

In uneasy silence, they checked out the rest of the inn. There was a den and a small bed and bath off the kitchen, and four bedrooms and two community bathrooms upstairs, all shabby chic minus the chic.

Next, they walked out to the marina. The small metal building was half equipment storage and half office—and one giant mess. Kayaks and tools and oars and supplies vied for space. In the good-news department, four of the eight boat slips were filled. "Rent," Maddie said, thrilled, making more notes.

"Hmm," was all Tara said.

Chloe was eyeing the sole motorboat. "Hey, we should take that out for a joyride and—"

"No!" Maddie and Tara said in unison.

Chloe rolled her eyes. "Jeez, a girl gets arrested once and no one ever lets her forget it."

"Twice," Tara said. "And you still owe me the bail money for that San Diego jet ski debacle."

Maddie had no idea what had happened in San Diego. She wasn't sure she wanted to know. They moved outside again and faced the last section of the "resort," the small owner's cottage. And actually, *small* was too kind. *Postage-stamp*-sized was too kind. It had a blink-and-you'll-miss-it kitchen-and-living-room combo and a single bedroom and bath.

And lots of dust.

"It's really not that bad," Maddie said into the stunned silence. They stood there another beat, taking in the decor, which was—surprise, surprise—done in blue and white with lots of stenciled ducks and cows and roosters, oh, my. "Mostly cosmetic. I just think—"

"No," Tara said firmly. "Bless your heart, but please, *please* don't think."

Chloe choked out a laugh. "Love how you say 'bless your heart' just before you insult someone. Classy."

Tara ignored Chloe entirely and kept her voice soft and steely calm. "Majority rules here. And majority says we should sell ASAP, assuming that in this economy we don't have to actually *pay* someone to take this place off our hands."

Maddie looked at Chloe. "You really want to sell, too?"

Chloe hesitated.

"Be honest with her," Tara said.

"I can't." Chloe covered her face. "She has Bambi eyes. You know what?" She headed for the door. "I'm not in the mood to be the swing vote."

"Where are you going?" Tara demanded.

"For a ride."

"But we need your decision—"

The door shut, hard.

Tara tossed up her hands. "Selfish as ever." She looked around in disgust. "I'm going into town for supplies to see us through the next couple of days. We need food and cleaning supplies—and possibly a fire accelerant." She glanced at Maddie and caught her horror. "Kidding! Can I borrow your car?"

Maddie handed over her keys. "Get chips, lots of chips."

When she was alone, she sat on the steps and pulled Lucille's recipe box from her bag. With nothing else to do, she lifted the lid, prepared to be bored by countless recipes she'd never use.

The joke was on her. Literally. The 3x5 cards had been written on, but instead of recipes for food, she found recipes for...

Life.

They were all handwritten by Phoebe and labeled *Advice for My Girls*. The first one read:

Always be in love.

Maddie stared at it for a moment, then had to smile. Years ago, she'd gotten the birds-and-bees speech from her father. He'd rambled off the facts quickly, not meeting her eyes, trying to do his best by her. He was so damned uncomfortable, and all because a boy had called her.

Boys are like drugs, her father had said. *Just say no.*

Her mother and father had definitely not subscribed to the same philosophies. Not quite up to seeing what other advice Phoebe had deemed critical, Maddie slipped the box back into her bag. She zipped up her sweatshirt and headed out herself, needing a walk. The wind had picked up. The clouds were even darker now, hanging low above her head.

At the end of the clearing, she stopped and looked back at the desolate inn. It hadn't been what she'd hoped for. She had no memories here with her mother. The place wasn't home in any way. And yet...and yet she didn't want to turn her back on it. She wanted to stay.

And not just because she was homeless.

Okay, a little bit because she was homeless.

With a sigh, she started walking again. About a mile from the inn, she passed the art gallery, waving at Lucille when the older woman stuck her head out and smiled. Snowflakes hovered in the air. Not many, and they didn't seem to stick once they hit the ground. But the way they floated lazily around her as the day faded into dusk kept her entertained until she found herself in town.

She suddenly realized that she was standing in front of a bar. She stepped back to read the sign on the door, tripped off the curb, and stumbled backward into something big, toppling with it to the ground.

A motorcycle. "Crap," she whispered, sprawled over

the big, heavy bike. "Crap, *crap*." Heart in her throat, she leapt to her feet, rubbing her sore butt and ribs and mentally calculating the cost of damages against the low funds she had in her checking account.

It was too awful to contemplate, which meant that the motorcycle had to be okay. *Had* to be. Reaching out, she tried to right the huge thing, but it outweighed her. She was still struggling with it when the door to the bar suddenly burst open and two men appeared.

One was dressed in a tan business suit, tie flapping, mouth flapping, too. "Hey," he was saying. "She was asking for it…"

The second man wasn't speaking, but Maddie recognized him anyway. Hot Biker from earlier, which meant—Oh, God. It was *his* motorcycle she'd knocked over.

Karma was such a bitch.

At least he hadn't seen her yet. He was busy physically escorting Smarmy Suit Guy with his hand fisted in the back of the guy's jacket as he marched him out of the bar.

Smarmy Suit pulled free and whirled, fists raised.

Hot Biker just stood there, stance easy, looking laid-back but absolutely battle ready. "Go home, Parker."

"You can't kick me out."

"Can, and did. And you're not welcome back until you learn no is no."

"I'm telling you, she wanted me!"

Hot Biker shook his head.

Smarmy Suit put a little distance between them then yelled, "Fuck you, then!" before stalking off into the night.

Maddie just stared, her heart pounding. She wasn't sure if it was the volatile situation, ringing far too close to home, or if it was because any second now, he was going to notice her and what she'd done. With renewed panic, she struggled with his bike.

Then two big hands closed around her upper arms and pulled her back from it.

With an inward wince, she turned to face him. He was bigger than she'd realized, and she took a step backward, out of his reach.

His dark hair was finger-combed at best, a lock of it falling over his forehead. He had a strong jaw, and cheekbones to die for, and disbelief swimming in those melted caramel eyes. "Mind telling me why you have it in for my bike?"

"Okay, this looks bad," she admitted. "But I swear I have nothing against you or your motorcycle."

"Hmm. Prove it."

Her gut clenched. "I—"

"With a drink." He gestured with his head to the bar.

"With you?"

"Or by yourself, if you'd rather. But you look like you could use a little pick-me-up."

He had no idea.

He righted his bike with annoying ease and held out a hand.

She stared at it but didn't take it. "Look, nothing personal, but I've just seen how you deal with people who irritate you, so…"

He looked in the direction that Smarmy Suit had vanished. "Parker was hitting on a good friend of mine and making an ass of himself. Yeah, he irritated me. You haven't. Yet."

"Even though I've tried to kill your bike twice?"

"Even though." His mouth quirked slightly, as if she

were amusing him. Which was good, right? Amused at
her klutziness was better than being pissed.

"And anyway, the bike's going to live," he said, directing
her to the door, the one whose sign read THE LOVE SHACK.

"This is a bad idea."

He flashed her a smile, and holy mother of God, it
was wickedly sexy. It might even have been contagious if
she hadn't been so damn worried that any second now he
was going to morph into an angry, uptight, aggressive LA
attorney who didn't know how to control his temper.

No, wait. That'd been her ex, Alex. "Honestly," she
said. "Bad idea."

"Honestly?"

"What, don't people tell the truth around here?"

"Oh, the locals tell the truth. It's just that they tell *all*
the truth, even when they shouldn't. It's called gossip.
Lucky Harbor natives specialize in it. You can keep a pile
of money in the back seat of your unlocked car and it'd
be safe, but you can't keep a secret."

"Good thing I don't have any."

He smiled. "We all have secrets. Come on, I know the
bartender. It'll help you relax, trust me."

Yes, but she was in the red on trust. Way overdrawn.
In fact, the Bank Of Trust had folded. "I don't know."

Except he'd nudged her inside already, and her feet
were going willingly. The place snagged her interest
immediately. It was like entering an old western saloon.
The walls were a deep sinful bordello red and lined with
old mining tools. The ceiling was all exposed beams.
Lanterns hung over the scarred bench-style tables, and the
bar itself was a series of old wood doors attached end to
end. Someone had already decorated for Christmas and

huge silvery balls hung from everything, as did endless streams of tinsel.

Hot Biker had her hand in his bigger, warmer one and was pulling her past the tables full with the dinner crowd. The air was filled with busy chattering, loud laughter, and music blaring out of the jukebox on the far wall. She didn't recognize the song because it was country, and country music wasn't on her radar, but some guy was singing about how Santa was doing his momma beneath the tree.

Shaking her head, Maddie let herself be led to the bar, where she noticed that nobody was here to drink their problems away.

Everyone seemed... happy.

Hoping it was contagious, she sat on the barstool that he patted for her, right next to a woman wearing sprayed-on jeans and a halter top that revealed she was either chilly or having a really, really good time. Her makeup was overdone, but somehow the look really worked for her. She was cheerfully flirting with a huge mountain of a guy on her other side, who was grinning from ear to ear and looking like maybe he'd just won the lottery.

Hot Biker greeted them both as if they were all close friends, then moved behind the bar, brushing that leanly muscled body alongside of Maddie's as he did.

She shivered.

"Cold?" he asked.

When she shook her head, he smiled again, and the sexiness of it went straight through her, causing another shiver.

Yeah, he really needed to stop doing that.

Immediately, several people at the bar tossed out orders to him, but he just shook his head, eyes locked on

Maddie. "I'm done helping out for the night, guys. I'm just getting the lady a drink."

The other bartender, another big, good-looking guy—wow, they sure grew them damn fine up here in Lucky Harbor—asked, "What kind of wing man just takes off without proper clearance? Never mind." He slapped an opened sudoku puzzle in front of Hot Biker. "Just do this puzzle in three minutes or less."

"Why?"

"There's a woman at the end of the bar, the one with the fuck-me heels—Jesus, don't look! What, are you an amateur? She said she'd do things to me that are illegal in thirteen states if I did the puzzle in less than five minutes. So for all that is holy, hurry the fuck up. Just don't let her see you doing it."

Hot Biker looked at Maddie and smiled. "Trying to impress a woman here, Ford."

Ford turned to Maddie speculatively. "I suppose you already know that this guy here has got some charm. But did he tell you that in our freshman year we nicknamed him Hugh because his stash of porn was legendary? Yeah, he had more back issues than eBay. And maybe he mentioned that he can't pee his name in the snow anymore because the last time he did, he gave himself a hernia trying to cross the X at the end of his name?" Ford turned back to Hot Biker and slapped him on the back. "There. Now you have no hope of impressing her, so get cranking on that puzzle—you owe me."

Hot Biker grimaced, and Maddie did something she hadn't in weeks.

She laughed.

Chapter 3

*"A glass of wine is always the solution.
Even if you aren't sure of the problem."*
PHOEBE TRAEGER

So you collect porn."

Jax Cullen took in the genuine amusement on the woman's face and shook his head. Fucking Ford. "Past tense," he corrected. "I sold the collection to an incoming freshman when I left for college."

"Uh-huh. That's what they all say."

Liking the way the worry had faded from her eyes, which were now lit with good humor, he leaned over the bar and whispered near her ear, "Want to swap stories, Speed Racer?"

She composed herself enough to grimace. "I'm just glad you can laugh about me almost killing you."

"As opposed to?"

"I don't know. Yelling."

Jax studied her face before she turned away from him, purposely eyeing the bottles of alcohol lining the back of the bar, trying to conceal her discomfort. "Not much of a yeller," he murmured and reached out to play with one of her dark blond curls. He couldn't help himself—they were irresistible.

So was she.

"I've heard that LA women are pretty aggressive in their pickup tactics. But this just might be one for the record books. You should probably just save us both some trouble and ask me out directly."

"Hey, I didn't nearly run you over on purpose. And I tripped on the bike trying to read the sign."

"Ah, but you don't deny the attempting to pick-me-up part." He nodded. "You want me bad."

She laughed and then shook her head as if surprised at herself. "If you plan to keep stalking me like this, we should be on a first-name basis. I'm Jax." He held out his hand. "Jax Cullen."

She slid her smaller, chilled-to-the-bone hand in his. "Maddie Moore."

He knew the name, more than he wanted to. She was Phoebe's middle daughter. Giving himself a moment, he rubbed her hands between his, trying to warm them up. Earlier when she'd been using the highway—and nearly his body—for offensive-driving practice, he'd gotten the impression of a sweet, warm, and very stressed-out woman, and that hadn't changed. He loved the wild, curly hair which was barely contained in a ponytail, but her long side bangs brushed across one eye and the side of her jaw, nearly hiding her eyes and her pretty face.

She'd dressed to hide her body, as well. Watching her squirm on her barstool under his scrutiny, he wondered why. "What's your poison?"

"A beer, please."

Jax grabbed two Coronas, lifted the walk-through, and took the barstool next to her. Ford, who was a coowner of the place—and until about two minutes ago also one of his best friends—came back and jabbed a finger at the sudoku book. "You haven't even started it? Killing me, Clark."

Maddie frowned. "Thought your name was Jax."

"It is, but Leno-wannabe here thinks he's being funny when he calls me Clark. As in Superman," he clarified, making Ford snort.

"As in *Clark Kent*," Ford corrected. "See him squint at the puzzle? Yeah, that's because he needs reading glasses and he won't wear them. He thinks he won't ever get laid again if he does. Because apparently squinting is sexier than admitting his vision sucks."

"Thanks, man," Jax said.

Ford clapped him on the shoulder. "Just keeping it real."

Maddie was looking at him. "Actually, you do sort of look like Clark Kent, if he were really fit. And tough. And edgy. What's your superpower?"

Ford grinned in approval at her and opened his mouth to answer, but Jax reached across the bar, put a hand on Ford's face, and shoved. "I try to keep the superpower on the down-low," he said. "Because the people here like to gossip."

Even with Jax's hand on his face, Ford managed another snort and tapped the sudoku book in front of Jax. "If he's a superhero, ask him why the puzzle's still blank. Tick-tock, bro. Tick-tock."

"Forget it. And maybe you could actually be the bartender and serve us." Jax looked at Maddie. "Food?"

She was too nervous to eat and shook her head.

"That's all right," Ford said. "This guy'll eat me out of

house and home all on his own." He leaned over the bar, smiling at her, pouring on the charm that got him laid so regularly.

"Hey," Jax said.

Ford grinned at Maddie. "He doesn't like to share. It's because I'm hotter than he is."

Maddie was smiling again. "You always make fun of your friends?"

"Hey, you can't make fun of your own brother, who can you make fun of?"

Maddie took a long pull on her beer, set it down, then once again turned to face Jax, eyeing him for a long beat. "You're brothers?"

Jax understood the question. Ford had lighter hair, lighter eyes, and more bulk to his muscle, like a football player. He mostly sailed these days and was, in fact, a world-class pro. When on the water, he moved with easy, natural grace, not that you could tell by looking at the big lug. "Not by blood."

"Yeah, by blood," Ford said. "We cut each other's palms and spit on them in the third grade, remember? Misfits unite."

Maddie was still dividing her gaze between them. "Neither of you look like misfits."

"Ah, but you didn't see us back then," Ford said. "Two scrawny, bony-ass kids. The best that could be said of us was we knew how to take a beating."

"And run fast," Jax reminded him.

Maddie looked horrified. "How awful."

"It wasn't so bad." Ford lifted a shoulder. "We had Sawyer."

"Sawyer?"

"Our secret weapon. He'd been wrestling with his older brothers since before he could walk. It's why we let him hang out with us."

Maddie finished her beer and set the empty down, looking infinitely more relaxed. "Another, please."

Ford obliged. "So is this a social second round or a get-shit-faced one?"

She pondered that with careful consideration. "Does it matter?"

"Only if I have to peel you off the floor and call you a ride."

She shook her head. "No floor peeling."

Ford nodded and smiled, then turned to Jax and pointed at the puzzle before moving off to serve his other customers.

Maddie sipped her second beer. "So you and Ford are close."

"Yeah."

"Do you two fight?"

"Occasionally."

"And how do you settle these arguments?"

"Depends. Fight night in town square usually works."

At that she gave him a long look, and he smiled, making her shake her head at herself. "You'd think LA would have beaten the gullible out of me," she murmured.

"Nah. I'm just good at pulling legs."

"So what do you and Ford argue about? Women?"

"We try to avoid that."

"Okay, not a woman. Something else. Would you solve it with, say, a diplomatic coin toss?"

"Probably not," he admitted. "Loudest usually wins. A well-placed punch is always a bonus."

When she narrowed her eyes in blatant disbelief, he smiled again. "See, you're catching on to me already."

"Actually," she murmured, "it's not a bad idea. But I'd lose a fight against my oldest sister. Tara's got some *serious* pent-up-aggression issues." She considered her beer for a minute, her fingers stroking up and down over the condensation, drawing Jax's full attention.

"Probably I could take Chloe on account of her asthma," she said. "But that'd be mean. Plus I'm out of shape, so..."

At that, he gave her a slow once-over, fully appreciating her real curves, and shook his head. "Not from where I'm sitting."

She blinked. Compliments obviously flustered her, which only stirred his curiosity all the more. "You could challenge your sisters to a street race in your Honda," he said. "My money's on you."

She choked out a little laugh, set down her beer, and pointed at the opened puzzle book. "Four."

"Excuse me?"

"Four goes there. And six goes there." Leaning in, she took his pencil and filled in the two spots while he found his mouth so close to her ear he could have taken a nibble. Instead, he inhaled her scent. Soft. Subtle. *Nice.*

She cocked her head sideways, concentrating, and he just breathed her in. Which was how she filled in the rest of the puzzle before he realized it. "Damn."

"Don't be impressed," she said. "I've got a little compulsive problem. I can't stand to leave anything unfinished." She hopped off the barstool. "Unfortunately, they don't have a twelve-step program for such things."

"Ford's going to owe you," he said, snagging her wrist to halt her getaway.

"You could have done it if you'd worn your glasses." She pulled free. "It was only a moderately hard one. Oh and FYI? Women think glasses are a sign of brains, and also, they're sexy."

Cocking his head, he took in the slight flush to her cheeks, the humor in her gaze, and felt something stir within him. She might be struggling with some demons, but she was sweet and sharp as hell and a breath of fresh air. "Are you flirting with me?"

"No. The porn thing was a dealbreaker."

That made him laugh, and even better, so did she, and something flickered between them.

Chemistry.

A shocking amount of it. Clearly she felt it, too, because suddenly she was a flurry of movement, pulling some cash from the depths of her pockets, setting it on the bar for Ford, and turning for the door like she had a fire on her ass.

"Maddie."

She turned back, looking a little frenzied again, a little panicked, much as she had when he'd first seen her across the expanse of highway. He wondered why.

"I have to go," she said.

"Puzzles to solve?"

"Something like that."

"It's not really a puzzle-solving night," he said, slipping her money back into her front jeans pocket, his knuckles grazing her midriff. She went stock-still while he pulled his own money out to cover the drinks. "It's more of a make-new-friends night," he said. "And Ford's putting out peanuts. We can throw them at him. He hates that."

She closed her eyes, and when she opened them again, emotion flickered there. "I'd really like that, but tonight I have to have that fight with my sisters."

She was clearly vulnerable as hell, and he needed to get away from her before he took advantage of that. But then her bright blue gaze dropped and homed in on his mouth, and all his good intentions flew out the window.

"I'm working on a new beginning here," she said.

"New beginnings are good."

"Yeah." Her tongue came out and dampened her lips, an unconscious gesture that said maybe she was thinking of his mouth on hers. Seemed fitting. He'd been thinking about her mouth on his since he'd seen her outside the bar.

It'd been a hell of a long time since he'd let himself feel something, far too long. That it was for this woman, here, now, was going to make things difficult, but he was good at difficult and wouldn't let that stop him.

Reaching for her hand, he pulled her in, lowering his head. His jaw brushed her hair, and a strand of it stuck to his stubble. He was close enough now to watch in fascination as her eyes dilated. Her lips parted, and—

"You two need a hotel room?"

Ford, the resident nosey-body.

Maddie jumped and pulled free. "I've really got to go. Thanks for the drinks." She whirled around and stumbled into a table. With a soft exclamation, she righted the spilled drinks, apologizing profusely. Then she hightailed it for the door, not looking back.

"You're an ass," Jax said to Ford, watching her.

"No doubt. So, you going to collect her, too?"

Jax slid him a look.

"Come on. Try to deny that out of guilt you collect the needy: the homeless dog, friends who need loans, the chick with the sweet eyes and even sweeter ass—"

"You know I'm not interested in a relationship." It wasn't that he didn't believe in the concept. In spite of his parents' failed marriage and Jax's own close call with his ex, he understood wanting someone, the right someone, in his life. But he wasn't sure he trusted himself. After all, his past was freely littered with the debris of his many, many mistakes.

"You don't have to have a relationship to get... *involved*," Ford said. "Not the naked variety of involved, anyway. But she did run out of here pretty darn quick. Maybe she wasn't feeling it."

No, that hadn't been the problem. There'd been chemistry, so much that they could have lit all of Lucky Harbor's Christmas lights from the electricity. And that chemistry had scared her. She'd been hurt, that was plain as day. Knowing it, hating it, Jax headed for the door, because bad idea or not, he felt compelled to get to know more about her.

"Hey, what about my tip?" Ford called after him.

"You want a tip? Learn to keep your big trap shut." And Jax stepped out into the night.

"Rule number one of drinking without a wing man," Maddie chided herself as she walked away from the Love Shack. "Don't do anything stupid."

She walked faster and found herself at the beginning of the pier, pushed around by the wind. But she hardly felt it. Nope, she was still all warm and tingly thanks to a certain gorgeous guy with a mischievous, bad-boy smile and an even better body—

You gave up men!

She had no idea why she kept forgetting that. She wasn't ready to let one near her. Not after leaving Alex six months ago now. She hadn't looked back. Hadn't looked forward, either, to be honest.

And yet she'd let Jax near enough to touch her.

Since going into the bar, dark had fallen. The main street was lit up like a Christmas card, and the quaint historical architecture was a great distraction.

She passed a beauty shop. It was open, the front chair filled with a client, the hairdresser behind her, and the two of them talking and laughing together like old friends. On the corner, where the pier met the street, came the delicious, mouth-watering scent of burgers from a little restaurant.

The Eat Me Café.

Her stomach rumbled. With good reason, as all she'd given it in the last few hours were chips and beer. She thought about a loaded burger, fries, and maybe a pie...

Instead, she had to go back and face her sisters.

Past the lights of the town stood a set of craggy bluffs, nothing but a dark, shadowy outline in the night sky now, most likely teeming with coyotes and bears. With a shiver, she turned and took in the coast, lined with impressive ancient rock formations and granite outcrops.

She hoped those coyotes and bears stayed up there and kept away from the beach. The pier was lit up by twinkling white lights strung on the railings. Someone had added red bows and mistletoe at regular intervals.

It could have been a movie set. Well, except for the realistic icy wind. Waves slapped at the pylons beneath her, far more real than any sound effect. She shivered in just her sweatshirt, but she shoved her hands into her pockets and kept walking because she needed another moment.

Maybe two.

She stopped at the base of the Ferris wheel and looked up. And up. Just thinking about riding it, sitting on top of the world, had the bottom falling out of her stomach.

Stupid fear of heights.

One of these days she'd conquer that fear, but it would have to get in line behind all the others, the ones she was letting rule her life—like her fear of being a mouse forever.

She passed the arcade and came to an ice cream shop. Just what the doctor ordered, she decided, and in spite of the chilly night, she requested a chocolate shake.

"How about a chocolate–vanilla swirl?" the guy behind the counter asked. He was young, early twenties, and had a smile that said he knew how cute he was. "It's our bestseller."

"Okay." But as soon as he turned away to make it, she smacked her forehead. "Don't let people make decisions for you! Dig deep and be like...Thelma. *No, wait. Louise. I want to be Louise.*" Crap. Which one had Susan Sarandon played? And did it matter? If she couldn't be strong, she was going to have to fake it until it sank in. "I'm *Louise.*"

"Ah, a fantasy. I like fantasies."

Heart in her throat, she whirled around and came face to face with Jax, looking dark and delicious, and instead of fear, something else entirely quivered low in her belly.

"But probably we should wait until after our first date to role-play," he said.

Jax and *fantasy* in the same sentence made her shiver. Jax slipped out of his jacket and offered it to her, leaving him in just a long-sleeved black shirt. She opened her mouth to tell him she wasn't cold, but then he drew the ends closed around her and her nipples pebbled as if he'd touched them, and she promptly forgot what she was going to say.

The leather held his body heat, wrapping her in it like a cocoon, and she murmured her thanks. "When I first heard you walk up behind me, I had visions of a wild animal from the cliffs dragging me off to its den to eat me, so I'm glad it was you."

"What makes you think you're safer with me?"

A laugh escaped her. "Well, it is true that you aren't looking so Clark Kent–like right now, not out here in the dark." Nope, he seemed much more like a superhero, all tall and dark and focused on her. It made it difficult to breathe, in fact. "I need to walk."

He gave her a single nod.

Apparently that meant he was coming along, because he kept easy pace with her. The back half of the pier was empty except for the occasional bench. There were no stars visible through the clouds, and, other than the pounding surf and gusts of wind, no interruptions. She slurped on her shake, then offered some to Jax.

He searched her gaze a moment, his own quiet and reflective. Then, instead of taking the cup, his hand enveloped her own as he leaned in to draw on the straw. Her fingers itched to run over his stubble to see if it would feel rough or silky. And then there were those sinfully long, dark eyelashes, practically resting on his cheekbones, wasted on a man. But her gaze locked in on the way the muscles of his jaw bunched as he sucked the shake. When his tongue released the straw, she actually felt an answering tug deep in her womb. She must have made a noise, because he sent her a curious glance.

"It's nothing." Well, nothing except she was all alone with a complete stranger on the far end of the dark, nearly deserted pier. No one to save her from herself.

"It's a different pace out here, isn't it?" he said quietly.

"From LA? A different world entirely." Her daily drive to work had been like riding the bumper cars at the fair. Funny thing was, she'd never really minded because *everything* in her life had been like a ride at the fair—fast and just a little out of control. Her commute, her job, her boyfriend...

Especially her boyfriend.

Alex had been all charm and sophistication on the outside. On the inside, though, he'd been a simmering Crock-Pot of negative emotions.

She drew a deep breath recalling her secret shame, that it had taken her so long to realize that she couldn't change him, that instead she'd slowly changed herself into someone she didn't recognize.

Standing up for herself when he'd started hitting her had been empowering. Unfortunately, he hadn't taken it well, and a couple of weeks ago, after *months* of trying to talk her into reconciling, he'd cornered her in her office at work. She'd taken care of herself, but it turned out that the brass frowned on anyone tossing hot coffee into the lap of their high-powered, expensive entertainment attorney.

Needless to say, Maddie no longer had her crazy daily drive to make.

Her mother had died that same week.

Maddie was working on being okay with all of it, but she hadn't gotten there yet. Maybe she'd schedule it into her Blackberry.

Jax was watching her, as if something didn't quite add up. She could have told him not to bother trying to figure her out. No one had managed yet, not even herself.

"You okay?"

"Working on it," she said and gave him a small smile.

He returned the smile and stepped a little closer to her, which is when she discovered several things. One, she still had to fight her automatic flight response and purposely hold her ground, not taking a step back. *Not all guys are capable of smiling, stepping close, and then hitting,* she reminded herself. But while her brain knew this, her heart still wasn't ready to buy it.

Two, and even more unsettling, he smelled good—sexy and alluring. Closing her eyes, she felt her body actually tingle, brought to a hyper-awareness that felt almost foreign as something zinged through her.

Desire. Bone-melting desire.

When she opened her eyes again, he was even closer. His eyes weren't the solid warm caramel she'd thought but had flecks of gold dancing in them, as well. She could have drowned in all that deliciousness.

Not a bad way to go, she figured—death by lust.

Taking the shake out of her hands, he put it on the railing. "Maddie," he said. Just that, just her name in a deep voice that promised things she no longer believed in. And suddenly the part of her brain that had dictated the whole giving-up-men thing went on a vacay somewhere on the other side of reality, probably sharing a suite with the same gray matter that thought she could make a go of the inn. So instead of taking a step back, she took one forward and met him halfway on wobbly legs.

And what happened next was the oddest thing of all.

Odd and scary and amazing.

A heavenly sigh drifted past her lips as his arms came around her, and then his mouth touched hers, warm and tasting like the chocolate shake and forgotten hopes and dreams, and then…

And then there were no more thoughts.

Chapter 4

♥

"Never sweat the small stuff.
And remember, it's all small stuff."
PHOEBE TRAEGER

Maddie's eyes had slayed Jax from the very start, but her mouth...Christ, her mouth. The kiss started out gentle, and he'd meant for it to stay that way, but then she pulled back just enough to stare up at him, all flushed and wide-eyed.

Lowering his head, he pressed his mouth to the hollow of her throat. Beneath his lips, he could feel her pulse racing, and he touched his tongue to the spot. At her gasp of pleasure, he made his slow way along her jaw, over warm, soft skin to her ear. When he finally lifted his face to hers, her eyes were huge, a sea of dazed heat as she clearly wondered exactly what he was up to.

No good. That's what he was up to.

Proving it, he kissed her again, her little whimper for more going straight through him. He heard her purse hit the pier at their feet, and then her arms wound around his neck and she was kissing him, an all-consuming, earthy, raw kiss, and he was a goner. He groaned into her mouth at the pleasure of her touch, at the rush of heat, at the anticipation that swam through him instead of good sense.

Again she tore free of his mouth and stared up at him, eyes feral, mouth wet, breathing wildly. He had no idea what she was looking for, but apparently she found it because she tugged him back down, her fingers digging into his biceps as if she couldn't get enough.

That made two of them.

He kissed his way down her throat, and she gave a low, sexy gasp when he got to the spot where her neck met her shoulder. Her eyes slid closed, and she shuddered with the intensity. "You taste good," he murmured.

"Like chocolate–vanilla swirl?"

He lifted his head as she opened her eyes, opaque with hunger and desire. "Like woman." Her hair was wild, a few curls clinging to her face and dancing in the wind, calling to him. Needing to touch her, he raised a hand to stroke her hair back, and she flinched, hard.

Shock had him going still, fingers hovering near her forehead, but she went even more still. Slowly he lowered his hand. "Maddie—"

With a quick, single shake of her head, she took a giant step back, her eyes shuttered from him. I have to go."

"Okay." His brain raced, trying to figure out what had just happened. She'd acted as if he'd meant to hit her, which was crazy—he wouldn't.

Ever.

But someone had.

That was clear. So was the heat that rushed to her

face, knowing her involuntary gesture had just given her away.

Feeling sick for whatever she'd been through, sicker still for reminding her of it if only for a second, he stepped back. "Maddie—"

Tightening her lips, she bent for her purse, then turned away, walking back toward the street. "I *really* need to go."

Letting out a long, careful breath, he gave her a head start. He was quite certain that she'd like him to vanish entirely, but he couldn't do that. There was nowhere to go but back up the pier. So he followed, doing his best to give her the space he figured she needed.

Maddie walked fast down the pier, not slowing until she came to the Ferris wheel. Too bad her life couldn't be as simple as going round and round...

"You okay?"

Turning, she faced Jax, who stayed about five feet from her, hands in his pockets. "I'm fine." A little white lie that didn't count because she *wanted* to be okay. "About that kiss. I shouldn't have—We can't—" She blew out a breath and went with honesty. "Obviously I'm not in a place to start anything up."

"I'm getting that. It's okay, Maddie. I've been there."

She doubted he'd ever let anyone take advantage of him or hurt him, but she didn't want to talk about it. He was giving her an out, which she was going to take. Turning, she started walking. Not surprisingly, he kept pace. "I'm going back to the inn," she said. "Alone." She glanced over at him, not knowing what to expect, but it wasn't the quiet intensity she found. And it certainly wasn't feeling her own heart skip a beat.

They passed the ice cream shop, and the guy who'd served her waved at Jax. "Hey, man. Hot chocolate tonight?"

"Sure. A large to go, Lance. Thanks." He paid, then exchanged the warm cup for Maddie's shake. "For your hands," he said and guided her off the pier and onto the main street in front of the Love Shack.

A cute blonde burst out of the bar, teetering a little on her heels, laughing with a pretty brunette. "...and he wanted to drive me home!" she exclaimed.

"Well, you said you wanted to get laid," the brunette said.

"Yes, but look at me! I'm a nine tonight, maybe even a ten. And nothing less than an eight takes *this* body home—" Catching sight of Jax, she threw her arms around him. "Hey, sexy! Haven't seen you around all week. You working hard, or hardly working?"

"A little of both," Jax said, steadying her.

"Join us for a nightcap," Blondie said, slipping her arms around his neck.

Maddie looked down at herself. Yeah, okay, so she was dressed as a four, tops, but she wasn't invisible.

A cab pulled into the lot, and Blondie smiled. "There's our ride. Jax?" she murmured throatily, tugging his hand. "You coming?"

He shook his head, and Blondie and Brunette sighed in joint disappointment, then slid into the cab and vanished into the night.

"You could have gone," Maddie said after a minute. "Wouldn't want to hold you back."

"From...?"

"A threesome."

He arched a brow. "Is that what you think I want?"

"Well, it does seem to be the top male fantasy."

"Maybe I'm content with my current company."

She felt herself soften in spite of herself and decided it was all the emotion of the day. The wind was kicking hard now, but Jax's jacket was protecting her, and she was content to just stand there. "Are you cold?" she asked, really hoping he wasn't.

"I'm good. Let me drive you to the inn." He gestured toward a red Jeep.

"What about your bike?"

"Both mine. But the Jeep'll keep you warm."

"I don't know."

He met her gaze evenly, his eyes dark and warm, quietly assessing. "It's a long walk."

"Yes," she agreed. "But taking a ride from a stranger would be even more stupid than kissing one."

"I can provide references if you'd like."

"From Blondie and Nine-Maybe-Ten?" she asked.

He burst out laughing, and the sound sent heat slashing through her. Sliding his hand to the small of her back, he walked her to the Jeep. "I think I can provide better than that for you." He opened the passenger door and waited while she hesitated. Gallant superhero, she wondered, or smooth bad boy who'd just managed to talk her into his lair?

Hard to tell.

She buckled herself in. The interior of the vehicle

was dark, and he wasn't giving any hints as to his thoughts while he put the Jeep into gear and headed out of the lot.

She stared out the windshield, thinking that so far, superhero and smooth bad boy seemed to be running neck and neck. Not that it mattered, not when deep down, she secretly wanted both.

Chapter 5

"Just when you think you've hit rock bottom,
someone will hand you a shovel."
PHOEBE TRAEGER

Jax pulled up to the resort, and they both eyed the dark buildings. "Problem with the electricity?" he asked, idling the Jeep.

She hoped not. "I don't know."

"Your sisters are here?"

"I don't know that, either."

Jax thrust the Jeep into gear again and drove around to the back of the inn. Maddie held on to the dash and gulped. "This isn't the part where the big bad wolf eats me, is it?"

He sent her a mischievous glance. "What is it with you and things eating you?"

A nervous laugh burst from her, and he let loose a smile that was just wicked enough to boost her pulse and scare her at the same time. "Tell you what," he said silkily. "If *I* ever get the chance to eat you, I promise you'll like it."

Her stomach quivered. Her body had other reactions, too, but she kept them to herself as he pulled up to the cottage, where the windows were lit.

"How did you know to come back here?"

"I spent time out here as a kid. Once, with Ford and Sawyer, I TP'd the entire place."

It didn't surprise her that he'd had a wild youth. She suspected he'd had a wild everything. "You did?"

"Yeah, and Sawyer's father beat the shit out of us when he found out, and then turned us over to your grandpa. Instead of handing out our second ass-kicking of the night, he made us clean up our handiwork and paint the entire inn. He was a good guy." He flicked his gaze to the cottage, and she followed his line of sight to where both Chloe and Tara stood inside, staring out the window.

"They don't look very happy," he noted.

"Yes, I tend to have that effect on people."

His callused hand slowly slid up her back. When she started because she was looking out the Jeep window and not expecting the touch, he very gently touched the back of her neck. Warmth engulfed her.

"I don't know," he murmured very quietly. "You did a decent number on me tonight." His thumb swept over her nape, urging her to look at him.

One of them leaned in, she wasn't sure who, but suddenly her hands were on his chest and his hands were sliding up her arms, pulling her in as close as she could get with the console between them. "My sisters—"

"Can't see inside the Jeep." He kissed her once, and then again—small, brushing kisses that weren't enough, not even close, but when she heard a soft moan and realized it was hers, she pulled back.

"Yeah," Jax said, studying her intently. "I like this look on you a lot better."

"What look?"

"Heat. Desire. Not fear."

It took her a second for the words to register. When they did, she turned to open the door to get out, but he gently pulled her back and kissed her again, deep and hot. Her eyes drifted shut as she gave herself over to it, to him, and what he made her feel. He was such a good kisser, and his taste, his touch, his scent, the heat off his body—it all combined together so that she couldn't talk herself out of having this moment. She *needed* this moment. She deserved this moment, and, giving herself permission to enjoy it, she slid her hands over every part of him that she could reach, absorbing the groan of approval that rumbled from his throat.

"Haven't made out in a car in a damn long time," he said when they broke apart, his voice low and gravelly.

"Me either." In fact, she wasn't sure she'd *ever* made out in a car. She looked around. "We steamed up the windows."

He slid a hand over her shoulder, up her throat, his thumb skimming her pulse point. "We steamed up a lot of things."

Yes. Her body was humming with it. She ran her gaze down his body, past his broad chest, the flat abs she wanted to lick, and the button fly of his Levi's, which were strained over an intriguingly large bulge. Her gaze flew to his, which was both scorching hot and just a tad bit amused.

"I have to go in." But she didn't move. Well, actually, she did. She moved to give his mouth better access to her throat, which he took full advantage of, his lips rubbing slowly back and forth over her skin. "B-before they . . . Oh, God," she whispered. "Before they come out here to investigate."

He had a hand at her waist, beneath his jacket and her sweatshirt, his fingers gliding over the bare skin of her belly, and she let out a shaking breath. "You're going to have to take your hands off me, or . . ."

He met her gaze, his eyes dark and heated. "Or?"

Or she was going to crawl over the console and straddle him. "You don't play fair."

"I don't. You should remember that."

Telling her body to behave, she extricated herself from both his hands and the Jeep. "Thanks for the ride."

And the kiss . . .

He opened his door. "I'll walk you in—"

"No, don't." She didn't want to explain this. She dashed out of the Jeep and made her way up the rickety porch, but the door opened before she'd reached it.

Chloe stood there, a small smile on her lips as she peered past Maddie at the Jeep. "Who's that?"

Maddie watched the brake lights of the Jeep as it vanished into the night. "Jax Cullen. And that's all I know," she said before Chloe could ask anything else.

Well, except that he had a voice that went down like smooth whiskey, a way of looking at her that tended to get her to say more than she should, and oh, yeah, he kissed like heaven on earth.

"I want a Jax," Chloe said.

"You didn't even see him."

"No, but I can see the look he put on your face plain enough. Nice jacket."

"I forgot to give it back." *Maddie, Maddie, Maddie,*

she told herself. *That's a big fat lie. You didn't forget. You wanted the excuse to see him again.*

"I drove through town three times," Chloe said. "I never found a Jax."

Maddie slid her a look. Perfect dark red shiny hair. Cute, sexy clothes. Tight, toned body. An arresting face with piercing green eyes that said Trouble with a capital T, and that she was worth it. "There's no way you have a hard time attracting men."

"It's not the attracting that's the problem. You ever try to have sex with a third wheel in the bed?"

"Um, no," Maddie admitted. "I've never—"

"I meant my asthma," Chloe said dryly. "But good to know how your mind works. My *asthma* is the third person in my bed. And it usually kicks ass."

"You mean you can't—"

"Not in mixed company, or I end up needing an ambulance for the ensuing asthma attack." She sighed. "I really miss co-partnered orgasms."

"Oh, my God, will you get over the no-orgasm thing?" Tara said, coming up behind them. "Some of us *never* get them."

"Never? But you're married."

"Okay, so never might be an exaggeration. The point is, there are more important things than sex."

"Name one," Chloe said.

Tara lifted a bottle of wine.

"A close second," Chloe admitted. They moved through the living room as the wind rattled at the living room windows. The shag carpet had once been some sort of blue but had faded to a dingy gray, looking like a dead lawn that hadn't been watered in two decades.

"The place needs Christmas decorations," Chloe decided. "And a tree."

Maddie plopped down on the faded blue quilted couch and a huge cloud of dust arose. Chloe joined her, immediately drawing the neck of her shirt over her mouth and nose to protect herself. "And possibly a fumigation."

Tara shook her head and pulled Chloe off the couch. "Kitchen. The dust in here will kill you, sugar."

Maddie followed her two sisters, musing on the odd dynamic between them. Tara clearly cared while pretending not to. Chloe soaked up that caring like a love-starved child, while also pretending not to. As for Maddie, she had no idea where she fit in, or even if she could.

A loose shutter slapped against the side of the house and made her jump. The lights flickered off and then, after a long hesitation, back on again.

The three of them grabbed each other's hands and eyed the kitchen. It looked like the one in the inn, minus the table and *many* square feet. They sat hip to hip on the Formica counter. Tara poured the wine, handing a glass to Maddie, then poured one for herself.

"Hello," Chloe said, holding out her hand for a glass. "What am I, chopped liver?"

"Too young," Tara said.

"I'm past legal by three years!"

"Do you need a bra to keep your boobs from falling?" Tara asked. "Do you need a pair of Spanx to keep the tire hidden?"

"Tire?"

"Yes, the tire, the spare tire around the middle that doesn't go away in spite of a rigorous workout regime."

Tara gestured to her stomach, which in Maddie's opinion looked damn fine. She'd like to have a "tire" like that.

And probably she could, if she gave up chips.

"Do you get hot flashes that keep you up at night? Then you're not old enough to drink."

Chloe rolled her eyes and snatched a glass for herself anyway. "You know, you have some serious anger issues. And resentment issues. And holier-than-thou issues."

Maddie braced for the yelling. "Listen—"

"*Excuse me?*" Tara tossed back her wine and poured another, topping off Maddie while she was at it as she whirled on Chloe. "Holier than thou?"

"If the shoe fits," Chloe said. "*Sugar.*"

"Never mind, Miss Perky Boobs. I'll talk to you when you're sober."

"And I'll talk to you when you're not a bitch."

"Yeah, well, that might be a while," Tara said.

Chloe shook her head. "And for the record, you're thirty-four, Tara, not seventy-two."

Maddie snatched the wine bottle, because it was going to be that kind of a night.

"And another thing," Chloe said, taking the bottle from Maddie. "Maddie's boobs are just as perky as mine."

Everyone looked at Maddie's breasts. They were full C's, and the only reason they were anywhere even close to *perky* was thanks to her clearance sale push-up bra. She blew out a breath and looked at her empty wineglass. "I should stop now. Beer and wine don't mix well."

Tara looked at her empty glass, then over at the garbage can, confused. "How did I miss the beer?"

"She drank with Hot Guy," Chloe said.

"Hey." Maddie tried to find the indignation but had

some trouble working around the alcohol. "He has a name."

"What is it?" Tara wanted to know.

"It's a really, really, really good name."

"Can you even remember it?" Tara asked wryly. "Or did he suck your memory out along with your tongue?"

No, but he'd sure had a nice tongue. "His name's Jax. Jax Cullen."

Tara choked on her wine.

"Know him?" Maddie asked.

Tara set her glass aside and tipped the bottle to her mouth, taking a long time to answer. "How would I know him?" She dabbed delicately at the corners of her mouth. "And what do you see in this guy anyway?"

Chloe held up her hands about ten inches apart.

At that, it was Maddie's turn to choke. "I didn't sleep with him! I gave up men," she added much more weakly. "And anyway, penises that size don't really exist."

"Then why did you come in grinning?"

Maddie sighed. "Has anyone ever told you that you're a tattletale?"

"Always has been," Tara said. "Once when I was fifteen and sneaking out the back door, Chloe told Mom on me. I was grounded for the rest of the summer."

Chloe grinned. "Good times."

Maddie had lived with Phoebe only until she'd gotten pregnant with Chloe. After that, Maddie's father had taken custody. Maddie had visited during vacations or whenever her father couldn't have her with him at work, but it hadn't been often. As a result, she had only sparse memories of her sisters. But Tara had spent most summers with Phoebe and Chloe.

"Where were we that summer?" Chloe asked Tara. "Northern California somewhere, right? In that trailer Mom rented on some river with friends?"

Tara nodded. "Sounds about right."

"You wouldn't take me with you wherever you were sneaking off to. That's why I told on you."

"You were a baby!"

"I was five. And I wanted to be fifteen like you."

And Maddie wanted memories with them.

Tara sighed and leaned back. "I completely wasted fifteen. Youth is wasted on the young."

Chloe snorted.

"I'm not kidding!" Tara said. "If I was fifteen again, I'd definitely know what to do with it now."

"Really," Chloe said with disbelief heavy in her voice.

"*Really.*"

Outside, the wind battered the windows, the storm in full swing. They all paused and glanced uneasily out into the dark night. "I hated being fifteen," Maddie said quietly, feeling the wine. "The doubts, the lack of confidence, the despair." And damn if much had changed. She sighed and held out her glass for more wine. Tara obligingly topped her off again.

"If you're having what-ifs," Chloe said, "you're *still* wasting life."

"Not me." Maddie shook her head. "I'm not wasting anything, not ever again. I'm on a new life's lease. I'm starting over." She emphasized this with a wild swing of her glass. Wine splashed out over her hand, and she licked it off. "No more letting anyone speak for me, roll over me, step on me, slap me..."

The shattering silence that followed this statement sobered her up a little. "See, this," she said. "This is why I shouldn't drink." Ignoring the startled look exchanged between her sisters, she held out her glass. She definitely needed a refill.

But Tara gently took it away. "Somebody hit you?" she asked softly.

"Slapped." Big difference. A slap was humiliating and hurtful, but it wasn't like he'd punched her. Or caused her real harm. Well, except for that last time, when the corner of a cabinet had broken her fall, requiring stitches just outside of her eye. But hey, she was single now. All was good. Or as good as it could be.

"Maddie—"

"It's over and done." She dropped her head and studied her shoes. Sneakers, scuffed and battered. That had to be symbolic somehow, she thought unhappily.

Chloe was wearing cute ankle boots, not a scratch on them.

Tara was wearing stylish heels, so shiny they could have been used as a mirror.

"I need new shoes," she said out loud.

Chloe reached out and squeezed her hand. "New shoes rock," she whispered, sounding like her throat was too tight.

Maddie squeezed her fingers back while her wine-soaked thoughts rambled in her head, not quite readily available for download. "Oh! I forgot to show you guys something." She pulled the recipe box from her bag and told them about Lucille. She flipped through for a random card. "Bad decisions make good stories," she read.

"Lord," Tara said.

"Not 'bless her heart'?" Chloe asked, grinning until a gust of wind hit so hard that the entire house shuddered.

This was followed by a thundering *BOOM*. The ground shook, the lights flickered, and all three of them jumped.

"Holy shit." Chloe scooted over on the counter until she was right up against Tara, nearly in her lap.

Maddie hopped down and opened the back door, flicking on a flashlight that didn't do much for cutting into the utter blackness of the night.

"Where did that flashlight come from?" Chloe asked.

"My purse."

Chloe looked at Tara. "She carries a flashlight in her purse."

"For emergencies," Maddie said, trying to see into the yard.

"You have any chocolate?" Chloe asked hopefully. "For emergencies?"

"Of course. Side pocket, next to the fork."

"You're good," Tara murmured, holding out her hand for some.

"Are you of age?" Chloe asked snidely.

Tara growled, and Chloe hastily handed her a piece.

"You are a lifesaver," Tara said to Maddie, who smiled. She'd learned at work to be prepared for anything and everything. She'd never given it a second thought, but sensing her sisters' relief, and maybe just a little bit of admiration, as well, felt good.

Even if they were chomping on her secret chocolate stash.

But she'd always wanted a true family, wanted to be counted on. Oh, she loved her dad, and he loved her, but she had always yearned for more.

That her family could be here after all this time, right here in front of her, gave her a warm fuzzy in spite of the frigid, windy night, slapping her in the face as she started outside. Sweeping her flashlight from right to left, Maddie stopped when she came to the newly fallen tree bisecting the yard. "We lost a tree," she called back to her sisters. "A big one."

"Come back before one of them falls on your head," Tara called out.

Maddie kept going until she stood where the very top of the fallen pine tree had landed, trapping a scrawny baby pine tree beneath it. And damn if the sight didn't break her heart. It took her a moment to free it, and then she hoisted the tree into her arms, turning back to the porch, where both her sisters still stood.

"Found us a Christmas tree," she said.

Chapter 6

*"Obeying the rules might be smart,
but it's not nearly as much fun."*
PHOEBE TRAEGER

They decorated the tree with what they had on hand, which turned out to be some kitchen items and a string of chili pepper lights left over from what Chloe claimed to remember as a wild block party in the nineties.

Tara found a stack of twenty-year-old *National Enquirers.* "Phoebe's gospel," she said with a fond smile, holding up one with Mel Gibson on the cover. She cut out the picture and hung it on a branch. "What?" she said when Chloe and Maddie just stared at her. "I'd do him."

"You do realize he no longer looks like that, right?" Chloe asked.

"Hey, *my* fantasy."

They spent the next half hour drinking another bottle of wine and cutting out pictures of all the guys they'd "do." Turned out there were quite a few. Maddie claimed Luke Perry and Jason Priestley—pre all their horrible movie-of-the-week specials. Chloe went for the boy bands. All of them.

"It can't be just a hottie tree," Tara decided.

Chloe nodded and hung a serving spoon, then cocked her head to study it critically, moving it over an inch like she was creating the *Mona Lisa.* "I once dated a guy who had a face like this serving spoon. He was ugly as hell, but man, *oh, man,* could he kiss. He gave me a nightly asthma attack for the entire week we dated." She sighed dreamily. "Ugly men make good lovers."

"Logan's gorgeous *and* good in bed," Tara said. "What does that mean?"

"Um, that you're lucky to be married to him?" Chloe asked.

"No." Tara shook her head with careful exaggeration. "Gorgeous men are flawed. Seriously flawed."

"Not all of them," Chloe said.

"*All of them.*"

Maddie found a doily. "My ex is good-looking. And good in bed. And..." The shame of it reached up and choked her as she carefully folded the doily so it looked like a star. "And, as it turns out, violent." She nodded to herself and set the "star" on top of the tree. Yep. Perfect. Especially if she scrunched up her eyes. "Which I guess makes him pretty damn flawed."

There was a long beat of loaded silence. When she managed to turn to her sisters, both were looking at her with shock and rage and regret in their eyes.

"Is that who hit you?" Tara finally asked quietly. "Your ex?"

Maddie nodded, and Chloe let out a breath. "You hit him back, right?"

"And then called the police," Tara said. "You called the police on him, didn't you, sugar? Put him behind bars so he could be some big bubba's bitch?"

No, she hadn't. And it was hard to explain, even to herself. But it'd happened slow, the gradual teardown of her self-esteem until she'd no longer felt like Maddie Moore. She'd felt awkward and stupid and ugly.

Alex had done that.

No, scratch that. She'd let Alex do that to her, one careful, devastatingly cruel comment at a time before she'd walked out on him.

Without her confidence, without her savings, without anything.

It sounded so pathetic now, which she hated. "I dumped his coffee on his family jewels," she said. "Ruined his new Hugo Boss suit, which was pretty satisfying, since he looked like he'd peed his pants." Too bad her bosses hadn't appreciated her show of feminism and she'd gotten fired.

Details. But for the first time, she shared them over a third bottle of wine, while they cleaned and decorated the cottage into the night.

And much later, lying under the tree together, the three of them stared up at the chili pepper lights and grinned like idiots.

Or that might have just been Maddie.

She couldn't help it. The top of her head was bumping up against the scrawny trunk of the tree, and she was breathing in the scent of pine. Above her, she could see a set of barbecue tongs dangling off the branches next to a picture of Jon Bon Jovi, a whisk, a Tupperware lid, and a near-naked shot of a very young Johnny Depp.

"I've never had a more beautiful tree," she whispered reverently.

"That's because you're drunk, sugar. Drunk as a skunk."

Chloe sighed dreamily. "I haven't had a tree in years. Not since I left Mom's when I was sixteen."

Maddie sighed, too. They were as much strangers to each other as she was with Jax, really, and yet since arriving in Lucky Harbor, she'd never felt less alone. "I know you guys are out of here as soon as possible, but—"

"Maddie, darlin'," Tara said softly. "No buts."

"Just hear me out, okay? What if we refinanced? We could hire someone to renovate, and we could run the inn the way it should be run. And we have a part-time employee already in Lucille! Sure, she's ancient, but Mom trusted her."

"Mom trusted everyone."

"My point is, we could probably even make decent money if we tried."

"Do you have any idea what it takes to refinance these days?" Tara asked, ever the voice of reason. "We'd need a miracle."

"Then we try to find out who Phoebe left all her money to in that trust. Obviously, it's someone she cared about, which means this person cares about her in return. Maybe they'd be interested in investing in the inn. We could—"

"No," Tara said harshly, and when both Maddie and Chloe stared at her, she closed her eyes. "Think about this logically, okay? Running an inn is a lot of work." She waved her arms and nearly knocked the tree over. "And the marina, good Lord. Do either of you even know the first thing about boats or the ocean or—" She stopped because a spoon had fallen from a branch and hit her in the nose. "*Ouch.*"

"Mom wanted this." Maddie reached up and removed a fork from the branches before it fell, too, and maybe poked out an eye. "She wanted this for us."

Tara and Chloe lay there, silent. Silent and contemplative. Or so Maddie hoped. Exhausted, she let her eyes close, her thoughts drifting. She wanted this to work. She wanted it bad. So maybe her mother hadn't tried to get close to her. Maybe her sisters hadn't, either, and maybe, possibly, she'd even *allowed* her mother to rebuff her because it'd been easier. But now, right now when she'd needed an escape, one had appeared. "It's meant to be," she whispered, believing it.

For a long beat, no one said anything.

"My life is crazy," Chloe said quietly. "And I like crazy. It doesn't lend itself to responsibilities, and I'm sorry, Maddie, so very sorry, but this is a pretty big responsibility."

"And my life is in Dallas," Tara said. "I'm not a small-town girl, never have been."

"I get that," Maddie said. "But maybe we can put it all into motion, and I'll run the place. Maybe I'll send you both big fat checks every month. Maybe by this time next year, we'll be celebrating."

"That's a lot of maybe-ing."

"It could happen," Maddie insisted. "With a little faith."

"And a lot of credit card debt."

Sitting up again, brushing pine needles out of her hair, Maddie went to the kitchen and came back with a

Lucky Harbor phonebook. "I saw a bank right next to the Love Shack in town. I'll go there tomorrow and see about refinancing."

"What do they sell at this love shack?" Chloe wanted to know. "Is it a sex shop?"

"It's a bar."

"Even better," Chloe said.

"I'm leaving here by the end of the week," Tara warned. "Sooner, if I can manage it, with or without refinancing."

"You really get hives in a place like this, huh?" Chloe asked.

"Sugar, you have *no* idea."

Maddie had put her finger on a list of general contractors. "Two of them say they specialize in renovations." She pulled out her Blackberry.

"Maddie," Tara said.

"Just calling, that's all." She dialed the first.

"Isn't it the middle of the night?" Chloe asked, looking out the window.

"Oh, yeah..." Still buzzed, Maddie grinned. "I'll leave a message." Except the number she'd dialed had been disconnected or was out of service. She punched in the numbers for the second listing, a JC Builders. "Hey," she said to her sisters. "I got an answering machine, and it says they have a master carpenter on staff. A *master!*"

"She's drunk dialing contractors," Chloe said to Tara. "Someone should stop her."

"Shh." Maddie closed her eyes as she listened to a deep, masculine voice instructing her to leave a message. "Hi," she said at the beep. "Potential new client here, looking for a master—er, renovation expert. We're at

Lucky Harbor Resort, at the end of Lucky Harbor Road, you can't miss us. Oh, and we're in desperate need of mastering. You're probably busy, seeing as you're the only master in town, but we're short on time. Like *really* short on time. In fact, we're sort of desperate—" She broke off and covered the mouthpiece because Tara was in her face, waving wildly. "*What?*"

"You said *desperate* twice. You can't tell him that—he'll raise his price! And what the hell is your fixation on being mastered?"

Maddie rolled her eyes—which made her dizzy—and uncovered the mouthpiece. "Okay, forget the desperate thing. We're not desperate. Hell, we could do the work ourselves, if we wanted. So come or don't come, no worries." She paused, turned her back on her sisters, and lowered her voice to speak extra softly. "*But please come first thing in the morning!*" And then she quickly ended the conversation and smiled innocently at Tara.

"Stealth," Chloe said with a thumbs-up. "Real stealth."

As always, Jax got up with the sun. Apparently, some habits were hard to break. Once upon a time, he'd have hit the gym and downed a Starbucks while racing his Porsche on the highway to take his turn on the hamster wheel with the rest of the city. As a very expensive defense attorney for a huge, cutthroat law firm in Seattle, where winning cases at all costs had been the bottom line, he'd gone by his given name, Jackson Cullen III.

It'd been comfortable enough, given that he'd been raised by a man with the same philosophy as his firm. Jax had spent his days doing his thing in court, schmoozing with the other partners in the law firm, and in general sucking the very soul from himself and others. And then repeating the entire thing all over again the next day.

He no longer owned the snooty condo, fancy Porsche, or even a single suit, for that matter, and he was five long years out of the practice of schmoozing anyone.

But he was still working on recovering his soul.

Just being back in Lucky Harbor helped. It was a slower, simpler lifestyle, one he'd chosen purposely. He'd gone back to his first love, rebuilding and restoration, while trying to help people instead of acquit them.

Until yesterday anyway, when for the first time in far too long, he'd actually felt something real. He'd felt it with shocking depth for a curly-haired, endearingly adorable klutz, a woman with unconscious warmth and an innate sexiness, and a set of sweet, haunted eyes.

Devastating combo.

He pulled on his running gear and nudged Izzy, his two-year-old mutt. She was part brown lab, part possum, and proved her heritage by cracking open a single eye with a look that said *Dude, chill.*

"You're coming," he said.

She closed her eye.

"Come on, you're getting a pudge."

She farted.

He shook his head, then dumped her out of her dog bed, no easy feat since she weighed seventy-five pounds.

They ran their usual three miles along the beach. Well, Jax ran. Izzy sauntered a hundred yards or so, then slowed, dragging her feet in the sand until she found a pelican to pester. Then, apparently exhausted from that effort, she plopped down and refused to go another step until Jax roused her on his return.

He entered his house through the back door and stepped into his office. Surprised to see a blinking light on his machine at seven in the morning, he hit play, then realized it was a call from last night. He stood still in shocked surprise at Maddie's soft voice.

"Hi," she said. "Potential new client here, looking for a master."

The loud knocking startled Maddie out of a dead sleep. Discombobulated, she blinked, and then blinked again, but all she could see was a sea of green and a flashing red that had her groaning and lifting her hands to hold her pounding head.

Taking stock, she realized that she was flat on her back beneath the tree, staring up at a string of obnoxious chili pepper lights.

Or maybe that was the hangover that was so obnoxious.

With another groan, she managed to sit up and nearly took out an eye with one of the low, straggly tree branches. Slapping a hand over it, she looked down at herself. Huh. She was completely tangled in red yarn. And she was pretty sure she had sap in her hair.

Even more odd, the cottage was spotless. Maddie had vague recollections of a tipsy Tara moving through the place with a broom in one hand and a rag in the other, bossing Maddie to assist as she went.

Which didn't explain the yarn. But she also remembered going through the cottage's bedroom, where they'd found some of their mother's things. There'd been a basket full of loose pictures, an empty scrapbook that Phoebe had clearly meant to use but never had, and another book, as well—*Knitting for Dummies*. Maddie had stared at the book and at the half-knitted scarf beneath it and felt her heart clench at the long-ago memory—she and her mom, sitting together, trying to learn to knit.

Trying being the operative word.

Phoebe had laughed at their pathetic efforts, saying how the fun wasn't in the final product, but in the journey. At the time, it'd frustrated Maddie.

Not last night. Last night, it'd been a precious memory, one of far too few, and she'd laid claim to the book, the knitting needles, and the half-finished scarf from all those years ago. While Chloe had sorted through the pictures and Tara had cleaned, Maddie had re-taught herself how to knit.

Loosely speaking.

Her sisters were still prone under the tree, out cold. Chloe was snoring. Tara was...*smiling?* Not a sight Maddie had seen often. Hell, none of them were exactly free with their smiles, she'd noticed. She shook her head, then groaned at the movement.

Note to self—*never drink again.*

At some point, they'd clearly decided pj's were a good thing. Maddie was wearing her favorite flannel Sponge-Bob drawstring pants and a Hanes beefy tee with the words BITE ME across the chest. Chloe's pj's had come from Victoria's Secret, but with her body, she could have worn a potato sack and looked good. Across her teddy the words JINGLE MY BELLS were delicately embroidered. Tara was wearing men's boxers, a cami, a silk bathrobe, and a pair of knee-high socks.

Maddie nudged Chloe's foot.

"No more, Juan," Chloe whispered. "My inhaler's too low."

The knock on the front door came again, and in unison Chloe and Tara sat straight up, conked their heads together, and moaned.

Maddie staggered toward the door, taking a second to stare in shock at their tree. Last night, it had been the most gorgeous tree she'd ever seen. This morning, it stood barely three feet tall and looked like... "A Charlie Brown Christmas tree," she whispered. She stepped over her sisters' legs, caught sight of herself in the small mirror over the little table in the foyer, and just about screamed.

Her hair had rioted. The little mascara she'd had on her lashes was now outlining her eyes, and she had a crease down one cheek from whatever she'd used as a pillow, which she suspected had been the yarn she was still wrapped in. "Never again," she told her pathetic reflection and then pointed at it for emphasis.

Her reflection stuck her tongue out.

With a sigh, she opened the front door, then stood there in a stupor. Standing on the porch, wearing faded Levi's, a black sweater over a black T-shirt, mirrored sunglasses, and a crooked smile was Jax Cullen.

Chapter 7

*"Experience is something you get…
after you need it."*
PHOEBE TRAEGER

Maddie stared up at Jax, who was not hung over and didn't have a crease on his face. He looked big, and bad, and so sexy it should be a crime, and she reacted without thinking.

She shut the door in his face.

Tara gasped.

Chloe laughed.

And Maddie covered her face. "Quick, somebody shoot me."

"Honey." Tara's hand settled on her shoulder. "Maybe you don't know this being from LA and all, but shutting the door on someone's nose is considered rude in almost all fifty states."

"You don't understand. It's him. *Jax.*" And maybe it was the fact that her brain was on low battery, but just looking at him made her hot and bothered. Her! The woman who'd decreed that the entire male race was scum. "What do I do?"

"Well, for starters," Chloe said, "You stop slamming door on guys who look like *that*."

"He has superpowers," Maddie said, nibbling on her thumbnail.

"Yeah?" Clearly fascinated, Chloe took another peek. "Like being hot as hell?"

Tara lightly smacked Maddie's hand from her mouth. "What does he want?"

"I'm going to guess SpongeBob Pants here," Chloe murmured, still looking at him.

Maddie pushed her away from the window so she could take her own look. "Oh, my God," she whispered.

On the porch, Jax turned his head and gave her a slow, mischievous wink, making her jump back as if he'd bitten her. "*Oh, my God.*"

"She's starting to repeat herself," Chloe said to Tara, who took her turn at the window.

"Oh, sugar." Tara took her time looking him over. "You're not ready for the likes of him."

"I hate to agree with her on anything," Chloe said to Maddie. "But she might be right on this one."

Drawing in a sharp breath, Maddie put her hand on the door handle. With a sister crowding her on either side—she wasn't sure whether it was for moral support or to make sure she didn't jump his bones—she opened the door.

She had to give Jax credit. Certainly, the three of them looked like wild, grossly unpredictable creatures from Planet Estrogen. But much as he had at the bar in the face of that pissed-off Smarmy Suit, he stood his ground. He even smiled.

"Hey," Maddie said, taking a step forward to give them some privacy, but she tripped over the yarn. It took her a few seconds and most of her dignity before she fought her legs free.

He pulled off his sunglasses to watch her, revealing those melted caramel eyes, which seemed to be both amused and heated. Amused, no doubt, because of the little yarn incident, not to mention the bedhead and SpongeBob pj's. As for why his eyes were also heated, she could guess—he was thinking of last night.

Which made two of them, because the kisses—oh, good Lord, the kisses—were suddenly all her brain would upload. The memory of those delicious, hot, deep, amazing kisses had kept her up most of the night. And then there'd been how his hands had felt all over her. Just remembering had something tingling behind her belly button and heading south.

"You okay?" he asked.

Sure. She was peachy. Or she would be soon as she cleared a few things up. Because as much as just looking at him put a big, goofy smile on her face, she had to be honest with him. Or at least as honest as she could. "About last night. I'm sorry if I gave you the wrong impression, but I'm really not in a good place for this right now."

He didn't say anything to this, and the silence was worse than the hangover.

"It's nothing personal, of course. But I can't, I just can't go there." Why wasn't he saying anything? "I'm… not interested." Okay, so that was liar, liar, pants on fire, but his silence was unnerving. "I mean, I realize that I probably didn't *seem* uninterested last night, but that was extenuating circumstances." Those being that he was far too good-looking and he'd tasted like chocolate—lethal combination.

Fighting a smile, he reached out and started unwinding some of the yarn still around her shoulder. His fingers brushed her collarbone and sent yippee-kayee messages to her nipples.

She snatched the yarn from him. "And as for the pier and then needing a ride, well, I'm not usually so helpless. In fact, you should probably know..." She drew a deep breath. "I've given up men."

At that, he arched a brow.

Be strong. Be confident. Be...Neytiri from Avatar. *Okay, so Neytiri was a mythical creature, not to mention animated, but still. She was strong and confident, and that's all that matters at the moment.* "It's true. At first, I was just going to give up attorneys, but that seemed immature—and far too exclusive, so I'm playing it safe and giving up all the penis-carrying humans." Because that was so much *more* mature.

Tara peeked out from behind the door with an apologetic wince in Jax's direction. "It's possible she's still tipsy," she explained.

"I'm not still tipsy!" She didn't think so, anyway. "So I'm sorry if you drove all the way out here looking for a repeat of last night, but it's not going to happen. I'm not interested." She held her breath in case karma was listening, ready to flatten her with a bolt of lightning for lying.

Nothing. Well, nothing but more silence, and this time she bit her tongue rather than try to fill it with more embarrassing chatter.

"Okay," Jax finally said with a single nod. "That's all ... very interesting. But I'm not here for a 'repeat.'"

A very bad feeling began to bounce around in her gut. "You're not?"

"No. You called and asked me to come here."

Maddie took a second, deeper look at him and his attire: the black sweater that upon closer inspection was really a North Face hoodie and had JC Builders embroidered on his pec. His jeans were baggy but still emphasized his long, hard body in a way that suggested they were old friends. He wore work boots, and, given the battered, beloved look to them, they were not for show. But most telling was the measuring tape sticking out of a pocket and the clipboard he held resting against his thigh.

In the yard behind him was his Jeep with a big, brown dog riding shotgun.

"You're the contractor," she said weakly.

"Uh-huh." He was definitely amused now. "Unless you're no longer interested in my ... *mastery.*"

Oh, God.

"After all," he said. "I am a penis-carrying human."

Chloe laughed.

Tara grimaced and shut the door on his face, but she did hold up a finger first and say, "Just a moment, sugar." Once a steel magnolia, always a steel magnolia.

"Jeez," Chloe said in disgust. "How is it the so-called baby of this family is the only one who knows *not* to shut the door on the unspeakable hottie? I mean that's just sacrilegious."

Maddie groaned. "I called him. Omigod. *I* called *him.* I'm such an idiot."

"Aw, honey." Chloe stroked a hand down Maddie's out-of-control hair, her fingers getting caught in the tangles and tree sap. "You're not an idiot. Not exactly."

"It's the kissing! It's the stupid kissing! It's like he kissed all the vital brain cells right out of my head!"

"A good kiss is a signature," Chloe said, and when both sisters looked at her, she shrugged. "Hey, don't blame me, it was on one of Mom's cards."

Maddie shook her head. "What do I do?"

"You stick with your resolve. You're giving up men," Tara reminded her. "Next problem. We're selling this property. We need to tell him so before we waste any more of his time."

Maddie held her breath—and her head. Damn, she really needed Advil. "Last night, we said we'd give this place a shot."

"That was three bottles of wine talking," Tara said.

Suddenly Maddie's heart pounded in tune with her head. "Give me a month. Until Christmas," she said. Begged. "We fix the place up a little, and if you still don't want to make it work, we'll sell. And with the improvements, we'll get a better price. You'll have lost nothing."

Chloe looked at Tara.

Tara sighed.

"You know I'm right," Maddie said, sensing their capitulation. This was it. She had to convince them. She wanted, *needed,* this month. "We'll be better off for it, I promise."

"But what will we use for money for the renovations?" Chloe asked. "All I have is a Visa card, and there's not much left on it after last month's trip to Belize."

"I have an unused MasterCard," Tara said slowly.

"Me, too." It was Maddie's entire emergency contingency plan, since Alex had so unsuccessfully "invested" her small nest egg. "It's a start, and it shouldn't take us more than a few weeks to refinance. And I'm still determined to find out about that trust and talk to—"

"Let the trust go," Tara said firmly. "Mom went to great lengths and expense to separate it and protect it, and it's none of our business. Besides, that's not our real problem."

"What's the real problem?" Maddie asked.

"That I don't want to be here," Tara replied.

"You don't have to be," Maddie said. "We put this into motion, and I'll stay. You two can go, and I'll handle it."

"Until Christmas," Tara said. "And then we'll sell."

Not a mouse...Fake the strength. "If that's how the majority votes," Maddie said carefully, forcing herself not to back off.

"And you're okay doing this by yourself," Chloe clarified. "Really?"

"Yes." Maddie looked at the closed door and drew a deep breath. "Well, maybe not *all* by myself."

"A partner will definitely help," Chloe said, nodding. "And I have a feeling that man knows how to *partner.*"

Maddie remembered how it'd felt to be in his arms and got a hot flash. No question, he knew how to *partner.* She'd be willing to bet her life on it. Not that it mattered.

"Sugar, how do you plan to get his help when you just rudely told him you weren't interested?"

Oh, yeah. That. "I'm going to wing it." With a steady breath, she pulled open the door while simultaneously attempting to tame her hair—a losing battle.

Jax had moved along on the porch and was hunkered

down, arms braced on his thighs, studying the dry-rot on a post. When she stepped out, he straightened to his full height and looked her over. "Everything okay?"

"Sure. We were just, um, discussing what we're going to have for breakfast."

"Really."

"Yeah. You know, pancakes or Cap'n Crunch."

"Cap'n Crunch. Always Cap'n Crunch. And you're going to have to work on your lying." Leaning in, he tweaked a curl. "Thin door."

And here she'd been worried that she wasn't going to make enough of a fool of herself in front of him today. She glanced over her shoulder for assistance, but her sisters had vanished. *Traitors.* "Okay, listen. I'm sorry."

"For?"

"The drunken phone call. Shutting the door in your face twice this morning alone. The whole spiel you just heard—pick one."

Jax looked out into the bright, sunny, icy-cold morning, and then back into her eyes. "And about the kiss. Are you sorry about that, too?"

She'd thought that she would be. After all, she'd been so easily drawn into Alex's ready charm, and look at what a nightmare that had turned out to be.

They both knew the truth. If she'd felt any more "interested," she would have spontaneously combusted.

At her silence, he stepped in a little closer. Close enough that her body tensed with the need to step back, but then his scent came to her, his soap or deodorant or whatever that delicious male scent was, and her nostrils twitched for more. "I don't want to talk about it," she whispered.

"You have a lot of things you don't want to talk about."

Last night, he'd been kind enough not to ask questions. She hoped that was still the case. "I know." She braced for the inquisition, but he didn't go there. He kept it light.

And sexy. God, so sexy.

"I understand," he said, nodding. "All that kissing was...awkward. Messy. Completely off."

It'd been deep and erotic and sensual, and even now, just thinking about how his mouth had felt on hers sent butterflies spiraling low in her belly.

No.

No, she wasn't sorry about the kiss.

Clearly reading her mind, his mouth slowly curved. "So no interest, and certainly no chemistry," he murmured, dipping his head to take in the fact that her misbehaving nipples were pressing up against the words BITE ME on her T-shirt.

"R-right," she managed. "No chemistry whatsoever." But then she took a step into him instead of away, and look at that, suddenly his mouth was right there, and her hands were fisting in his fleece hoodie.

How had that happened?

His eyes were heavy lidded now and locked on her mouth. Beneath her hands, he was warm and hard with strength, and she tightened her grip. To keep him at arm's length, she told herself. "You don't want chemistry with me," she said. "I have...faults."

"Like you can't hold your liquor?"

"Ha. And no. I mean..." She searched for something suitably off-putting. "I'm twenty-nine, and I keep a flashlight on me, just in case I need to hold the closet monsters at bay. I can't let foods touch on my plate, everything has to be in its own quadrant. And my go-to movie is *The Sound of Music*. I can sing every song." There. Didn't get more embarrassing than that. But just in case, she added one more. "I can also burp the alphabet. I won an award for it in college, and sometimes when I'm alone, I practice in the mirror."

"The whole alphabet?"

"Yeah, so it's for the best that we don't...you know."

"You're right. That *Sound of Music* thing is totally a dealbreaker. Thankfully, we have no chemistry at all." He was teasing her, but when she met his gaze, he wasn't smiling. Nope. His eyes were lit with something else entirely, and it wasn't humor.

And she knew something else, too. She hadn't scared him off. Not even a little.

Chapter 8

*"The easy road is always under construction,
so have an alternate route planned."*
PHOEBE TRAEGER

Maddie rushed through a shower with water that wouldn't
go past lukewarm, and worse, it looked suspiciously rusty.
She'd be worried except she'd gotten a tetanus shot just
last year when she'd stepped on a nail at a movie set in
Burbank. And anyway, it was hard to find room for worry
when her body was humming and pulsing.

And he hadn't even kissed her again.

Dammit, how dare he bring her body parts back to life
with nothing more than his presence after she'd decided
to go off men entirely?

It was rude, it was thoughtless, it was...

Not his fault.

Getting out of the shower, she stood in the bathroom
and rummaged through her duffel bag. She'd packed only
the essentials, leaving the rest in storage with her dad in
Los Angeles.

She pulled on a pair of Levi's and struggled with the top button. Damn chips. She pulled on a tank top, then added a big bulky sweater, not letting herself hear a certain ex's voice whispering in her ear that she should hit the gym. Instead, she didn't look at herself too closely in the mirror. Ignorance was bliss, right? Maybe she ought to put *that* on a 3x5 card and add it to the box.

As always, her hair had a mind of its own. Battling with the blow-dryer helped only marginally. She took a couple of swipes with the mascara wand and declared herself good to go.

Jax had offered to wait for her to take a quick shower and dress so that she could walk him around the property. She found him in the small kitchen, which was made even smaller by his sheer size. He was drinking something out of a mug and talking to Tara, but when she walked into the room they both fell into a silence of the shhh-here-she-comes variety. "What?" she said, looking down at herself. Nope, she hadn't forgotten her clothes.

"It's nothing, sugar." Tara handed her a steaming mug. "It's only instant from the store, and trust me, it's no Starbucks." She shot Jax a look like this was his fault. "I picked it up last night when I bought the cleaning supplies."

"It's good enough for me," Jax said. "Thanks."

Maddie told herself not to stare at him, that it was like staring directly into the sun, but she'd never been good at following advice. Plus she found she couldn't stop looking at his mouth. It was a good mouth and made her think about things she had no business thinking about. "So about why we called you."

A faint smile hinted around the corners of his mouth. "You needed a master."

"Well, your ad did say you are an expert." Look at that, she sounded cool, even smartass-like. She'd always wanted to be a smartass. *Nicely done, keep it up. Do not let him see you sweat.*

And whatever you do, don't look at his mouth.

Or at the way his jeans fit, all faded and lovingly cupping his...cuppable parts. "Does your expertise include dusty hundred-year-old inns decorated in early rooster and duck?"

"Ducks and roosters are no problem. The cows are new to me. And I specialize in fixing things up and restoring them to their former glory."

She wondered if that talent extended to humans, maybe even humans who never really had a former glory. "So how much can we get done between now and Christmas?"

"And think cheap," Tara cut in to say. "Aesthetic value only, for resale purposes."

"The inn didn't come with an operating account, unfortunately," Maddie explained. "Just a big fat mortgage payment, so money's a problem."

Jax's eyes flicked to Tara, then back to Maddie, and once again she wondered what she was missing.

"So you're going to sell?" he asked.

"Hopefully," Tara said.

"Hopefully not," Maddie said.

Jax nodded as if this made perfect sense. "I'll walk the property and work up a bid."

"And I'm off to shower." Tara turned back at the door. "Sugar, tell me you left me some hot water so I'm not forced to head to Alpine and bathe outside like a cretin."

"Alpine?" Maddie asked. "What's that?"

"There's a natural hot springs about three miles up the road," Jax said. "The locals think of it as their own personal hot tub."

Maddie looked at Tara. "How do you know about the hot springs?"

"Doesn't everyone?"

"No," she said, but Tara was gone. Alone with Jax, she pointed to his clipboard. "Better put a new water heater in that bid."

"All right."

The kitchen seemed even smaller now that it was just the two of them. She moved to the slightly larger living room and was extremely aware that he followed. "I don't think we'll waste any money in here," she said. "Just the inn." She reached up to shove her too-long bangs out of her face and realized what she'd done when she caught him staring at her right eye, at the scar on the outside of it that she knew was still looking fresh. Before she could turn away, he was there, right there, and gently—God, so gently it nearly broke something inside of her—brushed the hair from her face and stared at the mark.

For the longest heartbeat in history, he didn't say anything, but the muscles in his jaw bunched. From his fingers, so carefully light on her, she felt the tension grip his entire body. "What happened?"

"Nothing. I don't want to talk about it."

Another agonizing beat pulsed around them before he let go of her, allowing her bangs to fall over her forehead again.

He let out a long breath and eyed their Charlie Brown Christmas tree. When he spoke, his voice was low but normal. "You have an eyelash curler on your tree."

Grateful, so damn grateful that he wasn't going to push, she let out a breath, too. "We improvised."

He took in the pictures of their teen crushes and shook his head, not smiling but letting go of some of the tension racking him.

"You don't like?"

"Actually, I do like," he said, and when she glanced over at him, she found him looking directly at her.

"I meant the tree."

He just picked up his leather jacket from its perch by the front door, the one he'd given her to wear last night. Once again he held it open for her, then nudged her outside ahead of him.

The morning was clear and crisp, and the trees and ground glittered with frost. The sun was so bright it hurt her eyes and head, and also her teeth, which made no sense.

"Hangovers are a bitch," Jax said and dropped his sunglasses onto her nose.

He walked away before she could thank him, so she closed her mouth and pushed up the glasses a little, grateful for the dark lenses. She tried to remember the last time anyone had done such a thing for her without anything expected in return—and couldn't.

"Also going on the list," he said when she'd run to catch up with his long-legged stride. "Making sure no more trees are in danger of killing you in the next wind storm. We'll chop that up for firewood."

She stared at the massive tree bisecting the yard. "Where I come from, firewood comes in a small bundle at the grocery store, and you set it in your fireplace to give off ambience."

"Trust me, ambience is the last thing you'll want this tree to give you. It's going to keep your fingers and feet warm."

She hugged his jacket to her and not because it smelled heavenly. Okay, because it smelled heavenly. And did he never get cold? She looked at him in that slightly oversized hoodie and sexy jeans and boots, carrying that clipboard. She wished she had a clipboard. Instead, she pulled out her Blackberry to make notes, too. "Do I need to call a tree guy?"

"I can do it. Those two trees there..." He pointed across the yard to the left of the marina building. "They're going to need to be seriously cut back. I'm sure there's others."

They walked the rest of the property and outlined all the obvious problems. There were many. After discussing them in detail over the next half hour, they were back in the center of the yard, next to the fallen tree.

"So," he said. "Your sisters want out."

"Yesterday," she agreed.

"I think your mom hoped you three would stick around and take care of this place the way she always intended to. You know how she was."

"Actually, I don't," she said. "I didn't know her very well. I was raised by my father in Los Angeles. She sent postcards from wherever the Grateful Dead were playing, and we had the occasional whirlwind visit. But she never mentioned this place, not once." She realized how detached that sounded and just how much she'd revealed about their lack of a relationship, and it both embarrassed and saddened her. Having bared herself enough for one day, she turned away.

"Some kids might resent their parent in this situation," he said quietly.

"There's some of that."

She felt a big, warm hand settle at her back, and he led her to his Jeep. The huge brown dog in the passenger seat sat up and gave a single, joyous *woof!*

Jax opened the door and the lab mix leapt out, all long, gawky limbs and happy tongue. Two huge front paws hit Maddie in the chest, making her stagger back.

Jax's hands settled on her arms from behind, steadying her. Leaning over her shoulder, he gave the dog a friendly push. "Down, you big lug. You okay?" He turned Maddie around to face him, eyeing the two dusty paw prints on her chest.

She backed away and brushed herself off before he got any notions about helping. "She's very pretty."

"Pretty *something,* anyway." He sent the dog a look of affection. "I just haven't decided on what. Izzy, sit," he directed, and the dog promptly sat on his foot, looking up at him in clear hero worship.

Maddie bent for a stick and threw it. Izzy craned her neck, took in the stick's flight through the air, and yawned.

"She's not much for chasing sticks," Jax said dryly. "She'll chase her tail, though, all day long. She's a rescue. She didn't get the Labrador handbook."

Izzy nudged her head to Jax's thigh, and Jax crouched to give her a hug and a full-body rub, and Maddie felt a moment of jealousy as Izzy slid bonelessly to the ground in clear ecstasy, groaning loudly.

"She likes that," Maddie managed.

"I have a way with my hands."

She bit her lower lip to keep the words "show me" inside.

He laughed again, soft and sexy, as he straightened and apparently read her mind. "We don't have chemistry, remember?"

She closed her eyes. "Okay, here's the thing. We have *some* chemistry," she allowed.

"Some? Or supernova?"

"Supernova. *But,*" she said to his knowing grin. Good Lord, he needed to stop doing that. "I really did give up men."

"Forever?"

"My gut says yes, but that might be PMS talking. Let's just say I'm giving up men for a very long time."

"You going to try out women?"

He was teasing her. She pushed him back a step, knowing damn well he only went because it suited him. No one pushed him around unless he wanted to go—something she wished she could say about herself. "I'm trying to say I'm not cut out for this, for the casual-sex thing."

"But you've given up men," he pointed out, still teasing her. "Sounds like there's going to be no sex, period."

"None."

He merely arched a brow. "Aren't you going to miss it?"

"No."

"Not at all?"

"Not even a little."

He shot her a look of blatant disbelief. "How is that even possible, not missing sex? That's like saying you wouldn't miss having a cold beer on a hot summer night or the sound of the ocean pounding the surf while you run, or . . . air in your lungs."

She had to laugh at his adamancy. "Maybe sex isn't all that important to me."

"Then you've been doing it wrong."

His voice dripped with innuendo, and her body tightened involuntarily while the meaning behind his words thrummed through her veins. It was a foregone conclusion that the man knew how to use his muscular body and talented hands to make a living. She figured it wasn't a stretch to imagine he could also use those things to make a woman very happy.

"Still with me?" he murmured.

A warm flush spread through her body, and she lost her ability to speak.

His mouth was serious, but his eyes were laughing. With a quick playful tug on a lock of her wild hair, he walked off, heading toward the inn in that long-limbed, confident stride of his.

She stared after him, a little flummoxed by the funny something still happening very low in her belly, something she was pretty sure meant her body was *not* on board with the giving-up-men thing.

Not even close.

Chapter 9

♥

"If you're going through hell…
keep moving."
PHOEBE TRAEGER

By the time Maddie gathered her wits enough to follow Jax to the inn, he'd opened the front door. "Did your mom have a set of blueprints for this place?" he asked.

"I don't know. It looks like she kept all paperwork in the office in the marina. We could check there."

"You'll need it for the escrow contract, because anyone who buys this place is going to need to make sure the entire property passes inspection and is up to code. It's probably got more violations than you can count, and that'll all have to be dealt with at the building department. But I think Phoebe dated Ed for awhile, and he works there. He'll help you through it."

She paused, a little dizzy at his knowledge and the educated, professional way he spoke. Her first impression of him had been Hot Biker. Her second impression had been Hot Biker Who Could Kiss.

Now she was seeing yet another side. She asked the question she'd been dying to ask. "You liked her. My mom."

"Yes. You resemble her, you know." He took his time letting his gaze run over her, leaving her breathless. "It's in the eyes," he said. "She could see right through a person, right to their soul, and know."

"Know what?"

"What they were made of."

She'd had a knot in her chest since Phoebe's death, a thick ball of grief and regret, and it tightened now. "I don't have that ability. I'm actually a terrible judge of character."

He didn't say anything for a long moment. "Your mom was fun and a little flighty, but she had substance where it counted. She had heart."

"Yeah, well, the flightiness was self-induced."

A little smile crossed his face. "No doubt."

Given the fondness in his tone, she figured he'd known Phoebe well. Certainly better than she had, and the ball tightened a little more. "So what about you?"

"What about me?"

"I know next to nothing about you. Tell me something."

He shrugged. "Not much to tell. I was born and raised here. My mom died of a stroke a few years back. No siblings."

"Except for Ford and Sawyer," she said.

"Except for them."

"What about your dad?"

"He's in Seattle."

There was something there, something in his voice

that had her taking a closer look at him, but his face was calm. "You've always been a carpenter?" she asked.

"No. I went away to college, then stayed away for several years after that. I've been back five years now. Boring story."

She doubted that, but he took himself and his clipboard inside the inn, and she and Izzy followed. The dog sniffed at every corner as Jax and Maddie went through room by room. He showed her what could be done to update and modernize, sometimes stopping to sketch things out for her as he talked, his love of a challenge shining through.

Maddie had enjoyed her job, sometimes, and it'd fulfilled her. But she'd never loved it. It was fascinating to watch him. *He* was fascinating.

They finished the main floor and headed up the stairs, while Izzy slept in the sole sun spot on the kitchen floor, snoring like a buzz saw. Jax made suggestions for the bedrooms and bathrooms. At some point, he'd gone out for his tool belt. There was something disturbingly sexy about the way it sat low on his hips, framing everything. She did her best not to notice, but he sure had a very nice...everything.

Together they crawled through the attic space, looking for the source of a roof leak they'd discovered in the last bathroom. Jax was out in front, braving the spiderwebs. Maddie was behind him, working really hard at not looking at his butt.

And failing spectacularly.

So when he unexpectedly twisted around, holding out his hand for the clipboard she was now holding, he caught her staring at him.

"I, um—You have a streak of dirt," she said.

"A streak of dirt."

Yes." She pointed to his left perfectly muscled butt cheek. "There."

He was quiet for a single, stunned beat. She couldn't blame him, given that they were both covered in dirt from the filthy attic. "Thanks," he finally said. "It's important to know where the dirt streaks are."

"It is," she agreed, nodding like a bobble head. "Probably you should stain-stick it right away. I have some in my purse."

"Are you offering to rub it on my ass?" She felt the heat flood her face, and he grinned. "You're a paradox, Maddie Moore. I like that about you."

"Is that because I said nothing was happening between us, and then I..."

"...Wanted to touch my ass." He finished for her. "You can, by the way. Anytime."

She squeaked in embarrassment and covered her cheeks.

"See? Paradox."

"You know, you don't sound like a contractor. You sound like..."

"Like?"

"Well, before the ass comment, I was going to say professional. Educated."

"Maybe I am those things, as well."

She followed some more, crawling along behind him, her eyes automatically locking in on the way his jeans stretched taut when he moved. Which meant it wasn't even really her fault. It was his. His and his tight—

"I'm pretty sure," he murmured without turning

around, "that it'd be a lot easier for you to give up sex if you stop thinking about it."

"How do you know I'm thinking about it?"

He didn't dignify that with an answer.

"Because I'm not. I'm thinking about…" What? "About how hard it'll be to get your jeans clean."

He laughed softly. "Hold that thought. I found the leak. It's fixable."

"Good."

"But you're going to need a new roof next year."

Not good. "What else?"

"Besides the fact that I like to look at your ass, too?"

With a moan that was only half embarrassment, she shook her head. "Stop it."

"Stop the looking, or the telling of the looking?"

Oh, God. "You're not helping me with this giving-up-men thing."

"I don't intend to."

There in the dark, dusty attic she stared at him. "You have a stake in this, too. You said you weren't interested, either."

"No, I said I've been there. *There* being fresh out of a bad relationship and so sure I never wanted to be in another again."

She sucked in a breath and considered denying that, but in the end, her curiosity won. "What happened?"

"I got over myself. Sort of. And for the record, I am interested. Very."

Oh, boy. "Let's go back to talking about the inn," she said shakily.

"Safer?"

"Much."

His eyes smiled. "The windows are single pane. If you replace them with energy efficient and insulated, you'd make the place far easier to heat, plus get an updated look at the same time. Parts of the porch have to be repaired. It's not up to code, it'd never pass inspection. There's the leaking roof. You need interior and exterior paint, and the carpet is trashed. I'd suggest ripping it out and restoring the hardwood that's beneath it. You want to replace the water heaters. You could easily update the bathrooms by putting in new vanities and cabinets when you fix the leaking pipes."

"Sounds like a lot."

"No, a lot would also be renovating the kitchen and replacing the entire roof."

True.

Back outside, they headed to the marina with Izzy trotting along after them. The sun wasn't assisting much in warming the air, and their breath crystallized in front of their faces. A long, shrill whistle came from the water. "What's that?" she asked.

"A seine boat searching deep waters for crab."

As always, she walked quickly, almost running. Jax's stride was long-legged and sure but as unrushed as everything else about him. He liked to take his time, she was learning. He took his time measuring, he took his time talking, he took his time drinking the water bottle he offered her from the back of his Jeep, and he took his time giving Izzy a hug when she roused a very pissed-off squirrel and got scared.

Maddie couldn't help but wonder if he took his time in bed, too, and just the thought caused a rush of heat to places that had no business getting all heated up.

He slid her a look, and his mouth twitched. "Again?"

"So your superpower is reading my mind?"

"Anyone can read your mind, Maddie. You wear it—along with your heart—on your sleeve."

She blew out a breath. "That's going to have to stop. Soon as I figure out how."

"You could start by letting go of some of the stuff you're holding in."

"I'm not holding anything in."

"Do we need to go over the long list of things you don't want to talk about? Like your thing against educated and professional and...lawyerly?"

She put her hands on her hips. "What's your thing with my thing against lawyers?"

He did the brow arch. "Nice deflection. You're getting better at it, actually."

"Consider it step one in learning how to *not* wear my thoughts on my sleeve."

He laughed softly and tugged on a curl. "If you're not going to tell me any deep, dark secrets, let's do the rest of this."

Inside the marina, they decided there was nothing critical to be done here on Jax's part. But taking a look at all the gear—kayaks, canoes, paddles, and more—her thumbs itched to get busy itemizing and cataloguing on her Blackberry. She had a month to prove to her sisters that this could be a viable business for them, and she didn't intend to fail.

"You seem pretty comfortable out here," she said to Jax. "Even for someone who once painted the inn."

"See that fourteen-foot sailboat in slip three? And the thirty-two-foot one in four? They're both Ford's. He leases year-round and sometimes drags me out on the water with him. But even before that, we used to come out here late at night."

"To TP."

"Just the once. Trust me, we learned our lesson on that one. Look out past the slips, to the woods beyond the marina. There are trails leading up to the bluffs. It's rough going, and the bush is really overgrown. It's a deterrent for everyone except the occasional teenager who wants a quiet place to go make out. Gives a whole new meaning to the name Lucky Harbor."

The thought of a teenage Jax hiking out there with nefarious intentions should have made her laugh. Instead, she wished she'd grown up here in Lucky Harbor, and that maybe she could have been one of those girls. "Even in the winter?"

"All the better. There isn't any poison oak in the winter. It's hard to convince a girl you're sexy when you can't stop scratching your ass because of the rash."

She laughed. She'd done that a few times now, when up until yesterday, being amused at anything had seemed so far out of reach. How it was possible that just one day and one tall, dark, and enigmatic man had changed things, she had no idea.

The marina office was small and held an ancient couch, a huge, beat-up, old desk piled with papers, and a filing cabinet. Drawers were open, and files were in complete disarray.

Jax shook his head. "You've got your work cut out for you."

Maddie shrugged. "I've organized worse." And what was the alternative, going back to LA with her tail between her legs? Hell, no. The thought brought her up a little. She'd been faking strength for so long now that it was starting to stick. About time.

Jax pointed out the window beyond the marina to the thick, overgrown woods. "Shortcut to the bluffs is right past that isolated, small rocky beach. Another good makeout spot, FYI. Especially when you're sixteen and grounded from a car."

She smiled. "Were you grounded a lot?"

"Pretty much 24/7 until I left for college."

"And did you miss small-town living when you were gone?"

"Not even a little. I didn't just walk out of Lucky Harbor; I ran like hell."

There was that same something in his eyes that had been there when he'd mentioned his father. She wasn't the only one keeping her own counsel. "And yet you came back."

His gaze met hers, clear now. Relaxed. "And yet I came back."

"Why?"

"Funny what a couple of years' perspective can do."

Growing up on movie sets as she had, just about everything in her life had been an illusion. The illusion of friends, the illusion of home. The question was—was Lucky Harbor just another set, or would it turn out to be the real thing?

Back at Jax's Jeep, he opened the driver's door, set his clipboard on the dash, then gestured for Izzy to jump in.

The dog leapt up, limbs akimbo, and sat. "Scoot over," Jax told her.

Izzy grinned.

Jax shook his head, leaned back against the Jeep, and looked at Maddie. "I'll work up a bid and email it to you."

"Thanks."

He looked behind her to the inn. "Phoebe left you the property because it meant something to her. If you really don't want to sell it, stand your ground." He flashed her a smile. "Be Louise."

The smile was devastating and contagious, damn him. "I'm trying. But there are problems."

"Yeah. It's called life."

"The mortgage is in arrears. I think the property is actually upside down on its loan. Which is a mystery to me, because like you said, I believe this place meant something to Phoebe, sentimentally anyway. But if she wanted us to keep it, why did she leave every last penny in a trust for someone else?"

He paused, as if carefully picking his words. "There are things you can do. Talk to your original lender, for one. Get an appraisal and refinance. And have you actually verified that there are no funds other than the trust? You've talked to the probate attorney and have a list of Phoebe's assets and accounts? Because that might lead you to...other avenues."

"There you go," she murmured, a little surprised to find that even more attractive than his butt were his brains. "Sounding like more than a pretty tool belt again. Maybe even like a...lawyer."

"And that's bad?"

She didn't answer, didn't know how. It wasn't exactly a rational fear she was carrying around.

"Let me guess," he said. "It's one of those things you don't want to talk about."

"Definitely."

Their gazes collided.

Held.

Time seemed to stand still, which was not only odd, but silly. Time never stood still, not even for sexy superheroes. When he pushed off the Jeep and stepped close, her pulse immediately kicked into high gear. "Thanks for coming," she whispered. "I—"

Slowly, purposefully, eyes still locked on hers, he invaded her personal space bubble.

She sucked in a breath as heat spiraled within her.

"You..." he said, trying to help her along.

"I can't remember a single thought in my head."

Gentle but firm hands settled on her hips, and he backed her into the Jeep.

"What are you doing?" she asked breathlessly.

"Giving you a new thought." Leaning in, he covered her mouth with his and kissed her, his tongue teasing lightly, keeping it soft until she moaned. Then he deepened the kiss into a hot, intense connection that had her head spinning and her blood pumping as their bodies molded together. Unlike last night's tender kisses, this was a little demanding, and a whole lot wild, and when he slid a thigh between hers, she lost her ability to think.

Last night, he'd been seeking permission. Not this time. This time, he buried his fingers into her hair and claimed her mouth, pulling her in even closer, a hand caressing down her back as if to soothe as well as incite, claiming another little piece of her heart in the process.

Sneaky bastard.

She'd tell him so, but her tongue was a little busy. So were her fingers, first enjoying the play of the muscles on his back, then holding on tight just in case he had any ideas about trying to get away. Because she wasn't done, not even when Izzy gave a little whine of unhappiness at sharing her man.

Maddie slid her hands over Jax's shoulders, reminding herself that enough was enough, but she tugged a thrillingly rough groan from deep in his chest so she tightened her grip instead. By the time they broke apart, she was completely out of breath. If it wasn't for the Jeep at her back and the thigh he still had wedged between hers, she'd have dropped to the ground in a puddle of lust.

"Maddie."

His voice was low and gravely and sexy as hell. "Yes?"

"I'm going to touch your face now."

Remembering last night and her mortifying reaction, she should have been grateful for the heads-up, but she was still dizzy from the kiss. "Oh. Well, I—"

He ran his hand up her arm, to her shoulder, over her throat, going slowly, achingly slowly, so that by the time he cupped her jaw, she was quivering, all right, but not from fear. Lifting his other hand, he slid a curl from her temple, tucking it behind her ear. With her pulse somewhere at stroke level, she closed her eyes to better absorb his touch. His fingers were warm and callused. Strong, though not using that strength against her, but in a protective way. And in spite of her admittedly irrational fear of men, her body and heart wanted him.

Bad.

"Maddie."

"Huh?"

There was amusement in his voice. "Are you still giving up men?"

He was pressed against her, deliciously warm and hard. *Everywhere.* She wanted to give him a chance, but she'd meant it when she said she wasn't ready. She needed a clear head first, and her life straightened out. A relationship of any kind at this point would be ludicrous. "Yes," she said, but it came out as more of a croak. She cleared her throat and said it again. "Yes, I'm still giving up men."

He studied her face, then gave her a very small smile before backing away, pulling his keys from his pocket. "I'll be in touch."

"Just the minimum," she reminded him. "That's all I need."

With a nod, he got into the Jeep, nudging Izzy to the back seat. He rolled the window down for the dog, and Maddie reached in to stroke her soft, silky coat.

"Just the minimum," she repeated softly, taking a step back as two warm doggy eyes laughed into hers, silently calling her out as a big liar.

Chapter 10

"Smile…it makes people wonder
what you're up to."
PHOEBE TRAEGER

Two days later, Jax was in his home office plowing
through paperwork. He'd put together the bid for Lucky
Harbor resort and emailed it off to Maddie. He'd handled
all his city council duties, but being Lucky Harbor's
mayor for his second term now was a relatively easy position to manage and didn't take much of his time. He was
signing accounts-payable checks that his part-time office
worker Jeanne handed to him one at a time.

"Electric bill," she said, standing over him like a
mother hen, even though they were the same age. Her
headband had reindeer antlers with bells on them that
jangled with every bossy statement she uttered. "Gas
bill," she said, bells jingling. "Visa bill. And here's my
paycheck. Thanks for the raise."

He slid her a look, and she laughed. "Kidding. You
already pay me too much. Oh, and here's the bill for those

supplies you sent over to the Patterson family. Nice of you to do that, since they lost everything in the fire. So... who's the woman?"

Jax pushed all the checks back at her. "What woman?"

"The one you were kissing on the pier the other night."

He arched a brow, and she grinned. "Oh, come on. You can't be surprised that I know."

"Call me naive, but I'm surprised."

She shook her head, like *You poor, stupid man.* She gave him that look a lot. He put up with it because she ran his office with a calm efficiency that was a relief to him. He hated office work.

Jeanne was flipping through the checks, putting them in some mysterious order that worked for her. "Jake told his sister, who told Carrie at the grocery store, and I happened to run into my sister today when I was loading up your refrigerator. And by the way, you were down to an apple and a piece of leftover pizza. I also found what looked to be a science experiment growing in a Tupperware container. I made an executive decision and tossed it. How do you live like that?"

"It's called takeout. What did you put in my refrigerator?"

"Fruit, cheese, beer, and a loaded pizza."

"I love you."

She laughed. "If that was true, you'd tell me about the woman."

He smiled but kept silent. Mostly because it would drive her crazy, but also because he didn't feel like sharing. Truth was, he'd been thinking about Maddie for two days now, and not as a future client. He thought about strangling whoever'd hurt her. He thought about how in spite of that hurt, she'd seemed so honest and artless—not like the women in his past. She was obviously afraid but doing her damnedest to move forward. He admired that.

He'd also given a lot of thought—*a lot*—to how she'd looked after he'd kissed her: ruffled and baffled and turned on. It was a good look for her. So was how she'd looked when she'd opened the door to him, sleepy and hung over, no bra, just a very thin T-shirt, the one that invited the general public to bite her.

Christ, he'd wanted to do just that.

"Rumor has it," Jeanne said, shoving another check under his nose. "She's Phoebe's middle daughter. She was at the hardware store today, and Anderson rang her up. He said she was pretty and sweet, and even though she knocked over his entire display of five-gallon paint cans, she got a big thumbs-up. Oh, and because she has a nice rack, he asked her out."

Jax's pen went still. "What?"

"Hey, I didn't see the rack myself, I'm just passing on the information." Her smile went sly. "Betcha you want to know if she said yes."

He said nothing, and she grinned. "You want to know."

"I don't gossip. I'm a guy."

"You *so* want to know."

"No, I don't."

"Yes, you do."

"No, I—" *Fuck.* He pinched the bridge of his nose because yeah, he did. He wanted to know. "You used to be so sweet and meek."

"That was back in the days when your badass scowl used to do it for me." Delighted at whatever she saw in his face, she waggled a brow. "Okay, I'll tell you, but first you have to tell me how you met her, and how it is that you were kissing her on her first night in town, and if you plan to fight Anderson for the rights to her rack."

"Jeanne," he said in warning.

"Use that tough-guy voice all you want. I'm not married to you. I don't have to cave so that you'll keep my feet—and other parts—warm at night." With that, she scooped up all the signed checks and sashayed out of his office, humming "We Wish You a Merry Christmas."

"You know where I'll be," she called back. "Sitting at my desk working my fingers to the bone. Oh, and I'm decorating your place for Christmas, so be afraid. Very afraid. Anytime you want to come up with some answers for me, I'll be happy to do the same."

Shit. Shaking his head, he turned to something new, drawing up plans for a new client in Portland who wanted a handmade front door with cherry overlay and stained glass. It would take weeks to construct and was the perfect job for when the weather went bad, which it always did for about a month after Christmas. He needed work for when the weather went bad—not for his bank account, which was plenty flush—but so that he wouldn't be stuck with nothing to do but think.

Though all he could think at the moment was that Anderson had asked Maddie out.

He could hear Jeanne in the front room, talking to her computer. He'd gone to high school with her and had even briefly dated her—if one could really call it dating when all you did was climb the bluffs and make out. When he'd gone off to USC, she'd married Lucky Harbor's high school quarterback and given him three kids. She was still happily married but bored beyond tears. So when Jax had come back to town five years ago, she'd shown up on his doorstep one day and announced that she was his new, perfect, part-time office assistant. Perfect because she had no interest in his money or his bed.

Which was a lie. She'd been harping on his heart and soul, trying to save him, ever since she'd demanded the assistant position. Not that he had much of a heart and soul left after he'd detonated both in his last job practicing law. He'd talked himself into embracing the lifestyle: the big salary, the corner office, the penthouse condo, the trophy fiancée. And he'd reaped the benefits, plenty of them.

The firm he'd worked for had been the best of the best at getting people acquitted of their white-collar crimes. It was a multibillion-dollar industry, and Jax had been good at it. Good at twisting the facts, good at misdirecting, good at getting their clients off with their crime of choice, even when it meant that innocent people paid the price.

Jax's discontent over that had started small and slowly grown. And then came to a head when the wife of one of their clients had paid the ultimate price.

With her life.

Her husband had been guilty as hell, and Jax had known it. Hell, everyone had known it. Yet Jax had gotten the man acquitted of embezzling from his wife's family, a family with known mob connections, so there'd been little sympathy for either side.

Except for the wife. She'd grown up as a pawn, and she'd been married off as a pawn. She'd never known life as anything else. An increasingly disenchanted Jax had known her enough to understand that when this went down, in all likelihood her assets would be confiscated and she'd be left penniless and alone. Unable to live with that, he'd broken attorney–client privilege to warn her, but instead of heeding his advice and taking off for parts unknown, she killed herself.

Forced to face his own part in her self-destruction, not to mention just how ethically indecent he'd become, Jax had quit. His fiancée left him shortly after. Game over. He'd left Seattle without looking back. Alone, unsettled, even angry, he'd somehow ended up back in Lucky Harbor.

The last place he'd been happy.

That had been five years ago. Sawyer had come back to town, as well, and after a wild, misspent youth had become a Lucky Harbor sheriff, of all things. Ford was around, in between sailing ventures that'd included the world-class circuit. The three of them had gravitated together as if they'd never been apart.

His first year back, Jax had lived on Ford's second sailboat in the marina. He'd practiced a little law here and there, for friends only, and he'd hated it. So he'd gone back to basics, which for him had been building things with his own hands. As he'd worked on getting over himself, he'd designed and built the house he'd always wanted. He did what he could to give back to the community that had welcomed him without question, including somehow, surprisingly, being elected mayor two terms running.

He was jarred out of his musings when his father strode into his office and immediately set Jax on edge with nothing more than his stick-up-his-ass gait and ridiculously expensive suit. They hadn't spent much time together, mostly because his father was still good and furious over what he saw as Jax's failure in Seattle.

"Got a case for you." His father tossed down the file.

This wasn't surprising. His father often felt the need to manipulate his son's emotions. Which was ironic, since Jax had been trained by the man himself that emotions and business never mix. Hell, in their little family of two, emotions didn't even *exist*. "You haven't spoken to me since I refused to represent that charming Fortune 500 sex offender you brought me last time. That was three months ago. Now you walk in here like you own the place and toss me yet another case I don't want. I'm too busy for this, Dad. Jeanne and I have billings to go over—"

"He said I should go home," Jeanne said softly from the doorway. "I'm done for the day anyway," she said in silent apology, jerking her head toward his father, indicating that they should try to talk.

Fat chance.

Jax didn't often feel his temper stir. It took a lot, especially these days, but his father could boil his blood like no other. "Still minding your own business, I see," he said when Jeanne had left.

"Get over yourself, son. This is a simple, open-and-shut case."

Everything in Jackson Cullen's world was open-and-shut—as long as he got his way. "If it's so simple, you take it."

"No, they want someone young, an up-and-comer."

"I've up and come. And gone," Jax reminded him. "Now if you could do the same…" He gestured to the door.

"Jesus Christ, Jax. It's been five years since you let your job go. You let your fiancée go, too. Time to stop feeling sorry for yourself and get back on the horse."

Jax shoved the file back across his desk and stood up. "Get out."

"You're not listening. Elizabeth Weston is thirty, loaded, beautiful, and her daddy's going to be the next state governor."

"Which matters why?"

"She's looking to settle down. You'll do."

He choked out a laugh. "Now you're whoring me out? Not that this surprises me."

"What, you're not seeing anyone, are you?"

Was he? He'd like to say hell, yes, but the facts were simple. He was guessing Maddie's ex had been an attorney, and a real asshole, to boot. When she learned about Jax's past, she'd run for the hills. Even if he somehow managed to show her that he'd changed, he doubted she'd understand his morally and emotionally bankrupt history. He wouldn't expect her to.

Hell, just being a man was a strike against him. She wasn't in a place to trust any person with a Y chromosome.

"A wife like Elizabeth will be an asset when you take over my practice," his father said.

"I've told you, I'm not taking over your practice."

"You're a Cullen. You're my only son. You have to take over the practice. I spent the past thirty-five years building it for you."

"You built it for you," Jax corrected. "Come on, Dad, doesn't this ever get old? You bullying me, me refusing to be bullied. Hire an associate and be done with it."

"This is asinine." Jaw tight, his father scooped up the file and moved stiffly to the door. "No one can disappoint me quite the way you can."

Ditto. "Dismiss Jeanne or interfere with my work again, and you won't be welcome back."

When the front door slammed, Jax picked up a paperweight on his desk and flung it against the wall, where it shattered. There. Marginally better. And it seemed that he and his father had something in common, after all—sometimes Jax disappointed himself, too.

He was still struggling with his own temper when Ford strode into the office and kicked Jax's feet off his desk. "Get up. Water's calm. Wind's kicking. We're going sailing."

"Not in the mood."

"I'm looking for a first mate, not a sex partner. Besides, you need some tranquility."

Jax slid him a look. "Tranquility? A big word for you, isn't it?"

"What? The bar's been slow. I've been reading."

"You didn't get that word out of *Penthouse* Forum."

"Hey, I read other stuff." He paused. "Sometimes. Now get up. Jeanne's got the afternoon off, and so do you."

He looked at the one person who knew his entire sordid story and didn't seem to blame Jax for being an asshole. "How do you know Jeanne's got the afternoon off?"

Ford didn't answer.

"Shit," Jax said. "She called you."

"A little bit," Ford admitted. "She wanted me to give you a hug."

"Fuck off."

"Figured you'd say that. Also figured you'd be needing to get out."

Which is how Jax ended up on the water on Ford's thirty-two-foot Beneteau. It was late in the year for a leisurely sail. Far too late. Most sailing enthusiasts had long ago winterized their boats, but Ford being Ford, he never let a little thing like winter slow him down. He always thrived on pushing the envelope, and not just in sailing.

They were rewarded by an unexpected cold, hard wind that took their breath and every ounce of questionable talent they owned. The swells rose to nearly eight feet, ensuring that their planned easygoing few hours turned into an all-out work-their-asses-off-fest just to stay alive, much less afloat.

"Christ," Ford breathed when they'd made it back to the slip. He slumped against the hull, head back. "I sailed the West Indies and nearly died three times. That was nothing compared to this. What were you thinking, letting me take us out there?"

Jax didn't have the energy to kick Ford's ass, so he slid down the hull next to him and mirrored his pose, his every muscle quivering with exhaustion and overuse, even his brain. "Forgot what a drama queen you are."

Ford choked out a laugh. "If I could move, I'd make you eat that statement."

"You and what army?"

"Fuck you," Ford said companionably. "And when were you going to tell me about Maddie? I have to hear about some supposedly hot kiss on the pier from Jeanne, who heard it from—"

"I know this story, thanks." And in tune to Ford's soft laugh, Jax thunked his head back against the hull and closed his eyes. He wondered what she was doing right now, if she was working at the inn. He knew everyone, himself included, had found Phoebe fun and free-spirited, but having met her daughters now, Jax found himself angered at how Phoebe had neglected them.

Maddie deserved better. They all did.

"Did you know that Anderson asked Maddie out?" Ford asked.

"Yes!"

"Hell, man, sailing's supposed to relax you."

Jax *was* relaxed. He was easygoing and laid-back. It'd taken him five long years to get there. He no longer let things stack up on his shoulders until he was ready to crumple. He no longer kept secrets for a living, his clients' or his own, secrets that had the ability to burn holes in the lining of his stomach.

So why hadn't he told Maddie that he'd been a lawyer?

Because he was a dumbass.

And a chicken, to boot.

And because you know she'd stop looking at you like you're a superhero...

Oh, yeah, *that.*

Maddie and her sisters spent their days going through the inn and marina, each for different reasons. Chloe was bored. Tara didn't want to miss anything of resale value. But for Maddie, it was about sentiment and about learning how the inn could run. She'd hoped to have everything computerized by now, but she'd spent most of her time digging her way through just to see what she had to work with.

On the second day, she headed into town with a list of errands. When she saw Lucille out in front of the art gallery, she pulled over. Lucille was thrilled for the company and after hugging Maddie hello said, "I hear you've been kissing our Jax on the pier."

"Oh. Well, I—"

"You've picked the cream of the crop with that one, honey. Did you know he lent me the money to help my granddaughter stay in college? Don't let the motorcycle, tattoos, and aloofness fool you; he's a sweet, caring young man."

Maddie hadn't found him aloof. Big and bad and intimidating, maybe. Sexy as hell, certainly. And—Wait. Tattoos? He had tattoos? Just thinking of ink on that body of his had heat slashing through hers.

"Come in, come in," Lucille said. "I just put up my Christmas decorations. And I have tea. And brandy."

She wasn't sure what it said about her that she was tempted. "I'm on a mission for Tara, running some errands, but thank you."

"Going back to the hardware store?" Lucille cocked her head. "Heard Anderson asked you out."

Maddie had gone yesterday to get some organizational supplies. The guy behind the counter had been wearing a Santa hat, and was extremely cute and extremely funny, but she'd left with only her supplies, gently turning down the date.

She'd given up men.

Or she was trying. "Does everyone know everything around here?"

"Well, we don't know which guy you're going to date, Anderson or Jax. But if you could tell me, I'll be real popular tonight at bingo," she said hopefully.

Maddie's next stop was the pier for another shake, which she needed bad.

She smiled at the familiar guy behind the counter. "Lance, right? Straight chocolate this time."

He smiled and nodded. He was in his early twenties, small boned, and had a voice like he was speaking through gravel.

He told her that he had cystic fibrosis. He had family in Portland, but he lived here in Lucky Harbor with his brother, priding himself on his independence in spite of a disease that was slowly ravaging his young body.

Listening to him, Maddie decided she had nothing, absolutely nothing, to complain about in her life. And on the way back to her car, she stared up at the looming Ferris wheel.

Had her mother ever ridden it? From all that she'd read on Phoebe's "recipe" cards, Maddie had to believe her mom had lived her life fast, and just a little bit recklessly.

Chloe was a chip off the old block.

Tara hid her wild side, but she had traveled far and wide, as well, and she had a lot of life experiences under her belt.

Maddie...not so much. Sure, she'd lived in Los Angeles, but that was because her father had brought her there. Those adventures she'd had on movie sets were because of him, not because she'd had some deep yearning for the profession.

She'd fallen into it. She'd fallen or been dragged into just about everything she'd ever done.

Including the inn.

No, she decided. This was going to be different. She was going to make this adventure her own. Nodding, she walked along, listening to the rough surf slap at the pier. The slats of wood beneath her feet had spaces between them, and in the light of day that gave her vertigo and a fear of falling through.

"The trick is not to look at your feet when you walk."

Maddie turned toward the voice and found a woman busy nailing a sign to a post. Appearing to be about Maddie's age, she was petite and pretty, with dark waves of hair falling down her back. She wore hip-hugging pin-striped trousers and a business jacket fit for her toned figure, looking cool and composed and far too professional to be standing on a pier with a hammer and nails in her manicured hands.

"If you look straight out to the horizon," she told Maddie, "You won't feel like you're going to fall." Looking quite comfortable with the hammer in spite of her outfit, she pounded a last nail into the sign, which read:

Lucky Harbor's Annual Shrimp Feed
this Saturday at 6:00
The Biggest and Bestest in the State:
Dinner, Dancing, and
***Kissing The Mayor*—Don't Miss it!**

"You're new." Smiling, the woman thrust out a hand. "I'm Sandy. Town clerk and manager. I also run the library." She smiled. "You know, you look like your momma."

"You knew her?"

"Everyone knew her. Be sure to bring your sisters to the feed. Here." Reaching into the bag at her feet, she pulled out a round of what looked like raffle tickets. She tore off a long strip of them and handed it over. "On the house. A welcome-to-town present."

"What are these for?"

"The guessing tank. You write how many shrimp you think'll get dragged in on the shrimp boat parade that night. Winner gets to kiss Jax when he comes in off the jet ski leading the boat parade."

Maddie blinked. "Jax? Jax Cullen?"

"The one and only."

"Why does the winner get to kiss Jax?"

"Besides the fact that he is one *fine* man?" Sandy grinned. "Because someone always gets to kiss the mayor. We like to torture our own here. Especially someone as popular as Jax. Before Jax, it was me, actually. I was mayor for three terms. I got lucky one year—a board member won the raffle and he was a cutie pie. Couldn't kiss for beans, though. The other years I had to kiss frogs."

"But mayor?" Maddie shook her head. "Jax is a contractor. He restores things."

"He's a man of many talents." Sandy said this with a secret little smile, and Maddie knew a moment of horror.

Oh, God. "He's your boyfriend." She'd kissed another woman's boyfriend.

"No," Sandy said with a sigh. "Much to my utter dismay—and not for lack of trying—Jax and I are just friends." She dropped her hammer into her bag and smiled. "See you at the feed. Oh, and are you going to hand out coupons for the inn? Phoebe did that last year, and it was a big success."

"It was?" How was that even possible? The place was a complete wreck.

Seeing Maddie's expression, Sandy smiled. "Yeah, probably she didn't charge them, but the point is, she could have. She was a wonderful lady, your momma, but not much for business. Maybe she didn't mention that."

No, Phoebe hadn't mentioned that. Phoebe hadn't mentioned much of anything. "I'll talk to my sisters about it, but the inn won't be reopened until…" Well, maybe never, but since she was done with negativity, she said, "Hopefully right after the new year."

Sandy nodded. "Can't wait to see what you do in the way of updating and modernizing. The whole town is buzzing about it."

"How does anyone even know we're doing anything?"

"Well, you've asked Jax for a bid. Jeanne had lunch with Tracy, her best friend, who told Carla, my sister-in-law, who's the local newspaper reporter. Lucky Harbor prides itself on keeping up with the news, and you three are big news."

Maddie tried to wrap her mind around the thought that she was news. Maddie Moore, assistant to the assistant, was news. "We're not really that interesting."

"Are you kidding? Three new women in town, running the inn? It's the biggest news this month. Well, maybe not quite as big as the upcoming shrimp feed, or watching Jax freeze his most excellent butt off leading the parade, but big enough." She smiled. "Okay, I'm off to hang more signs. See you!"

"See you," Maddie said softly and sipped her shake. She wanted to think about all Sandy had mentioned. She needed to wrap her head around the Lucky Harbor grapevine, the possibility that people were excited to have her in town, and the inn, but her brain kept stuttering on one thing.

Jax—the mayor!—and his most excellent butt.

Chapter 11

"A sister is a forever friend."
PHOEBE TRAEGER

That's not a quote about men or sex," Chloe said, scooping up another piece of pizza. She was wearing a snug black hoodie, zipped to just between her breasts. There was a single bright white word emblazed across the front—NAUGHTY.

They were on the counter at the cottage having dinner, where they'd taken to pulling out a random Phoebe quote from the recipe box because otherwise they argued. They argued about the inn, about the sole bed in the cottage, about the cottage kitchen—mostly because only Tara could cook, but she refused, saying she was on vacation. They argued about Phoebe's wishes, clothes...there was no sacred ground.

Tara and Chloe were going back to their lives in a matter of days. Maddie was staying.

So the cards were just about the only safe subject.

Most of the cards were outrageous. Some were downright absurd.

But once in a while there was a treasure, something so real, it caught Maddie like a one–two punch. *A sister is a forever friend* was one of them. "I like that one," she said quietly. "I like it a lot."

Tara tapped her perfectly manicured nails a moment, clearly uncomfortable with Maddie's obvious emotion. Finally, she blew out a breath and spoke with more emotion than Maddie had ever heard from her. "I agree, it's a keeper."

"Aw, look at you." Chloe nudged shoulders with her. "Going all Ya-Ya Sisterhood on us."

When Maddie and Tara both gave her the stink eye, she rolled her eyes. "Jeez, just lightening up the moment so we're not reenacting a Lifetime movie."

Maddie sighed, then carefully put the card back in the box, hoping the quote proved to be true.

The next evening, Jax stood behind the bar drying glasses, waiting for Ford to finish his shift so that they could go grab a late dinner. Jax had spent the day finishing up a mahogany dining room set for a client, and though he'd showered, he still smelled like wood shavings. He had two splinters in his right hand that he hadn't been able to remove himself, and a pounding headache that he suspected was directly due to the scathing email his father had sent him earlier regarding his last visit.

He was starting to wish he'd snagged himself a shot of 151 instead of a beer.

Ford was down at the other end of the bar. He turned and looked at Jax, brows up.

Jax shook his head. He was fine.

Fine.

A breeze hit him as the door opened, accompanied by a sizzle of awareness that zinged straight through him.

Maddie walked in and slid onto a barstool. He took in her jeans and soft, fuzzy, oversized sweater the exact blue of her eyes and was powerless against the smile that crossed his lips. "Hey."

"Hey Mr. Mayor."

He grimaced and served her a beer. "Discovered that, did you?"

"I can't believe you didn't tell me."

"It never came up."

"It could have," she said. "Maybe between the 'so glad I didn't kill you' and, oh, I don't know, when we played tonsil hockey."

"Which time?"

She rolled her eyes. "You know what I'm saying. You've encouraged me to blab all about myself, but you seem to have managed to remain quiet about you."

Yeah, and he was good at it. He came around the end of the bar and sat next to her. "In a town this size, being mayor is more of a dubious distinction than anything else."

"A pretty *fancy* dubious title." She sipped her beer and studied him.

He studied her right back. It'd been two days since he'd emailed her the bid. Three days since the aforementioned tonsil hockey. He'd thought of her, a lot more than he'd meant to.

He wondered if she'd done the same.

"So what's the protocol here?" she wanted to know. "Do I curtsy when I see you? Kiss your ring?"

He felt a smile curve his mouth. "A curtsy would be nice, but you don't look like that kind of girl. And I don't wear a ring, but I have something else you can kiss." He tapped a finger to his lips.

She laughed, and he decided that was the best sound he'd heard all day.

She handed him a file folder.

He opened it and found she'd printed his bid. He looked at what she'd circled and signed and then into her face.

"I got my sisters to agree."

There was a world of emotion in her voice, though she was trying to hide it. She'd gone up against her sisters and stood her ground. "Proud of you, Maddie."

"Thanks. And you're hired," she said quietly. "Assuming you still want the job."

The job, the woman . . .

"I circled what we can afford to do right now. Some of the other stuff, like the interior painting and the hauling of any demo debris, I'm going to do myself."

"Yourself?"

"My sisters aren't staying, just me. When can you start?"

The days of working 24/7 and cultivating as many clients as he could handle, maybe even more than he could handle, were long gone. Happily gone. These days, he took only the jobs he wanted. At the moment, all he had waiting on him was a wood-trim job in town, but his materials hadn't come yet. He also had to finish a front door design and the final touches on the dining room set. "I can start the day after tomorrow."

"Fair enough."

There was something in her voice, something she'd held back until now, and he realized she'd been avoiding direct eye contact. Removing the beer from her fingers, he set it down, then put his hands on her hips. Gently he turned her on the stool to fully face him, waiting until she tilted her head up and met his gaze.

Yeah, there it was. *Damn.* Unhappiness. "You wanted this," he murmured quietly. "The renovation on the inn."

"Very much."

"Then what's wrong?"

She looked away. "That whole superpower mind-reading thing is getting old."

He let his fingers do the walking, up her arm, over her throat, giving her plenty of advance warning before he cupped her jaw. Just as slowly, he brushed her long side bangs away from her right eye.

Her breath hitched, but she didn't pull away. The scar there was fading, and he let his thumb brush over it lightly, hating what it represented. He wanted to know the story, wanted to know how badly she'd been hurt, and whether she'd managed to give as good as she'd gotten.

He realized that he'd tensed, and that Maddie had stopped breathing entirely. When he purposely relaxed, she responded in kind, her eyes drifting closed, and she surprised the hell out of him by tilting her head slightly so that his hand could touch more of her. His heart squeezed up good at that, and his fingers slid into her hair, and then around to cup the nape of her neck.

Obeying the slight pressure he applied, she slid off the stool and then, of her own accord, stepped between his legs, dropping a hand to his thigh. When her chest bumped his, she let out a soft sigh. "You touch me a lot."

"I like to touch you. That's not what's making you unhappy."

She shook her head. "This is still a bad idea." She looked at him then. "Just so we're clear. We are, right? Clear?"

He didn't take his eyes off hers. "Crystal."

She nodded, then backed away from him. "Then I'll see you the day after tomorrow."

"Yes, you will." He snagged her wrist. "Maddie—"

"Listen, I'm not trying to be coy, or play a game, I promise. It's me. I'm just…" She shook her head. "It's me," she repeated softly. "I'm just trying hard to be who I want to be, that's all. I'm okay, though. Really."

"Good." He slid his hand to hers and stroked his thumb over her palm. "One more thing."

"What?"

He covered her mouth with his. He kissed her until his headache vanished and so did his bad mood. He kissed her until he felt her melt into him, until she was gripping his sweatshirt like a lifeline and kissing him back with enough passion that he forgot what the hell he thought he was doing.

Lifting his head, he ran his thumb over her slightly swollen, wet lower lip and struggled to put his brain into gear. "Saying that this isn't going anywhere doesn't change the chemistry problem we have. Just wanted to make that clear, as well."

Eyes huge on his, she licked her lips and made him want to groan. "Crystal," she whispered breathlessly and pulled free. This time she didn't stumble into a table— instead she plowed over some poor sap at the door. Apologizing profusely, she vanished into the night.

"Always in a hurry," Ford said conversationally, leaning on the bar.

"Always," Jax murmured.

"Ah, so you do still have a tongue. For a minute there, I thought maybe she sucked it out."

"Fuck you, Ford."

"You keep saying that, but you're not my type. And do you realize you're still looking at the door?"

"Just reminding myself to keep my distance," Jax said. "Distance is good."

"Yeah, that was some nice distance you had going there a minute ago."

Jax opened his mouth, but Ford held up a hand. "I know, fuck me, right? So tell me this, is keeping your 'distance' why you bid the inn renovation? Or why you stopped by the hardware store earlier to what, *chat* with Anderson? Because I heard you set him up on a date with Jeanne's cousin. Smooth, by the way. Real smooth."

"Okay, so the distance thing has gone out the window," Jax admitted. "I don't know when or why, but it has."

Ford laughed, easily vaulted over the bar, and clapped a hand on Jax's shoulder. "Maybe because she's hot and sweet? Or because you two have enough chemistry to light up this entire town? Because karma's a bitch?"

Jax shoved him off. "This isn't funny."

"Yeah, it is. Come on, I'm starving. You can brood over a burger."

Five minutes later, they walked into Eat Me Café to grab burgers. Maddie was at a semicircular booth with her sisters, the three of them bent over a stack of paperwork. Jax looked at her frown and figured they were going over the inn's outstanding bills and the refinancing forms.

Jax stopped, fighting the urge to yet again hint that she should approach her current note holder, but she hadn't asked his opinion and probably wouldn't.

Tara sat on Maddie's left, facing Jax and Ford. Her eyes locked on Ford, then widened right before they darkened. If looks could kill, Ford would be six feet under. Then, smooth as silk, she cleared her face until it was blank, got up from the table, and headed in the opposite direction, slipping into the restroom.

Jax looked over at Ford, who was watching Tara go with a tight look to his mouth, eyes shuttered.

What the hell?

He was unable to ask Ford about it, because they were now even with Maddie's table. Jax greeted her and then introduced Ford to Chloe.

While Maddie and Chloe made casual pleasantries with Ford, Jax took in the paperwork on their table.

Yeah, bills. And by the looks of things, lots of them.

The waitress came by to seat Jax and Ford, and they ended up on the other side of the café. Tara came out of the restroom, and Ford followed her with his eyes.

"What's going on?" Jax asked him.

"What? Nothing."

"You're staring at Maddie's sister."

"Maybe Tara's staring at *me*."

Jax leaned back and studied his oldest friend. "I never said which sister, and I sure as hell didn't say her name, either. *And* I was under the impression you didn't know any of them."

"I'm a bartender. I know everyone."

"You're an athlete who happens to own half a bar. Cut the shit, Ford. What's going on?"

Ford just shook his head, silent. Since Jax had given up destroying souls for a living, he'd admittedly become more easygoing and laid-back, but even so, Ford was just about catatonic in comparison. He was so chill that sometimes Jax felt like checking him for a pulse.

But nothing about Ford looked chill now. His mouth was grim, his eyes inscrutable, and he seemed shaken.

Except nothing shook Ford. *Nothing.* "What the hell's up with you? You bleeding from where her eyes stabbed daggers into your sorry ass?"

Instead of smiling, Ford shook his head. Thing was, if Ford didn't want to talk about something, then Jax would have better luck getting answers out of a rock. He looked at the table where the three sisters sat, Tara on one side of Maddie, looking tense enough to shatter, Chloe on the other, slouched back, a little distant, a little bored, and clearly frustrated.

Between them, Maddie was talking, probably trying to make everyone happy. Ever the peace maker. Even as he watched, Maddie looked at Tara, then over at Ford.

She'd noticed the tension, too.

Ford slumped in the booth a little, face turned to the window.

"Ford."

"Let it go, Jax."

"I will if you will."

Ford was silent a long moment. "You ever make a stupid mistake, one you think you can run from, only no matter how fast and far you run, it's still right there in front of you?"

"You know I have."

Ford let out a long, shuddery breath. "Well, chalk

it up to that. One I don't want to talk about now, maybe not ever." The door to the café opened, and a uniformed sheriff strode in. He was built almost deceptively lean. Deceptive because Jax knew that the guy could take down just about anything that got in his path. He'd seen him do it. Actually, he'd seen him do it to Ford.

And okay, also himself. The guy was a one-man wrecking crew when he wanted to be, and the three of them had gone a few rounds with each other over the years.

Sawyer, the third musketeer.

He made his way directly to their table and sprawled out in the chair Ford kicked his way. "Shit, what a day." He turned down the radio at his hip and looked around. "I'm starving."

The guy had been born starving. He ate like he had a tape worm, and he eyed the burgers lined up on the kitchen bar, waiting to be served. Both Jax and Ford gave him space. You didn't want to get any key body parts, like, say, a hand, in between Sawyer and grub when he was hungry.

Jax waved over their waitress, and between the three of them, they ordered enough for a small army. Sawyer didn't speak again until he'd put away two double doubles. Finally, content, he sighed and leaned back. "So. Why are we staring at the sisters?"

Not much got by Sawyer.

"What do you know about them?" Ford asked him.

"Other than Jax going at it with the middle one on the pier the other night? Which, by the way—nice, man."

Jax let out a long breath and felt a muscle bunch in his jaw. "People need to mind their own business."

Sawyer flashed a rare grin and helped himself to Jax's fries. "Not going to happen in this town. As for the other sisters, I know the oldest has a sweet ass to go with her sweet-ass accent when she's pissed, and she was pissed earlier at the post office when she found out that we don't have guaranteed overnight from here. And the youngest, she might be hot, but she's also crazy. I clocked her at seventy-six on a fucking Vespa 250. When I pulled her over and wrote her up a ticket, she said I was committing highway robbery because there was no way she'd been going a single mile per hour over sixty-five. She chewed out me, my radar gun, and my mama, and I gotta tell you, that girl has a mouth on her. Oh, and apparently I need some sort of guava shit facial because my skin is dry in my 'P' zone. Like I care about my P zone. She's going to be trouble, big trouble."

"I think it's a 'T' zone," Ford said, pointing to his own.

Sawyer sent him a look of banality. "Is there something you want to tell us?"

"Yeah, I'm fucking gay." Ford shook his head, confident in his sexuality. "And *all* women are trouble, man. Every last one."

At this, Sawyer raised a brow. Ford loved women. Always. *Period.* Sawyer looked at Jax for answers.

Jax shrugged. "It's a sucky day in Mayberry," he said and took another look at the table of sisters.

Tara was saying something through tight lips to her sisters. Chloe downed her drink and raised her hand for another.

Maddie shoved the stack of papers aside and reached into her purse, pulling out two knitting needles and a bright red skein of yarn. Jax wondered if it was the same one he'd seen wrapped around her the other morning.

Biting her lower lip between her teeth, she slowly and awkwardly worked the knitting needles, murmuring to herself as she did, clearly talking her way through each stitch with heartbreaking meticulousness. It got him right in the gut.

She got him right in the gut.

"Earth to pussy-whipped Jax."

Jax slid Ford a long look. "Pussy-whipped?"

"I thought you gave up that shit when you ran away from Seattle."

He hadn't run away from Seattle. He'd walked. Fast.

Sawyer was looking like he'd found a bright spot to his day. "So exactly how many women do you figure have thrown themselves at you since you've been back in Lucky Harbor?"

"I don't know."

"All of them," Sawyer said. "But this is the only one to hold your interest, and don't even try to tell me I'm full of shit." He hitched his chin to indicate Maddie. "So basically, it's Murphy's Law now. Sheer odds say you're about to make an ass of yourself." He said this as if it was Christmas morning and Santa Claus had delivered.

"And this makes you happy?" Jax asked in disbelief.

"Oh, fuck, yeah."

Jax took another look at the sisters. The three of them were talking, but Tara was looking at her watch. Chloe was now making eyes at the busboy's ass. Maddie still had her brow furrowed in fierce concentration as she carefully talked herself through another stitch.

"Christ, you have it bad," Ford said in disgust.

It was entirely possible that for once, he was right.

Chapter 12

*"You're as happy as you make up
your mind to be."*
PHOEBE TRAEGER

For the third morning in a row, Chloe whipped the blanket off Tara. Maddie knew this because Tara's distinct screech echoed in the small bedroom they'd been sharing in the cottage.

Where there was only one bed.

At least it was a queen-sized, and it'd been cold enough that they hadn't minded being packed in like a litter of kittens. Well, they minded Chloe talking in her sleep, because it was usually things like "harder, Zach, harder," which both Tara and Maddie could do without hearing.

Tara was still complaining about being woken up, her drawl thick and sweet as molasses. This was in direct opposition to the words she was saying, something about Chloe's questionable heritage and the turnip truck she rode in on.

Cocooned in between the wall and a pillow, Maddie snickered and burrowed deeper into her own warmth. And then the blanket was rudely ripped off her, as well. "*Goddammit!*"

Looking disgustingly cheerful and put together in black, hip-hugging yoga pants and an eye-popping pink sports bra, Chloe smacked Maddie's ass. "Get up."

"Touch *my* ass," Tara said, sitting up and pointing at her, "and die."

Chloe grinned. "Two minutes."

When she'd left the room, Tara gritted her teeth and rolled out of bed, wearing only a cami and boxers, looking annoyingly fabulous with her hair only slightly mussed. "I intensely dislike her."

"You seem to intensely dislike a lot of people. Like Ford, for instance—who I didn't realize you knew."

Tara stiffened. "I don't."

"Your accent definitely thickens when you lie. You might want to work on that."

Tara let out a long, shaky breath. "What do *you* think of him?"

"Ford?" She thought of him standing behind his bar, tall and sexy, that easy grin charming anyone in its path. "I like him. What's going on, Tara?"

"Nothing."

Maddie understood that sentiment. She had a lot of stuff that she didn't want to talk about, either. She sat up in bed and patted her hair, knowing it resembled something from the wild animal kingdom. She sighed and staggered off the bed. By day, they'd been doing their own thing. She'd been going through the "office" in the marina, trying to make sense of the wacky accounting system—which seemed to be one step above a shoebox. Tara had been cleaning. Chloe couldn't do either. She'd decided she was going to create a line of skin care products with the inn's name and give away baskets to their customers when the time came. And when they sold the inn, she hoped the new owners would want the line.

It was a great idea, unique and perfectly suited for a small, cozy beachside inn—assuming they got customers.

When Chloe wasn't working on that, she spent her time looking for trouble—and, given the two speeding tickets she'd already racked up, she'd found it.

At night, they ate as a family, which meant they fought. Maddie had discovered that it didn't matter what subject they tackled. Tara and Chloe could argue about the sky being blue.

Mostly they fought over the inn. Tara wanted a commitment from her sisters to sell. Maddie wanted a commitment to give the place a fair shot. Chloe wanted... well, no one really knew. But one thing was certain, she still didn't want to take sides.

So the tension mounted and manifested itself in stupid little disagreements. Like over yoga.

"Sixty seconds!" Chloe yelled from the living room.

Maddie tied back her hair. "Coming!"

"Liar!"

For being such a tiny thing, Chloe was a purebred pit bull. Maddie staggered to the living room, where Tara was already sitting obediently, legs crossed.

As they'd learned the hard way for three mornings running, Chloe took her yoga seriously. For the next forty-five minutes she chided, bossed, demanded, and bullied myriad poses out of them until Maddie was dripping sweat and barely standing on muscles that were quivering. "I need food," Maddie gasped.

"*Eat me?*" Chloe asked.

"If I have to eat one more greased up, heart-attack-on-a-plate meal from that place," Tara said from flat on her back, "I'm going to kill myself. *I'm* cooking."

"*Finally,*" Chloe said with relief. "What took so long?"

"I don't do it for people I don't like."

"But *sugar,* you don't like *anyone.*"

Maddie shook her head at Chloe, then looked at Tara.

"It's more that I've decided I don't *not* like you," Tara said.

Even flat on her back and sweaty, Tara exuded confidence. Maddie flopped down and sighed. She'd been working on her own confidence, but even faking it, it was still hard to go toe-to-toe with her sisters.

Half an hour later, Tara had food spread in front of her sisters that blew Maddie's mind. Blueberry wheat pancakes, egg-white omelets, turkey bacon, and fresh orange juice.

"Not a river of grease in sight," Tara said. "Chloe, stop wrinkling your brow or your face will stick like that."

"I don't like wheat pancakes—they taste like dirt." But she took a bite, chewed, then shrugged. "Okay, never mind. These don't taste like dirt."

"I don't give a flip," Tara said, mixing up more batter.

"Well, flip this," Chloe said and gave her oldest sister a middle finger.

"No, that's what I call them—'I Don't Give a Flip'

Pancakes. I could make peace on earth with those pancakes."

"You should really work on that self-esteem issue you have," Chloe said dryly, gathering ingredients of her own into a bowl—almonds, jojoba oil. "Making a cracked-heel treatment today. Because Maddie's feet need help."

"Hey," Maddie said.

"You keep rubbing those babies against my legs at night, and it hurts. And," Chloe said, looking at Maddie's plate and the way she'd carefully arranged her food, nothing touching, "you're a freak."

Maddie looked at her large plate of food and tried not to get defensive and failed. "I'm hungry. I just burned a million calories doing yoga."

"The way you do it? Not quite. And I was talking about how you're trying to keep your syrup off your eggs, not about how much food you have on your plate."

"I don't like my foods touching."

"Like I said...freak."

"Hey, I don't mock you."

"What's to mock? I'm normal." Chloe began whisking up the ingredients in her bowl for her balm, or whatever it was. "Oh, and I know I told you I was leaving tomorrow, but good news. I'm not leaving for two days, because my thing got pushed back."

"Yay for us," Tara said dryly.

Chloe ignored her. "First up is New Mexico, and then I'm thinking about going to meet a friend in Houston, who's interested in buying some of my recipes." With a sly look in Maddie's direction, Chloe set down her whisk to turn to her plate, where she purposely mixed her eggs with her pancakes, smeared it all in syrup, then dipped

a huge bite...into her orange juice. Watching Maddie
squirm, she sucked it into her mouth, making "mmm-
mmm" noises.

Maddie couldn't even watch. "You're disgusting."

Chloe just moaned in pleasure. "This is damn good
food. Boggling really."

"Why is it *boggling* that I cook well?" Tara asked in a
tone that had the air around them going frosty.

"First off, you don't cook 'well,' you cook *amazing,*
and it's boggling because I thought I was the only one
who got Mom's artistic streak. Not to mention that people
who can cook are usually more outgoing and friendly
than you are, and—"

"And," Maddie said, quickly jumping in because she'd
learned that was the best way to keep things from escalat-
ing, "you just don't seem like the cooking type."

Ignoring Maddie, Tara narrowed her eyes at Chloe.
"Finish your sentence."

"Are these blueberries fresh?" Maddie asked desperately. "Cuz they taste fresh."

"You seriously think that you're the only one who got
anything from Mom?" Tara asked Chloe.

"I know I'm the only one who liked her."

"You didn't even know her, not really!"

"And the orange juice," Maddie interjected into the
very tense room. Her first instinct was to find a hole to
crawl into. Her second was to grab her knitting, which
she'd discovered was not only a sentimental escape, but
was also a great relaxation technique. Better than chips.
Problem was, she couldn't look away from the impending
train wreck. "The orange juice is amazing, Tara. How did
you get out all the pulp?"

"I knew her better than you," Chloe said to Tara. "At least I called her."

"I called." Tara's voice was pure South, dripping with fury. "She screened me!"

"Well, maybe there was a reason."

"Like what?"

"Like maybe because you're controlling and anal and a b—"

Tara slammed her hands down on the counter.

Maddie nearly leapt out of her skin, and her elbow hit Chloe's bowl of . . . whatever concoction she'd been making. The contents flew out, splattering across Tara's face.

After a horrendous, thundering beat of silence, Tara scraped herself clean and glared at Chloe. "This is because I asked you to leave my house when you visited me for Easter last year."

"Hey, it's Maddie's elbow that got you all covered in liquid, not me."

"I didn't mean to," Maddie said, gaping at the goop dripping off Tara's nose. Maddie had some of Chloe's foot balm on her, as well, but she didn't look at it because she had a burning question. "And how come I never got an Easter invite?"

"You were somewhere on a movie set, I think," Tara said. "This year I'll ask you instead of her, believe me."

"And you didn't ask me to leave," Chloe said. "You *kicked me out.* Because your husband's friend kissed me!"

Tara was holding a ladle full of pancake batter, and she pointed it violently in Chloe's direction. "He was *my* friend, too. And *you* kissed *him!*"

Chloe jumped to her feet. "I knew you didn't believe me!"

Tara tossed her plate into the sink with enough violence to splash soapy dishwater all over Maddie.

"Great!" Maddie said, pulling her shirt away from her skin with a suction sound.

"I'm done talking," Tara informed them loftily, which was hard to pull off with some balm on her face, but she managed.

"Good tactic," Chloe said. "Ignore all your problems—because that seems to be working out so well for you."

Maddie stood up. *Quiet strength,* she told herself. *Just project quiet strength, like ... Julia Roberts in* Erin Brockovich. Okay, so Erin wasn't always quiet in her strength, and you know what? She didn't have to be, either. So with a deep breath, Maddie said, "Shut up."

Both sisters stared at her.

"We all know what we're really tense about."

The inn. How the final vote between the three of them would go. What would happen ... With a sigh, she picked up her knitting instead of inhaling any more food and continued from where she'd left off last night. "In, wrap around," she said to herself. "Pull out."

"You know," Chloe said, licking some batter off her thumb. "The way you knit always sounds a little dirty. I bet if you knitted in earshot of a guy, you'd get laid for sure."

Tara was tossing breakfast dishes into the running sink, each harder than the last, if that was possible.

Chloe responded by cranking up her music via her iPod Touch parked in the dock on the counter. Hip-hop thumped out of the speakers. Tara hated hip-hop, and her head whipped around like the possessed victim in a horror flick.

"In, wrap around," Maddie said, trying to find the calm. "Pull out—"

The back door opened, and all three of them swiveled to look as Jax filled the doorway. He looked like sin on a stick in faded Levi's, a long-sleeved graphic Henley, and—there went her pulse—that damn tool belt slung low on his hips.

Izzy was at his side, alert and panting happily until she caught the tension in the room. With a soft whine, she sat on Jax's foot. Jax set a hand on her head as his gaze went straight to Maddie. "Problem?" he asked over the booming bass.

Yep, Maddie thought, more reading his lips than actually hearing him. A big problem, actually. Because whenever she so much as looked at him, no matter what was going on around her, her body got all quivery. Some parts more than others.

"No problem, sugar," Tara drawled, a polite smile on her face as she slapped the power button on the iPod dock, forcing a sudden quiet over all of them. "Blueberry pancakes?"

With a sound of disgust, Chloe pushed her way to the door. "They're both nuts," she warned Jax as she passed him. "Freaking nuts. I'm going for a ride."

Giving up the pretense, Tara wiped her hands on a towel, her dignity somewhat ruined by the sole blueberry left in her hair. "Me, too. I need to get out."

Maddie handed over her car keys.

"Thanks, sugar." And then Tara was gone, too.

Still covered in a sticky, wet combo of batter and soapy water, Maddie remained seated, carefully holding her knitting so it didn't get dirty. To her left, the water was still running in the sink, bubbles rising high. Jax came toward her in that easy, steady stride of his. The singular intent in his gaze had her faltering on the next knitting stitch, partly because she couldn't look at him and knit at the same time. Much like how she couldn't look at him and breathe, either.

Two big, warm hands pulled the large plastic needles and yarn out of her fingers and set them on the counter in the sole clean spot left in the whole kitchen. "Want to talk about it?"

Which—that her sisters were crazy, and she might be, too? Or that she'd been dreaming about him, nightly fantasies involving a lot of nakedness with all his good parts getting intimately acquainted with all her good parts?

"I . . . it's . . . No," she finally managed. "Not really." She looked down at herself. "I need to take another shower."

Grabbing a chair, he spun it around and straddled it directly in front of her. He gazed at the batter and water splattered on her, taking his time about it, too. "Ford and Sawyer are never going to forgive me for missing the girl-on-girl fight. Can I at least lie and say I saw a little of it? And that you guys were all wearing tiny tank tops and panties?"

A reluctant smile tore from her lips, and, given the warmth that filled his eyes at the sight of it, that's what he'd meant to happen. "Guys are perverts," she said.

"Mmm-hmm." He was busy watching a glob of batter make its way down the curve of her right breast, disappearing down the front of her shirt.

Maddie swiped at it with a finger, but before she could wipe it on a napkin, Jax took her hand and, still holding eye contact, sucked it off her finger.

At the strong pull of his warm, wet tongue, she shivered.

"You taste good enough to eat," he said, eyes darkening as he watched her nipples pebble against her T-shirt.

"Shower," she said out loud, reminding herself. "I need to shower."

His fingers sank into her hair, his thumb gliding softly along her jaw. "I'm good in the shower, Maddie."

She shivered again, heat swamping her. "Do you always say everything that comes to your mind, no holding back?"

"Usually, but I'm holding back right now."

"You are?"

He nodded with eyes so hot they scorched her skin. "If I told you what I was thinking," he said, voice low and seductive. "You'd probably run for the hills."

She shuddered again. Strength... "Tell me anyway."

"Maddie—"

"*Tell me.*"

Leaning on the back of his chair, he was so close now that when he spoke, his lips lightly brushed hers with every word. "I want to put my hands all over you. I want to..."

Her breath caught, and she felt herself go damp. "What?"

"Touch. Kiss. Lick. Nibble. And then—"

At that moment, the sink—still running—finally overfilled, and water splashed to the floor. Jumping up, she cracked her head on Jax's chin. Staggering back, she held her head. "Ouch!"

Jax shut off the faucet. His boots squeaked in the water on the floor as he turned back to her, a red spot already blooming on his chin.

Staring at the spot in horror, she took a step backward
out of sheer instinct. "I'm sorry, I'm so sorry—are you
okay?"

"Your head isn't that hard." Calmly, he crossed the
room to her, not allowing space between them. "You
have two choices." His tone was light and easy, his hands
going to her hips to gently squeeze. "You can kiss it better, or you can go take your shower."

It was as if her body took over the decision-making
process from her brain, because she went up on tiptoes
and pressed her lips to the spot she'd hit. He had a
little stubble going, just enough to feel deliciously male
beneath her lips, and she slowly inhaled against him,
breathing him in.

A low groan rumbled from his chest, and his hands
tightened on her, just as Tara walked back in.

She took a moment to glare at Jax, who held her gaze
with an even look of his own.

"Sugar," she finally said to Maddie, grabbing the
jacket she'd forgotten off the hook by the back door.
"You can either fuck him or hire him, but you shouldn't
do both. That's the advanced class, and you're not ready."
She walked back out, and a minute later they heard the
car start up.

Maddie let out a long, shaky breath. Tara was usually
the voice of reason, but this decision was not majority
rules. This decision was hers alone.

Jax was still in her space, quiet, watchful.

Sexy as hell.

Patient.

He wanted her. His body was tight with the wanting,
but it was her decision.

Alex had made all the decisions. Maybe not in the beginning, but somewhere along the way with him she'd lost herself. She'd let it happen. That was another thing that was going to change. If she wanted something, she was going to get it. If she wanted someone, she was going to take him.

She wanted Jax. She wanted the oblivion, she wanted to feel good, she wanted...

To be wanted. And a little bit of ravishing and cherishing would be good. Love would be better, but as Tara had noted, she wasn't ready for that. She was, however, ready for this, this one time. And even if she wasn't, it didn't matter. She wanted him.

Grabbing his hand, she pulled him with her out of the kitchen. Allowing it, he brushed his big, hard body up against her back.

In the small bathroom, she dug through Chloe's bathroom bag on the counter and came up with a condom, which she handed to Jax, who hit the lock on the door.

She started the shower, then reached for the hem of her shirt. He took over, slowly pulling it off, tossing it to the floor. Then he repeated the gesture with his own shirt.

She found the tattoos, which made her weak in the knees. A tribal band around a biceps, another down one side from the top of his ribs to his oblique muscle.

She wanted to lick them.

"Maddie."

She couldn't stop staring at him, all hard and warm and delineated with strength. "I don't want to talk," she said.

Amusement crowded for space with the hunger in his gaze. "What do you want?"

"You. Now. Fast. Maybe hard, too."

"You got me. But not fast, not hard." He ran a long finger over the front hook of her bra. "Not our first time."

"Our *only* time," she corrected.

"Hmm," he murmured noncommittally, and with a flick of his wrist, her bra fell to the floor. He covered her mouth with his and unbuttoned her jeans, slowly sliding them to the floor.

"Christ, Maddie. Look at you. You take my breath away." His dark gaze took her in and got darker as he kicked off his boots and shucked his clothes, revealing the rest of his mouthwatering body in its entirety, including the part of him she wanted inside her, *yesterday*.

Leaning past her, he checked the temperature of the water while she checked out his perfect ass. As usual, he caught her at it and sent her a heated smile that dissolved her bones as he tugged her into the shower with him. In contrast to the hot water, his hands were still a little chilly from being outside, giving her a zing when he slid them up to cup her breasts.

Her eyes drifted shut and her other senses took over. His body was unyielding, strong, rippling with power against hers. He was hard, and huge.

It should have made her nervous. Instead, it turned her on, and she pressed closer, wrenching an appreciative male growl from him.

"Be sure, Maddie."

She opened her eyes. The steam from the shower was fogging the tiny bathroom, making it hot and humid. "If you even think about stopping now, I'm going to have to hurt you."

He stared down at her for a beat, then murmured her

name before kissing her, slow and deep. She'd never felt more aroused, more wanted, and it made her tremble.

Jax pulled back, his hands threading into her hair, holding her gaze. She had no idea what he was looking for, but something in her expression must have reassured him, because he brought his mouth back to hers, his tongue flicking out over her bottom lip. His hands slid down her body, cupping her bottom, lifting her to grind his hips to hers. He was hard and thick against her, straining between them. Pushing her back further into the shower, he kissed his way over her, starting with her throat and working his way down. He had a nipple in his mouth, sucking it hard between his tongue and the roof of his mouth when she reached down and wrapped her hand around his hard, pulsing length. When she stroked him, he groaned and covered her hand with his, moving with her, showing her what he liked, until suddenly he stopped her.

"You don't like that?" she asked.

"I love that." His voice was hoarse, unsteady. "But it's been too long." With the water washing over their bodies, he nibbled at her neck, cupping a breast, rasping his thumb over her nipple, none of which deterred his free hand from slipping between her thighs. When he felt how ready she was, he dropped his forehead to hers and said her name in a jagged whisper.

She clutched at him. "Now, Jax. Please, now."

His finger was tracing over her, stroking, teasing. "I love how wet you are," he murmured against her ear, sucking the lobe into his mouth as he slid a finger inside her.

With a strangled cry, she rocked to him. "It means I'm ready."

He brushed his lips against hers. "Just making sure."

"I'm *sure!*"

He added another finger, gliding deep while brushing his thumb over her in just the right rhythm until she came with a rush. While she was still shuddering, he rolled on the condom and slid inside of her with a single, sure push of his hips.

She gasped, arching helplessly as it extended her orgasm. When she could open her eyes, she blinked him into focus. His eyes were solid black and locked on hers, intense and fierce. As he began to move within her, she felt the tile at her back, warm from both her own body heat and the hot water pulsing down over them. His strokes were strong and steady and sent her spiraling. He came with her, the both of them rocking together, gasping for breath. Unable to stand, they slid to the shower floor, still entwined.

Completely spent, Maddie dropped her head to his chest, managing a smile when he drew her in against him with a wordless protective murmur, pressing his face in her hair. At the tender touch, something came over her, something new. It was both warm and wonderful.

And terrifying. Because he'd given her just what she wanted.

Only she already wanted more.

Chapter 13

"My momma always said that two rattlesnakes living in the same hole will get along better than two sisters. So I had three daughters to improve the odds."
PHOEBE TRAEGER

The next day Jax spent most of his time at the inn, stripping old windowpanes and carpeting.

And watching Maddie.

She'd pretty much kicked him to the curb after yesterday's shower. It was a first for him, not being the one to need space, and he hadn't known what kind of reception to expect this morning.

She'd greeted him with a sweet, warm smile, and because she wasn't one to fake anything, that had told him that they were okay. "How about dinner tonight?" he asked her midday.

Maddie glanced at him, then back to her task of hauling out the debris. She was looking hot and just a little bit breathless. Her hair was wild, her shirt untucked, and the seat of her jeans was dirty.

He couldn't take his eyes off her.

"Can't," she said.

He tossed the load in his arms into the back of the Dumpster they'd had delivered and brushed his hands off on his jeans, catching her arm before she could turn away. "Can't? Or won't?"

She closed her eyes but then surprised him by dropping her head to his chest. "I'm all dirty and sweaty, Jax."

"I like dirty and sweaty," he said, drawing her into his arms. "And it's just dinner, not a ring or a white picket fence."

Choking out a laugh, she pressed in even closer, sighing when he kissed her temple. But then after a moment, and far before he was ready, she backed away from his touch and met his gaze. "But no condom on this dinner date, right? Because…"

"…Because you're not ready for this."

"I just need…I really need to take a step backward from anything serious."

And sex for her was serious. He understood. Hell, what they'd experienced in the shower was so serious, he still hadn't recovered. "Take the step back if you need it. Hell, take two. Just don't go running away."

That brought a small smile. "I no longer run."

"Good," he said and went back to work, for the first time in five years wanting something he couldn't have.

Maddie divided her time between the marina office and painting the inn's bedrooms. Tara helped with the painting. Chloe couldn't do much because of her asthma. Maddie got that, but the way she held herself separate from them, working on her skin care line instead of the inn, was more worrisome than annoying. At some point, Chloe was going to have to exercise the swing vote, and Maddie had no idea which way she'd go. With a sigh, Maddie watched Tara walk across the yard, gingerly carrying paint supplies. Tara had at least deigned to get her hands dirty, risking her manicure. Not because she believed in the cause.

Nope, what Tara believed in was saving money.

Over the past few days, Maddie had finished the paperwork for refinancing their loan and filed it at the bank. Her fingers were crossed. Tara and Chloe were both leaving tomorrow, and Maddie would be on her own. But that was a worry for later, she told herself. For the moment, she was covered from head to toe in paint.

"I'm changing my penny-pinching stance," Tara huffed at her side, with hardly any paint on her. "We should have hired someone to do this part."

Maddie had no idea how her sister had managed to stay clean, but it was really annoying. Perhaps it was the invisible bubble of righteous perfection that clearly surrounded her. "We should have hired someone? You did not just say that."

Tara sighed. "I hate being peasant stock." She swiped her brow, but Maddie didn't see a drop of sweat on her. Maybe she had a sweat-gland disorder or something. That thought made her smile a little. Only Tara could have a medical condition that aided her perfect southern belle image.

"You okay?" Tara asked.

"Yes, why?"

"Because for the past few days, you've been . . . different somehow."

Yes. Multiple orgasms tended to do a body good.

"You went out with Jax last night."

"Just for dinner." And a few hot-as-hell kisses. Turned out, she didn't really want to take *too* many steps backward, only a little one. A real little one.

"So you're okay?"

"Yep."

Tara nodded and looked at her hands. "You know, I'm not normally one to gripe." She narrowed her eyes when Maddie snorted. "But I would like to make an official complaint that *I* didn't get the asthma in the family."

Maddie had to give her that one. Chloe was sitting a hundred yards away on the dock, free of the chemicals that would have sent her into asthma hell, surrounded by bowls and containers filled with ingredients like eggs and honey and almonds. "What is she making today?"

"Some facial to clean out our pores when we're done," Tara said. "And she's brewing some sort of soothing homemade sun tea that reduces stress." Her tone said this was as likely as them making a go of the inn. "She said it'd be better than a spa day."

"I've never had a spa day," Maddie said on a sigh.

"And you have the pores to prove it."

"What? I do not." Maddie moved to the hallway and stared at herself in the full-length mirror leaning against the wall, the one they'd pulled off one of the interior guest room doors. Oh, boy. Her hair looked like she'd stuck her finger in a live electrical socket, and her skin was shiny with perspiration, but she didn't see any pores. Probably because she was layered in a fine dusting of paint. She paused, searching for a natural transition to the question she wanted to ask and found none. So she jumped right in. "Why are you mad that Chloe kissed Logan's best friend?"

"Because *she* wanted Scott for herself," Chloe said from behind them, having come inside without either of them noticing. She was wearing leggings, a miniskirt, and a sweater that said DEAR SANTA, LET ME EXPLAIN. Eyes inscrutable, she handed them each a small vial. "Try this. Let me know if you notice a difference in the next twenty-four hours."

"But you're both leaving in the morning," Maddie said.

Chloe shrugged.

Tara didn't say anything. Done painting, she pulled on her sweater and wrapped a red scarf around her neck. Maddie had finished the scarf the night before, when she couldn't sleep because she'd been too busy reliving Jax's hands on her body.

The scarf was crooked, but just looking at it gave Maddie a little tug of pride. Her next project, started this morning, was with the green skein of yarn she'd commandeered from her mother's stash, which made it feel just as special as the red one. It wasn't quite as crooked— yet—but give her some time.

"You can text me," Chloe told them, voice flat.

Tara sighed. "I didn't want Scott for myself."

Chloe just gave her a long, level look.

"I didn't. I was just jealous because…well, because you make it so damn easy. You make friends in the blink of an eye, and I don't. This may come as a surprise to both of you, but some people find me…unapproachable."

Chloe was quiet for a long moment, and it wasn't clear if she was trying to fight a grimace or a smile.

"You shouldn't be here," Tara told her. "You'll get an asthma attack."

"I know but the bank just called. You and I each missed signing one of the loan docs. I'll take you on the Vespa."

"Are you going to promise not to kill me?"

"Only if you promise not to irritate me."

They left, and Maddie figured the odds were fifty–fifty that they'd both survive the short trip. She stared at herself in the mirror. She was wearing a long-sleeved knit tee and jeans, and she realized that for the first time in recent history, the button on the jeans wasn't cutting into her belly. Huh. She lifted the hem of the shirt and stared at her middle. It might have been wishful thinking on her part, but it seemed flatter. "Maybe I should forget to eat potato chips more often."

Two big, warm hands slid beneath hers, callused palms flat on her stomach. Her gaze collided with Jax's warm, amused one in the mirror.

For two days, he'd found a way to have his hands and/ or his lips on her every chance he got. Yesterday morning, he'd been wielding a huge power saw like a sexy lumberjack, cutting the fallen tree in the yard. When he'd caught her watching him, he'd pressed her up against the stack of cut wood, slid his hands beneath her shirt, and kissed her senseless.

Yesterday afternoon, he'd backed her into the upstairs linen closet and she'd spent the best five minutes of her life making out like they were teenagers.

Except she was fairly certain that a teenage boy couldn't have brought her to orgasm with nothing more than a touch of his fingers.

"Mmm," Jax murmured now, those magic fingers stroking lightly across her stomach. "Soft and warm."

"But not hard and ripped like you." She tried to say this critically, but it was difficult not to sound breathless with his hands on her bare skin, his chest plastered to her back, and his hips snuggled to hers.

"I've definitely got the hard taken care of." Still holding her gaze in the mirror, he rubbed his jaw to hers as he slowly rocked into her.

He was right. He had the hard taken care of. She thrust her bottom into him, moaning when he thrust back. At the sound, he whipped her around to face him, slowly pressing her back into the wall.

"You've had a rough morning," he murmured, his mouth descending to her neck.

"Yes. I'm dirty, Jax."

"Don't tease me."

That got a low laugh out of her, and she shifted closer. She felt him smile against her skin as she obviously acquiesced, not caring as long as he didn't stop.

He didn't. His lips brushed just beneath her ear, and his hands headed north.

"You're tense."

"A little," she admitted. Her fingers were in his hair. He had better hair than she did, the bastard, all soft and silky.

"A lot," he murmured against her, spreading hot, open-mouthed kisses along her jaw and down her throat, which he then gently bit.

A gasp escaped her, and she clutched at him, moaning when he licked the spot to soothe the slight sting. His hands slid up her ribs and very lightly grazed the undersides of her breasts. "I'm excellent at relieving stress," he said, and his thumbs glided over her nipples, wrenching a shocked, aroused cry from her that he swallowed with his mouth, kissing her until they had to tear apart to breathe.

"Still need space?" he asked.

"Maybe later."

His smile was sheer sex. "Are we alone?"

"Yes, but—" She looked around the hallway. "Here? You want to do it here?"

"Yes or no, Maddie."

"*Yes.*"

He kissed her again, slipping a hand between her thighs, his fingers pressing on just the right spot to drive her even more wild. It'd taken him four and a half minutes to get her to the toe-curling point yesterday. Right now she was pretty sure he could have her there in half the time, which was more than a little embarrassing.

"Jax—"

His fingers began to move, but a low growl conveyed his frustration with her jeans. A second later, he'd unbuttoned them and slid a hand inside. "Jesus," he murmured reverently.

Lost, she ground her hips against him and heard him swear roughly into the side of her neck. All this while his fingers continued to give her exactly what she needed. Like yesterday, it took shockingly little to topple her over the edge. She burst with a shudder and a soft cry and would have fallen to the ground if he hadn't supported all her weight.

When she stopped panting and her vision cleared, she realized she had a death grip on him. "Sorry," she managed a little hoarsely.

"Christ, are you kidding? I'll be thinking about that all day." Tucking a damp curl behind her ear, he buttoned and zipped her back up, and then studied her face. "Better. You look a lot less tense now."

"And you look more tense."

"I'll live."

"Or I could..." She pulled him toward her and placed her lips on his jaw. "Repay the favor."

He groaned and pulled her in tight, but they both went still as a car pulled up in the yard.

Jax looked out and groaned, dropping his head to Maddie's shoulder. "Material delivery."

When he was gone, Maddie sat down right there on the floor. He had a way of filling her with mind-blowing pleasure. She wanted to lose herself in it, but she wouldn't. She'd made that mistake before and still wasn't ready to trust herself.

Fifteen minutes later, Tara walked back inside the inn and executed a double take at Maddie sitting on the floor in the dirty foyer. "What are you doing?"

Waiting for her bones to reappear. "Nothing."

"So why do you look like you either just ate a bag of chips or got lucky?"

"What?" Maddie dragged herself upright and looked in the mirror. Flushed. Damp. Glowing.

Well, hell.

"Don't let Chloe know you're still eating chips," Tara said on a sigh. "She'll triple our yoga regimen."

Maddie nodded. "Okie-dokie, I won't tell Chloe about the chips..."

Or the orgasms...

Chapter 14

"Life is short. Eat cake."
PHOEBE TRAEGER

Their last night together, Maddie and her sisters ended up at Eat Me Café. Silver and blue tinsel hung everywhere, and cut-outs of Santa's reindeer were hanging from the rafters. Tara was, as usual, overdressed in designer jeans and a blazer. Maddie had gone with her decidedly not-designer jeans and her thickest sweater in deference to the chilly weather. Chloe was wearing denim leggings, kickass boots, and a long-sleeved shirt that read I MELTED FROSTY.

"Now we're going to get along," Maddie told them, walking through the decorated café. "Or I'm going to let my pores get big and go back to eating potato chips three meals a day."

"I don't believe you," Tara said, cool as a cucumber. "You're going to hit the Love Shack, get trashed, and do something extremely inappropriate with our master renovation expert."

Chloe raised her hand. "Can I vote for that? I think getting mastered by our sexy carpenter is a good idea."

Maddie's good parts all stood up and voted for that, too.

Tara shook her head. "Bad idea, sugar. Still not ready."

"Are you saying he's out of her league?" Chloe asked.

"I'm saying he's so far out of her league that she can't even *see* his league." Tara looked at Maddie. "No offense. I don't mean he's too good for you. I mean he's too..."

"Hot," Chloe supplied.

"Yes," Tara said. "Hot. You have to work your way up to a man like that. Maybe start out with a basic model." Her eyes roamed the bar and landed on a good-looking man who was pulling a bag of tea leaves from his plaid coat pocket and signaling the waitress for a cup of hot water. "Someone like him," she said. "A training-bra version of Jax."

Maddie sighed. "Subject change, please." She lifted her water glass. "How about a toast to Mom, for bringing us together."

Chloe and Tara lifted their glasses. "To Mom," they said in unison.

"Aw." Maddie smiled. "You two are so cute when you're in accord." Empowered, she lifted her glass again. "To our new venture, the three of us."

Silence.

"To our new venture," Maddie repeated, giving them the evil eye.

"To our new venture," they murmured.

"*The three of us*," she said firmly.

"The three of us," they muttered.

"But we're still selling," Tara said.

"Maybe selling," Maddie said, looking at Chloe. "You going to pick a side anytime soon?"

"Soon," she said noncommittally.

"Admit it," Tara said. "You like being the swing vote."

"Well, I do live to annoy you."

Thirty long, awkward minutes later, they still hadn't been served. The tension was rising. Tara and Chloe had a limit on the amount of time they could spend in close quarters, and they'd met it. "So about that weather, huh?" Maddie asked.

Both sisters just stared at her.

Cripes. She searched her brain for a joke and came up empty. Desperate, she flagged down the only waitress in the place.

"Sorry," the waitress huffed out, not stopping. "Our chef quit, and we're going nuts."

"*Chef,*" Tara said under her breath. "That guy wasn't a chef. He was a short-order cook trained at Taco Bell, bless his heart."

"Hey, I like Taco Bell," Maddie said.

"You would, darlin'."

Chloe snorted. "You are *such* a food snob."

"I beg your pardon." The South dripped from each word. *Delta Burke save us.* "I'd work here."

"Right," Chloe said. "*You'd* work *here.*"

"Absolutely."

"Admit it, you'd *never* lower yourself to work in a place like this, with real people and real food," Chloe said.

Tara's jaw began to spasm, and Maddie's belly matched it. Instead of pulling out the Tums, Maddie grabbed the half of a green scarf and knitting needles. True to form, this scarf was already crooked.

"Food. Snob," Chloe repeated softly to Tara, who abruptly stood, tugged on the hem of her perfect little blazer, and strode purposely toward the kitchen, heels clicking on the chipped linoleum.

"Holy shit," Chloe said, watching her go. "She's going to do it." She grinned and leaned back, like she'd just completed a job well done. "God, she's so easy."

"Why?" Maddie asked, baffled. "Why do you mess with her?"

"Because it's fun?"

Tara talked to the owner and vanished into the kitchen. In twenty minutes, the bell started ringing, accompanied by Tara's voice demanding that the waitress hustle because she didn't want the food served cold.

In another hour, the owner of Eat Me Café was begging Tara to sign on until they could get a permanent replacement. Maddie and Chloe had left their table and were in the kitchen now, staring in shock at how fast the chaos had been organized.

"I suppose I could stay a little longer," Tara said. "If they get me *real* garlic, no more of this dried crap."

"So you're *not* leaving in the morning?" Maddie asked.

"No." Tara was chopping onions at the speed of light. "I'm not leaving."

"But your husband. Your great job. Your perfect life."

Tara never even looked up as her hands continued to move so fast they were a blur. "Truth?"

"Please," Maddie said, confused.

"I don't have a great job. I do inventory for a chain of hotel's cafés and restaurants, and I hate it."

Maddie blinked. "And Logan?"

Pain and wistful regret came and went in Tara's gaze. "He's driving NASCAR, he's on the road 24/7. I gave up traveling with him two years ago. I was jealous of his career and bitter about being relegated to third place in his life behind his car and crew. I divorced him. I'm alone and have been for a year and a half."

"There's been no one else?"

"Well, for a little while I thought maybe I could start a thing with a close friend, but *someone* else got in the way."

"Me," Chloe said softly. "I got in the way."

Tara sighed. "I don't blame you for it. I was still missing Logan. It wouldn't have been right."

"Excuse me, girls."

The three of them turned to face Lucille. She wore her eye-popping pink track suit, minus the white headband. Today it was a rainbow-colored knit cap. Maddie introduced her to her sisters.

Lucille smiled at Chloe. "The wild one."

Chloe saluted smartass-like, but with a genuine smile. "At your service."

"And you," Lucille said, pointing to Tara. "You're the Steel Magnolia who sometimes forgets to breathe. Just wanted to say that was the best turkey club I've ever had, thank you. You're gifted. Oh, and I hear the inn's coming along. Looking forward to working for you girls."

Tara blinked as the older woman smiled and walked away. "I don't forget to breathe."

"Sometimes you do," Chloe said. "Can we rewind a minute? Back to the you-don't-blame-me thing? Cuz I gotta tell you, it feels a little like you do."

Tara took a deep breath, her fingers still chopping, chopping, chopping. "I might have a few anger issues."

"*No*," Chloe said in mock disbelief.

"And maybe some misplaced resentment."

"How long is it going to be misplaced?"

Tara grimaced and stopped chopping. "I'll let you know. But I am sorry for being a bitch, if that helps. And I'm sorry for any future bitchery."

Chloe cupped a hand behind her ear. "I'm sorry, what was that?"

"*I'm sorry!* Okay? I'm very, very *sorry!*" she yelled.

Chloe grinned. "I heard you. I just like hearing you say sorry."

Tara narrowed her gaze and tightened her grip on her knife, but Maddie stepped between them. "We'll just get out of your hair now," she said quickly, grabbing Chloe by the back of her shirt. She turned and bumped into Jax.

Ford was with him, and they were both eyeing the mountain of food with interest. "Heard there was a new chef," Ford said and met Tara's shocked gaze.

An awkward silence filled the kitchen. Maddie decided it wasn't the mouse who needed to fill it, but the new, improved, strong Maddie. So even though Tara and Ford obviously had some connection, she went with the benefit of the doubt. "Tara" she said. "Have you met—"

"Ford," Tara said calmly, her eyes anything but.

"Tara," Ford said just as calmly.

"So you two *do* know each other," Chloe said.

"No," Tara said.

"Yes," Ford said.

Maddie could have cut the tension with the knife in Tara's hand, the one that was currently looking a little white-knuckled for her taste. She reached out to try to take it, but Tara began slicing a tomato.

Actually, *slicing* was too gentle a word for what Tara was doing with deadly and lethal precision. More like making ketchup.

"Everyone who wants to keep all their body parts needs to get the hell out," Tara drawled coolly.

"Tara," Ford said quietly.

"No." She pointed the knife at him, not threateningly, necessarily, but not exactly gently, either. "No talking in my kitchen."

Ford's jaw bunched as he turned to Jax. There was some silent communication thing, and Jax opened the kitchen door, nudging Maddie and Chloe out ahead of him.

Ford shut the door.

On the other side of it, Maddie looked at Jax, who shook his head. "I don't know," he told her. "I don't know any more than you."

"Yeah, well, I hope you weren't that fond of him," Chloe said.

But Ford came out three minutes later, unscathed. At least physically.

"You going to explain that?" Maddie asked him.

Looking uncharacteristically tense, Ford shook his head. "No."

No. Of course not.

The next morning, Jax was on the second story of the inn sanding the wood floors into submission when he heard the rumble of Chloe's Vespa start up.

Setting down the sander, he walked past a snoozing

Izzy to the window. In the yard below, Chloe sat on her bike. Tara was on one side, hands shoved in the pockets of her long coat. Not Maddie. Nope, she stood directly in front of the Vespa, hands on hips.

Chloe said something.

Maddie said something.

Tara didn't.

Then Maddie removed the god-awful green scarf she wore, the one she'd been making for the past few days, and wrapped it around Chloe's neck.

Chloe looked down at it and grinned. Whatever she said had Maddie throwing herself at Chloe and hugging her tight. After a single beat of hesitation, Chloe returned the hug, awkwardly patting Maddie on the back.

Maddie craned her neck and sent Tara a *get-your-ass-over-here* gesture.

Jax watched Tara fight with herself, then capitulate to the "Mouse," who'd never really been much of a mouse at all. Tara stepped forward and nudged Chloe in the shoulder. Chloe nudged back, and then Maddie yanked them both closer and into a hug.

Afterward, Chloe drove off, and Maddie swiped at her eyes like a mother seeing her baby off on the first day of kindergarten.

Tara went into the cottage, but Maddie stayed there on the driveway, watching until the Vespa vanished from view.

Without taking the time to drop his tool belt, Jax headed for the stairs with a sleepy Izzy at his heels. He half expected Maddie to have vanished by the time he got outside, but she still stood in the same spot. Her eyes were wet but no longer leaking, for which he was infinitely grateful, though his heart clenched hard at the sight of her misery. "You okay?"

At the sound of his voice, she angrily swiped her nose on her sleeve. "No, and don't be nice." Her voice cracked, and she turned away. "Not yet, not until I . . . get this thing out of my eye."

"Aw, Maddie. Come here."

With a soft sniff, she whirled and threw herself at him, making the tools on his belt jangle as his arms came around her hard.

"I'm going to miss her," she whispered, her hands fisted in his shirt and her face plastered to his neck. "Which is ridiculous. We hardly know each other—"

"It's not ridiculous." Sliding a hand into her hair, he tugged her head up so he could see her eyes. "You love her."

"Every pissy, sarcastic, bitchy inch." She dropped her forehead to his chest and sniffed again.

He squeezed her tight and gave her a few minutes. Finally she relaxed and lifted her head.

"She'll be back," he said.

"Yes," she agreed, sounding better, much to his relief. "She'll be back." She shifted against him, then sucked in a breath when his hammer jabbed into her hip.

"Sorry," he said. "Let me drop the belt—"

"No." She held on when he would have pulled away. "Don't. I like it."

Again, he lifted her face, and he smiled. "The tool belt turns you on."

"No." She closed her eyes and thunked her forehead to his chest. "Little bit."

Delighted and also immediately aroused, he laughed,

and she groaned. "Don't judge me. Apparently *everything* turns me on here in Washington. I think it's the ocean air." She rubbed her forehead back and forth over his chest. "Or…"

"Or…" He tightened his grip on her hair when the tip of her nose brushed over his nipple.

"Or learning to stand up for myself." Going up on tiptoe, she pressed her face into his throat and inhaled, her hips bumping his.

His eyes drifted shut as he held her to him. "Try again," he murmured against her mouth.

She stared into his eyes. "It's you."

"*Us,*" he corrected and kissed her, hot and insistent. She responded with a satisfying, soft whimper of need that went straight through him. He still held her ponytail, controlling the angle of her head, but he didn't have anything to do with the way she melted against him, trying to climb into his skin to get closer. Their tongues slid together in a rhythm that made him groan, as did her hands, which were all over him, slipping beneath his shirt, gliding over his back as if she couldn't get enough.

He sure as hell couldn't, but he wasn't going to get what he wanted out here in the yard, even when her hands came around to his front, playing with his abs, then with the waistband on his jeans, which were loose enough to allow the tips of her fingers to slip inside. He held his breath and wished she'd go south another half an inch—

"Oh, for the love of God."

Tara was hands on hips when they broke apart. She glared at Jax. "So was that tongue lashing you just gave her included in the bid?"

Chapter 15

*"Men are like parking spots. All the good ones are
taken, and those that aren't are inaccessible."*
PHOEBE TRAEGER

Maddie rounded on Tara. "You'll have to excuse me,"
she said. "Since I didn't get the memo about you having
the right to butt in on my business."

"How about I just remind you that you gave up men
for a damn good reason. You need to slow down and
think before acting."

"I spent my life doing that. It hasn't worked out so
well. I'm trying something new."

"At our expense," Tara said.

"Well, excuse me for lacking the *perfect* gene from
the Traeger pool."

Tara nearly choked at that. "Sugar, if you think my
life is perfect, you need to take off the rose-colored
glasses."

"Hey, until last night, you wanted *all* of us to
believe it."

Tara stared at her, myriad emotions dancing across her face, with hurt leading the pack. "Well," she finally said a little stiffly. "Nobody's perfect." And with a final glare in Jax's direction—one that he didn't need translated—she stalked off.

Maddie blew out a breath, then looked at Jax. "Tell me why I feel like I just kicked a kitten."

He gave a slow shake of his head. "A wild tiger, maybe. Not a kitten."

She smiled grimly and backed away. "I need something to do. Work, maybe."

"You could help me sand the floors."

"Tempting, but I need something more physical. I need to tear something up. You got anything like that?"

You could tear me up. In bed. For a minute his head actually spun with that image, but he shook it off and grabbed her hand. "I've got just the thing."

"Is it X-rated?"

He nearly smiled at the slightly hopeful tone in her voice. "Maybe later."

In less than five minutes, he had her suitably protected and holding an ax. He pointed to the pile of huge wood rounds he'd created from the fallen tree earlier in the week. "Have at it."

With a tight, thankful smile, she gripped the handle but then hesitated.

"Problem?"

She gave him an apologetic glance. "Feels weird with you watching."

"I like to watch."

She rolled her eyes and shoved a few curls out of her

face. "I know it's silly, but this feels like a...solo thing." She paused. "I'm used to doing things on my own."

"Solo isn't all it's cracked up to be. Maybe it's time for a new tactic."

No doubt. She gestured for him to step back a little.

"Go for it," he said.

Trinity in *The Matrix,* she decided. That's whose strength she was going for. She wriggled her hips a little, getting into position, and then swung the ax. It barely budged, much less flying through the air in slow-mo like in *The Matrix.* Damn, the thing was heavy.

"Put your weight into it."

She narrowed her eyes and looked at Jax. "Maybe you should go first and show me how it's done."

"Sure." He came close, moving with his usual innate and easy grace even in the tool belt. He was wearing Levi's again. This pair had a hole in one thigh and on the opposite knee. He had on an opened flannel over a caramel brown Henley that brought out his eyes.

Their fingers collided as he took the ax from her, and then he set his open hand low on her stomach, the hot, callused palm gently pushing her out of harm's way. As always at his touch, heat slashed through her, and for a minute, she closed her eyes and wavered.

She should have chosen sex. Note to self: *always* choose sex over physical labor!

"It's not too late," he said very softly.

Afraid to speak and give herself away, she pointed to the wood. With a knowing smile, he lifted the ax and swung it. Muscles bunched and worked with an effortless ease that left her mouth dry and other parts of her not quite so dry. He swung for five straight minutes without faltering in his rhythm, then stopped. He shrugged out of the flannel, leaving him in just the Henley, the sleeves of which he shoved up to his elbows. "You ready to try?" he asked.

Hell, no. Not when she had a view like this. She shook her head. "Watching you do it is helping a lot. Keep going."

He gave her an amused look but turned back to the wood.

"Um, Jax?"

He glanced over his shoulder.

"You look..." *Hot.* "Overheated. Probably you should take off your other shirt, too."

"You think?"

Oh, yeah. Not trusting her voice, she merely nodded.

His lips quirked, but he said nothing as he reached up and behind him, tugging the shirt over his head in one smooth, very male motion.

And then he stood before her in those low-slung jeans, tool belt, and nothing else but a gleam of sweat.

"Better," she tried to say, staring at his tatts, but it came out more as a squeak. She was lucky not to be a puddle on the ground. Honest to God, the man shouldn't be allowed to look like that. It just wasn't fair to all the other men on the planet.

Turning back to his task, he went at the wood for a while. Maddie backed up to a large wood round and plopped down. After a few minutes, Tara came out with a peace-offering tray of iced tea and glasses. "Oh, sweet merciful Jesus," she whispered, eyes locked on Jax as she sank to the log next to Maddie.

The two of them sat there in companionable, lust-filled silence watching Jax like he was must-see TV until finally he stopped and gave them a long glance, swiping his brow on his forearm. "Your turn, ladies."

Tara jumped to her feet. "Oh, not me, honey. I have a thing in the thing..." She waved vaguely behind her. "Enjoy the rest of the tea. There's plenty." And then she was gone.

Maddie poured him a glass, which he downed in a few gulps while she watched a drop of sweat slide down his chest. "I don't think I can pull that off," she murmured, nodding to the wood.

"That's okay. I have something better for you."

Oh, boy. "Is *this* X-rated?"

He flashed that badass grin, grabbed his shirts, and took her to the second floor of the inn, in one of the bedrooms that had been used as a storage room, gesturing to the stack of wooden crates that someone had piled there. The plan had been to tear them up and use the wood for kindling. Jax handed her a much smaller ax than the one he'd used outside and nodded for her to have a go.

So she gave it a shot and found that she could do this. She swung and chopped until she was shaking and sweaty and feeling much better. "Whew," she said, dropping the ax. "How long was that?"

"Two minutes." He laughed at the look on her face and stepped up right behind her, dipping his head so that his mouth brushed her ear. "You look overheated. Probably you should take off your shirt."

He was playing with her and thought she wouldn't dare. Something came over her at that—the exhilaration that came from discovering a man found her sexy, maybe.

In any case, she took a deep breath and stripped out of her sweatshirt, leaving her in just a cute little baby blue tank that she'd borrowed—okay, stolen—from Chloe.

He went still, his eyes eating her up.

With a small smile, she put a hand to the middle of his chest and pushed him back, once again grabbing the ax.

She lasted a whole minute before dropping the heavy tool and gasping for breath.

"Feeling better?" His eyes were lit with heat, amusement, and something even better. Pride.

"Getting there," she murmured.

Stepping forward, eyes locked on hers, he swiped at a smudge on her jaw. "What would make it even better?"

She closed her eyes for a beat, swaying toward him. *You,* she thought. *In me.* That's what would make it alllll better.

From somewhere below, Izzy barked. She was looking for her human. "You going down?" Maddie asked him.

His eyes flamed. "Any time."

And just like that, her nipples did their Jax Happy Dance. Much as she hated to admit it, Tara had been right. He was out of her league. She grabbed her sweatshirt and turned to go downstairs to open the door for the dog herself, but he reeled her in until she was up against him, her back to his front. "Remember this place," he said, voice low. "Remember where we are. Right here, this very spot."

"You mean here in this room, all hot and sweaty?"

His teeth nipped her ear, and she shivered.

"You keep taking those steps back," he said. "Not enough forward." Turning her in his arms, he lightly brushed his lips over hers before pulling back to meet her gaze. "Save our place," he said quietly, all signs of teasing gone, and turned to go.

He cared about her, he liked her, just as is. Her hands caught him, brought him back, pulling him down to her. "I won't forget." And then she kissed him, loving the ragged groan she wrenched from his chest. She loved the way he kissed, too. He tasted warm and tangy sweet from the iced tea, and it was intoxicating. So was the solid feel of his body pressing into hers, making her want to forget about her to-do list, about Tara just next door in the cottage, the dog wanting in, everything. "We have to go," she said.

"Uh-huh." Dropping her sweatshirt back down to the floor, she accepted that she was making the slippery descent into oblivion and slid her arms around his waist, losing herself in their connection.

In him.

With a rough sound, he took control, backing her to a beam. He palmed her breast, thumbing her already erect and straining nipple over her thin tank top.

"God, you're soft," he said. "Soft and warm and perfect. I have to feel you again, Maddie." His hands slid beneath the tank. Pushing the material up, his mouth took itself on a tour along her collarbone and down, his tongue gliding over the lace of her bra, right over her nipple as he ground his pelvis into hers.

He was big, which no longer scared her, and extremely aroused, which excited her beyond belief. "Jax."

"I know. I can't get enough of you." Tugging the cups of her bra down, he licked her again, over her bared flesh this time so that she clutched at his biceps and arched up into him. "Not even close," he said. He gripped her bottom, squeezed, then brought his hands around and was heading for the button on her jeans when the dog barked again.

Their eyes met, and Jax let out a breath of male frustration. "She's got timing, I'll give her that." They were still both breathing erratically when he stepped back, his eyes blazing with heat.

He wanted her. Again. *Still.* It was a powerful feeling.

"Save our place," he repeated in a soft but direct command and was gone.

For two mornings running, Maddie and Tara did yoga. Chloe's legacy, they decided. Plus it burned calories.

They did it in silence. Well, Tara was silent. Maddie had been asking questions like "Why did you agree to the job at Eat Me when you wanted to leave?" and "Are we celebrating Christmas together?" and "How do you know Ford?"

None of which Tara answered.

Finally one morning Maddie sat on her yoga mat and refused to do a single pose. "Not until you answer at least one question."

Tara sighed. "Fine. Regarding Christmas, I don't think we should exchange gifts that cost any money, not when we're spending every spare penny we have on this place."

"Fair enough," Maddie agreed. "But expect another scarf, probably crooked. And that wasn't the question I most wanted answered and you know it."

Tara sat and faced her, stretching her long, perfectly toned body. "If I answer another, you have to do the same."

"Deal. Why didn't you tell us about Logan?"

Tara's cool expression crumpled. "I don't know, probably because I didn't want to look like a loser."

"We're sisters. Sisters are supposed to tell."

"Yes, but I'm the oldest." She went into some complicated upside-down yoga pose. "Oldest sisters are supposed to be perfect."

"Says who?"

"Older sisters." Tara sighed and changed positions with ease. "And I realize it's no secret that when we first got here, all I wanted was to get back out again. I really can't explain why I agreed to stay. I don't know. Temporary insanity."

"Or...we're growing on you."

"Or I'm enjoying the weather."

Maddie sighed. "So about Ford."

"Oh, no. I just answered *two* questions. Now you. What are you doing with Jax?"

"Huh," Maddie said. "Suddenly I'm seeing why it's more fun to be the one asking the questions. Would you believe me if I say I have no idea? I mean you saw me when I first got here. I didn't want to even think about men." She hesitated. "Problem is, he's hard *not* to think about."

"If I looked like him," Tara said. "I'd want to have sex with myself. All the time."

Maddie laughed. "Now you sound like Chloe."

"No need for insults."

"She should have stayed with us."

"Aw, you missed me."

They turned in shock to face *Chloe.* "Hi, honey," she said with a wave. "I'm home."

"Already?" Tara asked. "What about New Mexico?"

"Didn't quite get there." Chloe rolled out her yoga mat.

"Texas?" Maddie asked, mimicking Tara's pose so it looked like she'd been working hard all morning.

"Didn't get there, either. Decided you two were going to have too much fun without me. Besides, I love the natural sea salt here. I came up with an idea for a body lotion. Maddie, focus. Hold your pose."

What, was she kidding?

"You're moving too fast, as usual. You're always in a hurry. Got to take a moment to smell the roses." Chloe began to stretch, bending in one fluid movement to lay her palms flat on the floor, legs straight.

"I'm working on other things," Maddie said.

"Like?"

"Like changing my moniker from 'the Mouse.'"

"To?" Tara asked.

"Actually, I'd like to be more like you. You know, the strong, take-no-shit Steel Magnolia."

Chloe chortled, then zipped it when Tara sent her a narrowed gaze before turning to Maddie with clear surprise. "Sugar, you don't want to be like me. I'm as messed up as they come."

"Yes, but you pretend not to be. And you, too," Maddie said to Chloe. "I like that. And I'm starting to see it's all in the pretending. And the attitude. You know, act tough, be tough."

"You going to be bitchy, too?" Chloe asked. "And say 'bless your heart' and do the holier-than-thou shit?"

"Or maybe she could just get whiny," Tara said smoothly. "Or better yet, take off on her Vespa when the going gets a little rough."

The tension ratcheted up a notch. "Maybe I'll do a combination," Maddie said. "Bitchy *and* whiny, with only a dash of anxiety. We'll call it 'the Blend' and make a recipe card about it for our kids."

Both sisters stared at her for a shocked beat, then looked at each other. That was the only warning Maddie got before they both tackled her down to the yoga mat for a wedgie.

Yeah, Maddie thought, lying there with her underwear twisted in places it shouldn't be as Tara and Chloe got up and bumped fists. They were really starting to gel together as a family.

Chapter 16

"Never leave a paper trail."
PHOEBE TRAEGER

Maddie sat at the desk in the marina office. It was beginning to become clear why the inn hadn't been successful. Phoebe hadn't charged enough for any of the services, and sometimes, when she'd known her customers, she hadn't charged at all.

That would have to change—assuming they got their financing, that is. And assuming that by fixing the place up, they got customers. And that both of those things helped Maddie convince her sisters to keep the inn instead of selling. She dropped her head to the desk and hit it lightly a few times as a man let himself into the marina building.

He was six foot four, at least two hundred and fifty pounds, and looked like Sully from Monsters Inc., minus the smile and blue fur.

"Need to rent a boat." His voice thundered like he'd spoken through a microphone. "Fully equipped."

She jumped in automatic response. "Have you rented here before?"

"Yes."

Good. So one of them knew what they were doing.

"Name's Peter Jenkins." He pounded his finger on her desk. "And I get a deal. Phoebe always gave me a deal."

Since Maddie had just yesterday organized the accounts receivables, she was proud to be able to go right to the file cabinet and locate a stack of boat rentals, where she pulled out one with his name on it. *Please have notes, please have notes...*

"Make sure it's gassed up," he boomed. "And I'm in a hurry here."

Yes, she was getting that. And she was getting something else—nervous as hell. He yelled when he talked. It was making her fingers refuse to work and her brain uncooperative. Plus, she hadn't yet studied any of their rental agreements or learned the procedure.

"What the hell's taking you so long?"

"I'm sorry." She reached for the file of blank rental agreements, looking for one for the fishing boat. "I'm new at this, so—"

"Oh for fuck's sake." He slapped some cash onto the desk, making everything on the surface bounce. Maddie nearly jumped out of her skin. She took a careful breath, working really hard to find her nerve. She located it about the same time she put her fingers on the right form. "Got it—"

But he'd taken the keys off the hook on the wall and was already out the door and on the dock, stalking toward the boat.

"Hey," she called out, grabbing the cash and stuffing

it into her pocket to add to the cash box later. It wouldn't be difficult. The cash box was currently empty. "Excuse me!"

He'd boarded the boat by the time she caught up to him. "Mr. Jenkins, I need you to sign—"

Ignoring her, he untied the rope and pissed her off. She hopped on board before he could pull away, but as she jumped down, the boat pitched violently.

"Stern!" he bellowed. "Stern!"

Gripping the side of the boat, Maddie crouched low and looked at the very cold water, trying not to panic as they rocked hard. Logically she knew *stern* had to mean right or left, or maybe front or back. For all she knew, it meant go to hell, but with no idea which direction to move, and with the boat still pitching side to side and threatening to capsize, Maddie dropped to her butt.

"Get *off* the goddamned boat!"

Oh, hell no. "Not until you sign!"

Mr. Jenkins sent her a hard, long look, but she didn't cower.

Much.

Instead she whipped a pen out of her pocket and offered it up. He snatched the paper from her, signed it, then tossed it in her lap. Gee, guess he was in a hurry to get rid of her. She very carefully climbed out of the boat and stood on the dock as he headed out of the marina, muttering something about suing her for stupidity.

Rude. She stalked back to the office, talking to herself.

"Did you skip the caffeine again?" Jax asked.

She took in the unexpected sight of him standing in the doorway, palms up on the wooden frame above him.

Just looking at him made her feel better.

A lot better. He was watching her with a little smile on his face, wearing his usual uniform of a pair of jeans and battered boots, today with a merino wool hoodie sweatshirt.

And his tool belt.

Let's not forget the tool belt. "I've had caffeine," she told him. "And a blast of Mr. Jenkins. He called me an idiot."

Jax's lazy smile vanished. "What?"

"Yeah, I didn't know stem from stern. Hell, I barely know what horses have to do with engines." She smiled, but he didn't.

Instead, he pushed off from the doorframe and came close. "He's an ass."

"Agreed. But he's a paying ass. Why would my mom have given that man a deal?"

"I think she dated him briefly, but even her sunny nature gave up trying to cure his chronic grumpiness. Tell me you kicked him out of here when he mouthed off at you."

"I was tempted. But truthfully, it was my own fault."

Jax stilled, his expression going very quiet, very serious. "Maddie."

She stared at him, her stomach pinging hollowly. "Dammit," she whispered. "It *wasn't* my fault. I did it again." She closed her eyes. Whirling, hands fisted, she flew to the marina door with some half-baked idea about climbing back onto that boat and—

"Maddie."

"No, I have to go. I have to give him a piece of my mind and maybe a foot shoved up his—"

Two warm arms surrounded her, pulling her back against a solid chest. "I'm all for that," he said in her ear. "In fact, I'll hold him down for you if you'd like. But unless you want to go for a swim to retrieve him, you're going to have to wait a few hours."

She turned to face him. He was still dangerously quiet, and there was an anger in his eyes she'd not seen since he kicked that patron out of the Love Shack that first night. It gave her yet another heart lurch, even though she knew he wasn't mad at *her*. "Being the strong female lead star of my own life is harder than I thought."

"You're doing good. You're doing real good."

She let out the breath that she hadn't realized she was holding and tipped her face up to his. "Yeah?"

His eyes warmed. "Yeah."

She managed a little smile. "Would you really hold him down for me?"

"In a heartbeat."

For some reason, that gave her a warm fuzzy, and her smile spread. "It's not exactly...politically correct."

The look he gave her said he didn't give a shit about being politically correct, he only cared about what was right.

And God, even from here, he smelled delicious. How was it that he always smelled so good? But rather than grabbing his sweatshirt and pulling him in, she stepped around him to her desk. "I've got to finish getting all this straightened out. I don't want to lose money because I don't know what I'm doing. And Mr. Jenkins threatened to sue me for stupidity, which would really suck."

"Tell him you're going to countersue for emotional damages."

She smiled at the thought. "Can someone really do that?"

"If you could prove you were negligently injured."

"You sound like a lawyer." She grinned. "Good thing you're not, because then I'd probably not like you as much."

"Come here," he said softly and pulled her in for a hug. "Kiss me, Maddie. Show me you remember our place."

She went up on her tiptoes and kissed him until she couldn't remember her own name, then pressed her face to his throat, feeling an odd tug in her chest at how much this meant. At how much he meant.

"Maddie—"

"I love how open you are," she said. "How honest. Do all the women you date appreciate that?"

"I'm not dating anyone else right now. Tell me that you know that we wouldn't have had sex if I was seeing someone else."

"Well, you'd think I'd know that, but I've made some bad choices," she said. "I no longer trust my judgment. It's easier for me to hear it straight from you, because I can believe what you say."

That odd something crossed his face, coming and going so fast she couldn't identify it. For a long moment, he watched his thumb glide along her jaw. "How about what I don't say?"

"What?"

"I haven't been in a relationship for five years," he said. "Since before I moved back here. Opening up isn't exactly second nature for me, Maddie."

"Five years is a long time to go without sex."

His eyes cut to hers. "I didn't say I'd gone without sex."

"Oh." *Oh.*

"But before you, it'd been a while for that, too."

"There's plenty of women in town."

"Yes, and most of them take their dating far more seriously than I do. Maddie, you need to know something about me."

God. "You're married. You're a felon. You're—"

"A lawyer. Before I moved back to Lucky Harbor, I was in Seattle. I was practicing law."

Jax spent a few days building new bathroom vanities at his own home wood shop on the other side of town. Maddie hadn't said much about his revelation, but then again, she'd made herself scarce.

There was nothing Jax could do about his past, it was written in ink. And he'd done the right thing by telling her. Especially since he'd held back other things—secrets that weren't his to share.

He only hoped Maddie saw it the same way. He kept telling himself that she would, that what they were beginning to feel for each other would be stronger than extenuating circumstances.

As he made his way through his house to leave for the shrimp feed, he shook his head at all the decorations Jeanne had put up, complete with mistletoe hanging from his doorways. It was clear that she was optimistic for his shot at having a woman in the house. Probably he'd blown that.

He drove to the pier. In a few hours, just about everyone in town would arrive for the annual event. The money raised tonight would supplement the funds for the police and fire departments, which was important but definitely not the first thing on people's minds as they paid to get in.

Nope, that would be the events. First up was the parade of shrimp boats, always led by the mayor on a decorated jet ski. Then the person who came closest to guessing the amount of shrimp brought in would get to kiss the mayor.

Man, woman, or child.

With Jax's luck, it'd be Ford or Sawyer. Last year it'd been his mail carrier—much to everyone's utter delight. Hopefully this year, plenty of the other two thousand people in town had bought tickets.

Afterward, they'd eat until their guts hurt and then dance to the Nitty Gritty, the local pop-rock band. People would probably still be dancing as the first pink tinges of dawn came up on the horizon.

Sawyer arrived right after Jax. He was in uniform, there on official crowd-control duty. And to make fun of Jax, of course. Ford showed up, too, setting up a booth for the Love Shack from which beer, wine, and eggnog would be floating aplenty.

Jax eyed the jet ski waiting for him. It was a loan from Lance and his brother—when they weren't manning their ice cream shop, they were big jet skiers. In the summertime, like normal people.

Not many were crazy enough to go jet skiing in the dead of winter, but tradition was tradition.

Lance was grinning when he handed over the key. The kid was facing a virtual death sentence with his cystic fibrosis, but he knew how to enjoy life. He'd lavishly decorated the jet ski with Christmas lights. Sawyer had helped him, and both had promised that everything was battery operated and waterproof so Jax *probably* wouldn't get electrocuted.

Good to know his friends had his back.

Out on the water about two hundred yards, three shrimp boats waited, also lavishly—aka garishly—decorated, ready for him to escort them in parade-like fashion. "Good times," Lance said and grinned.

Jax turned his face upward. Lots of clouds, but no snow or rain. That was good. But it was forty-eight degrees, so "good" was relative. He pulled on the thick, waterproof fisherman gear the shrimpers wore so at least he wouldn't freeze off any vital parts.

The crowd woo-hoo'd as if he was stripping instead of putting on gear, and he rolled his eyes. Looking out into the faces, he locked gazes with Maddie.

She shook her head. Obviously, she wasn't over the whole lawyer thing—not that he blamed her—and just as obviously, she thought he was crazy.

He'd have to agree there. He smiled at her. She didn't return it. Ouch. He'd have to work on fixing that, but one problem at a time. Stepping into the water, he straddled the jet ski and took another look at the shore.

Ford and Sawyer were grinning. So was Chloe.

Bloodthirsty friends.

Maddie had her hand over her mouth, so he wasn't exactly sure what her expression was now. He hoped it was sympathy, and he also hoped that he could get that to work in his favor in a little bit when he needed warming up.

As he'd imagined, the next ten minutes passed in a frozen blur as he rode the jet ski and lead the shrimp parade. Then he was back on shore, being warmly greeted and wrapped in blankets. Sandy shoved a mic into his hand and a piece of paper. The crowd hushed with expectant hope.

"Eight hundred and fifty-six shrimp," Jax called out.

No one had guessed that exact amount, but one person had come close at 850. He accepted another piece of paper from Sandy with the winner's name. He read it silently and looked at Maddie, who stared back, thoughts closed but a little pissiness definitely showing.

Trying to convey both apology and self-deprication, he smiled at her. "Maddie Moore," he said to wild cheers.

Maddie's mouth fell open.

Chloe helpfully shoved her forward.

"But I didn't put any tickets in," Maddie said as Jax grabbed her hand in his and pulled her up onto the makeshift stage.

Ford and Sawyer were cracking up. So was Chloe, and Maddie narrowed her eyes at her. "How many tickets in my name did you enter?"

"Fifty."

"Me, too," Ford called out.

Sawyer grinned. "A hundred from me. Good cause and all."

Okay, Jax thought, so maybe sometimes his bloodthirsty friends came in handy.

"I entered my name one hundred times," Lucille called out, disappointment clear across her face. "Damn. Maybe next year..."

"*Kiss, kiss, kiss,*" chanted the crowd.

Jax had stopped shivering, but he still had some serious warming up to do. Both his own body, and Maddie, because her eyes were on him, cool and distant.

Yep, definitely needed some warming up. Kissing sounded like a great way to do that. Holding Maddie's very resistant gaze in his, he tugged her close, looking forward to this for the first time all day.

"You're freezing," Maddie whispered.

"Yes."

She sighed and slipped her arms around his waist, tipping her face up to his. "I'm still mad at you."

"I know." He stared down into her beautiful eyes and felt his heart catch with all the possibilities he felt, not to mention hope—an extremely new emotion for him. "I plan on changing your mind about me."

"Jax—"

"I'm sorry, Maddie. I'm sorry I didn't tell you sooner, but you have to know, I'm not a lawyer now. That was my past."

"I know."

"Kiss!" yelled the crowd.

Maddie fidgeted in his arms, clearly not thrilled with having an audience for this. He ran a slow hand up her throat before cupping her jaw, leaving his other hand low on her back in what he hoped was a soothing gesture. "You okay with this, Maddie?"

Surprising the hell out of him, she answered by cupping his icy face in her hands and going up on her tiptoes to reach him. He met her halfway, bending low to cover her mouth with his. He heard her suck in a breath and knew his lips were icy. Apologizing with a soft murmur, he changed the angle to get a better taste of her.

Then she surprised him again.

Her mouth opened for his, and the sweet kiss turned into something else, something sensuous and intense.

Heat exploded within him, melting all the iciness from the inside out.

Around them, the crowd whooped and hollered, and Maddie began to pull back, but he held her tight.

"Need a minute?" she whispered, a hint of humor behind the heat in her eyes as she brushed up against his erection.

"Maybe two—" He broke off with a jagged groan when she put her mouth to his ear. "Maddie, that's not helping."

But then she whispered something that did help.

"Just think," she whispered. "It could have been Lucille."

Ford was bartending, serving beer on tap to a line of customers. Jax, warmed up now, was behind the bar getting cups and restocking the alcohol. The booth was good for Ford because it made the Love Shack even more popular, which in turn was good for Jax because he owned the other half of the bar.

In fact, Jax coowned several businesses in town. It was what he'd done with his money when he'd come back to Lucky Harbor. He'd bought up properties in a sagging market to help the people who'd known and loved him all his life.

They were thankful, but he was the one who felt the gratitude. They'd welcomed him back, given him a sense of belonging when he'd so desperately needed it.

"Wake up," Tara said with a little wave in his face. She'd come to his end of the bar, away from the line and the crowds, and was looking at him expectantly. "Yeah, hi. I'm looking for a drink."

"The line's over there. I'm not serving, I'm just—"

She tapped the bar. "Listen, sugar. Lucille just asked me about the stick up my ass, okay? I need a drink pronto. Make it a double."

He grimaced. "Beer, wine, or eggnog?"

"Well, hell. Wine."

Jax poured her a very full glass and handed it over, watching as she tossed it back like a shot of Jack. "Tara."

"Yeah?"

"You have to tell her."

Tara stared at him, then sat and dropped her head to the bar. "I'm going to need more alcohol for this. And something far stronger than wine."

Jax reached beneath the bar for a shot glass and a bottle of Jack that Ford had squirreled down there for... hell, he had no idea.

"Bless your heart," Tara said fervently as he poured her two fingers.

"You can't keep this from Maddie any longer."

"Watch me."

Jax shook his head. "When Phoebe asked me to draw up the blind trust five years ago, she also asked me for a promise. That you be protected at all costs."

"Not me." Tara shut her eyes. "My secret. She wanted my *secret* protected." Her eyes flew open. "Which means you *can't* tell." She sounded relieved. "You can't, you promised—"

"But *you* didn't," he said.

"Jax."

Who'd have thought that a promise to a dead woman would result in betraying a person he'd come to care for so deeply? "I don't break my promises, Tara. Ever." Not to mention professional confidentiality. "But when Phoebe put all her liquid assets into that blind trust—"

"It left her in a precarious position when she needed cash. And then you gave her the loan against the inn." Tara's eyes filled with misery. "I never meant for either of you to have to be in that position—"

"I know," he said quietly. "But now I'm sitting on *two* secrets from a dead woman. Secrets that aren't fair to either of your sisters."

"You care about Maddie."

"Yes, I do."

"A lot." She leaned in and looked deep into his eyes. "She's not just a quick lay to you."

Hadn't been for a while now, the knowledge of which had pretty much sneaked up on him. "You have to find a way to tell her," he repeated softly. "Or I'll find a way for you."

Tara stared at him, then thrust out her glass.

He obligingly refilled it, and she drank it down with a shudder. "I haven't told anyone," she whispered. "Ever."

"This isn't just anyone. It's Maddie. She deserves to know what you're holding back and why. And she deserves to know the domino effect of it all, the inn, the loan, the trust, all of it."

Tara closed her eyes and let out a long, slow breath. "I'm just so…ashamed."

Understanding that all too well, he covered her hand with his. "You were just a kid, Tara. You got in over your head and paid dearly. There's no shame in that. You're giving it more power by keeping it a secret."

"I know." She pulled her scarf closer around her neck.

It was green and sparkly, and very, very crooked. "She's making you one now," she said, seeing where his gaze had gone. "It's multicolored. And ugly as sin, bless her heart. I need another shot, sugar."

He poured, then watched her toss that back, as well. "You okay?"

"Fan-fucking-tastic."

"Liar."

Tara blew out a breath. "She made me this scarf with love, and lots of it, even though I'm the one who stresses her out when I fight with Chloe."

"So stop fighting with Chloe."

"She wants us all to be together." She closed her eyes and pushed the empty shot glass his way. "Here in this town where I made my biggest mistake."

"Maybe it's time to stop looking at it as a mistake. There's got to be *something* you like about being here, or you'd have left when you had the chance."

She stared down at the scarf, fingering the yarn. "I've been cooking."

"And damn well. I'm partial to those bacon bleu cheese burgers, myself."

"I am good," she said, looking both proud and a little surprised. "And somehow I agreed to work at the café and stay for the rest of the month, which is crazy, given how badly I want to be anywhere other than here. I'm working at Eat Me Café, for God's sake." Lifting her head, she leveled her baffled gaze on his. "Let me repeat that. *I work at a café called Eat Me.* What kind of idiot does that make me?"

"The good-sister kind," he said. "Tell her, Tara."

She closed her eyes, then opened them. They were

shiny now, and he feared that she was going to cry. But he should have known better.

"I can't, Jax," she said. "Not yet. I'm not ready."

He let out a long breath. Not what he'd wanted to hear. He ached for Maddie, ached for what he was beginning to feel for her knowing that they'd all held so much back from her. Taking Tara's shot glass away, he poured another glass with water.

"She wants things we can't give her, Jax. She wants us to be a family. I don't know anything about family."

"You're wearing the scarf she made for you," he pointed out. "That seems like a sisterly thing to do."

"She's been so alone. Her father's a good man, but he's a set designer. She spent most of her childhood on location, in the makeup and hair trailer or the production office. Her friends are all transient by the very nature of her job, changing from one project to the next. None of them have called her that I can tell. Her closest friend was her boss, and he dropped her like a bad habit when she got laid off due to the...situation." She put her hand over his, making him realize he was squeezing the bottle of Jack with white knuckles. "He wasn't the one who hurt her physically," she said softly.

"Someone did," he said flatly. "Someone hurt her plenty."

Tara nodded and sipped her water. "Past tense, though. She's getting stronger. You should have seen her giving poor old Mr. Jenkins what-for when he tried to rent another boat this morning." She smiled fondly. "She got all up in his grill, made him sign the form at her desk and say please and everything."

He would have enjoyed seeing that. "She was down

a quart in self-esteem and confidence when she first got here."

"And that's changing, in good part thanks to you." She stared into her glass. "She wants to make a go of this place. Only a complete bitch would turn her down."

"Then don't turn her down."

Chapter 17

*"Learn from others' mistakes. You don't have
enough time to make them all yourself."*
PHOEBE TRAEGER

A few days later, Maddie headed into the tiny laundry
room of the inn carrying a load of rags and towels. As an
afterthought, she added in her filthy sneakers.

"That's a pretty flimsy excuse to get some dryer therapy," Tara said, folding her clean clothes into perfect piles.

"Dryer therapy?"

"Sugar, everyone knows the shoes-in-the-dryer trick.
But the dryer's got nothin' on the spin cycle." She gave a
wicked smile and left.

Maddie shook her head, then added detergent. While
the load ran, she padded to the linen closet to continue
cataloguing sheets and towels on the computer for inventory purposes. She'd downloaded several new programs
designed specifically for running a small inn and was
having more fun than she'd thought possible organizing
and modernizing the place. Both Tara and Chloe were

amazed and thrilled at her skills but baffled as to the happiness it gave her to organize.

That was okay. She didn't understand enjoying cooking or practicing yoga or making spa treatments, either. Hell, she barely enjoyed *using* the spa treatments.

She glanced at her watch. For two days running, Ford had been giving her boating lessons. He was teaching her about all the marina's equipment, how to use and care for it, but her favorite part had been learning what *stern* and *stem* meant.

Take that, Mr. Jenkins.

Jax was still building their new vanities at his shop, so he'd not been around during the day. She realized he was giving her the space he thought she wanted. But she'd come here to Lucky Harbor not wanting her past to count against her—which meant she had no right to count Jax's against him.

That was logic.

Her heart wasn't feeling so logical. She knew that Alex's law degree wasn't what made him an abusive asshole, and a lying one at that.

Jax hadn't lied, but he had held back. She'd be the liar if she said that it didn't bother her.

But then there was the biggest problem: was she ready to trust herself again with a man? Blowing out a breath, she went back to the laundry room to check on the loud clunking sound coming from the washer. Her tennis shoes. Tara's words floated in her head—*the dryer's got nothing on the spin cycle.*

Suddenly it hit her what Tara had meant. Surely she couldn't—could she? She glanced out the small window. No cars in the yard. She was alone.

As usual.

She stared at the shuddering washer and bit her lip. Then she hopped up on it. Just to disprove the theory, of course.

Wow.

Gripping the sides of the machine tightly as the ride began, she had to admit that Tara had been on to something.

The thing had great rhythm.

Eighteen minutes later, she shuddered in brief ecstasy then slumped back against the wall. Eyes closed, she stayed there catching her breath. Not nearly as good as Jax's fingers—or other parts—but it had definitely taken the edge off—

The washer suddenly stopped.

In the jarring silence, she opened her eyes. Jax stood in front of her as if she'd conjured him up, his finger on the off button.

Oh, God. Arousal and embarrassment warred for space inside her, but she managed both with equal aplomb—she was nothing if not an excellent multitasker. "How long have you been there?"

He stroked a damp curl off her forehead and pressed a single soft kiss to the pulse racing at the base of her throat. "Just got there. You okay?"

Lord, the things he could do her with those lips. "Y—yes."

"Sure?"

"Uh-huh." She tried to look innocent. Like maybe she always just sat around. On a washer. While it was running. "Why?"

"Because you're all breathless and a little sweaty." His

eyes were darkening, his voice lowering in timbre. "And you're sitting on a washer."

"Well, look at that, I am. There's a perfectly good reason, actually."

"Yeah?" he asked huskily.

"Yeah." She bit her lower lip. "Except I don't want to say."

He looked at her for a long moment, his eyes hot enough to fry her brain. Bracketing her hips with a fist on either side of her, he ran his tongue along the outer shell of her ear, his voice soft and thick. "Was this one of those solo expeditions, Maddie?"

"No." She closed her eyes and shivered when he lightly bit her earlobe. *Oh, God.* "Maybe."

He groaned, and she drew in a shuddery breath. "And other than you, it's my most successful expedition in a long time."

He let out a soft bark of laughter and ran his thumb along her lower lip until her mouth trembled open, then leaned in for a kiss. "There's nothing wrong with solo," he murmured against her mouth. "But *not* solo is preferable."

"Oh," she breathed, trembling as he ran his hands down her body, his fingers grazing the sides of her breasts, then her hips and thighs.

"Are you still thinking, Maddie? About us? Still taking a step back?"

She stared up at him, wanting him more than her next breath, but…but. He'd held back, and she couldn't help the feeling that there was more.

"Ball's in your court," he said, and before she could finish catching her breath, he hit the power button. The clunking started up again, and she let out an involuntary gasp, gripping the sides of the washer for all she was worth.

Flashing her a slow, heated smile, he left her alone.

Two weeks. Maddie had been in Lucky Harbor for two weeks, and they'd been the best fourteen days of her life. Now she had two weeks left until Christmas to do what she had to do.

All along, she'd hoped that she'd be able to convince Tara and Chloe to give the inn a real shot.

She'd believed she could.

But that belief had just died with one shake of her loan officer's head.

Denied.

With a rough sigh, she left the bank, got into her car, and dropped her head to the steering wheel. She had the start of a headache pounding behind her right eye, her stomach was in knots, and the interior of her car felt like it was closing in on her as the loan officer's words echoed in her brain.

I'm sorry, Ms. Traeger, but you've been turned down for the refinancing. In today's economy, we have to work up against tougher regulations and qualifications, and you and your sisters didn't qualify.

Didn't qualify…

You're a loser…

Okay, so she hadn't said that last part, but Maddie had felt like a loser. Dammit, they'd needed that loan, both for the renovations and to get the inn up and running.

Not to mention paying off the credit card debt the three of them were racking up.

A shuddery sigh escaped her, but she refused to cry. *Couldn't* cry. She hadn't told her sisters that she'd had the bank meeting this morning. They thought they wouldn't be hearing until the end of the week.

Now she was glad she hadn't told them. Mostly because she wasn't quite sure they'd be as devastated that it was over.

She pulled out her cell and called her dad. She had no idea why, other than she needed to hear the voice of someone who loved her.

"Hey, sweetie," he yelled into the phone, sirens and screaming in the background. "How are you?"

"Dad?" Her heart stopped. "What's going on, are you okay?"

"I'm terrific. I'm on a set in New Orleans, filming a horror flick."

"Oh." Like a dope she nodded, even though he couldn't see her. His voice helped though, a lot. "Miss you."

"Well, then come on out here. We could always use another hand."

The thought was oddly tempting. "I might do that." Since she'd be homeless soon enough.

They spoke for a few more minutes, and then she hung up without telling him about the mess she'd made of her life.

And her heart...

God, she needed some chips. An entire bag. With a sigh, she drove to the inn, but neither sister was there, and Chloe's Vespa was gone. Turning around, Maddie headed to the café and found Tara working the lunch shift.

"Go away," Tara said from the chef's window. "I'm snowed under."

Okay, so that took care of telling Tara now. "I need something warm and fattening." *To ease the hot ball of anxiety choking the air out of me.* "And if you remind me that my jeans are finally fitting, I'm going to knit you another scarf."

To her credit, Tara merely nodded. "I've got just the thing—Life Sucks Golf Balls casserole. Eggs, bacon, cheese, and veggies for a healthy touch."

"But it's a *casserole.*" Maddie shuddered. "The ingredients will all be touching."

"Don't be a child."

"*Touching,* Tara."

"Yes, the ingredients are all touching, good Lord, but I'll put the bread waaaaay on the other side of the plate, okay? Maybe even on its *own* plate if you stop your bellyachin'. Now sit down and shut up, and I'll bring it out to you."

"Fine. But I also need hot chocolate and extra whipped cream. *Extra* extra." Because whipped cream was a solve-all. It would ease the dull throb of bitter discontent and swirling anxiety in her gut. She was counting on it.

In a few minutes, she was inhaling the amazing casserole and simultaneously spraying more whipped cream into her hot chocolate when she felt a shiver of awareness race down her spine.

Jax.

Already horrifyingly close to losing it, she didn't dare look up when his boots and denim-clad legs came into her line of vision. "How?" she asked, nose deep into her hot chocolate. "How do you always know?"

"That you're OD-ing by whipped cream? I didn't. I have a business meeting with a potential client." He nudged her over and slid into the booth next to her. She felt his long, searching look, then his warm palm sliding along the back of her neck at the same time as he pressed a hard thigh to hers, making her want to crawl into his lap and inside his opened jacket.

Instead, she squirted whipped cream directly into her mouth. She swallowed the mass and licked her lips, then happened a glance a Jax.

Whose eyes were locked on her mouth.

It was interesting, watching him watch her. Her life was in the toilet. Circling the drain, in fact, and he still wanted her. She hadn't thought that could matter, or that it could help, but somehow it did. "Thought you had a meeting."

"He can wait a minute. Talk to me, Maddie."

"About what?" She shook the nearly empty can of whipped cream. "How I just ran out of my drug of choice, or that I failed at yet something else?"

Her only defense at letting that last part slip was sugar overload. She read the label on the whipped cream, but nowhere did it say that mainlining this substance might cause low self-esteem and diarrhea of the mouth.

He took the can from her fingers. "What do you think you failed at?"

Life. She closed her burning eyes and swallowed past a thick throat. The beginning of a headache had turned into an entire percussion band sitting on her right lobe. "I need some chips," she whispered. "Layered in greasy, salty goodness. It soothes being rejected." Downing her hot chocolate, she went to stand, but Jax grabbed her wrist.

"Rejected?"

Rejected. Stomped on. Decimated… "You have a meeting."

"I do," he said, but didn't let go. She tried to tug free, but he reeled her in, then lightly kissed the corner of her mouth.

"Whipped cream," he explained.

She drew a shaky breath. She wanted him, bad, but even that wouldn't soothe the ache from knowing her dream was in its death throes. "I think your client is waving at you," she whispered.

He turned and eyed the man two booths over trying to get his attention. Jax nodded his head and held up a finger, and then turned back to Maddie. "Talk to me," he repeated firmly.

"The bank turned us down for the refinancing." Just saying it out loud made her want to be sick, but that might have been all the junk food she'd consumed. She shot a guilty look in the direction of the kitchen. "And I still have to tell Tara and Chloe, but we should cancel the new interior doors we ordered. Obviously, we need to put in the new windows when they come and fix the roof to sell, and I'll finish the painting, but little else. And your client's about to fall out of his chair trying to overhear us. You have to go."

"Maddie."

Oh, God, that low, husky voice filled with all that empathy was going to break her into a million little pieces. *Not here,* she told herself sternly. *You will not fall apart in a public place again.* Besides, this time there was no one to dump coffee on.

"Gotta go," she choked out. She'd used up all the fake strength in her arsenal. She needed to reboot, that was all. Pulling free, she got up and walked out.

• • •

Back at the inn, Chloe's Vespa was still gone, so Maddie headed directly into the marina office. If the ship was going down, the books were going to be balanced when it did.

Less than a minute later, she heard the marina building door open and shut, and then the slide of the lock, and she looked up into Jax's caramel eyes. Her heart skipped a beat. "What happened to your meeting?" she asked.

"Suddenly cancelled."

By him. God. She was costing him work left and right. "Jax—"

He came around the desk and leaned back against it, facing her, with his long legs stretched out in front of him. "You can try to get a revolving line of credit as a second mortgage. Or try another bank. Or your current lender, who's far more likely to—"

"If we go to the current lender, they'll know we're in trouble."

"Maddie, in this market, *everyone's* in trouble, not just you. This doesn't have to be over." His voice was low and serious. "I can help—"

"No." She swallowed hard and shook her head. "Thank you. It's incredibly kind of you to even think it, but—"

"Jesus, would you stop trying to figure this out all on your own? You're not on your own, not anymore, not unless you want to be."

Suddenly uncomfortably aware that he'd never gotten frustrated with her before, she stared at him.

He stared right back, unwaveringly. "Maddie, remember when you listed all your faults for me?"

"Jax—"

"*Do you?*"

"Yes," she said tightly, hating that her stomach had knotted at the first sign of his frustration. He wouldn't hurt her, she told herself. He'd never hurt her.

"I'm going to guess you're still using a nightlight for the closet monsters. And I know you still don't like your food touching." He cocked his head. "What else was there?"

"*The Sound of Music,*" she said, then rolled her eyes. "And the burping the alphabet."

"You forgot one."

She'd forgotten many. On purpose. But hey, if he wanted to think she had only one more fault, she wasn't about to dispel that notion.

"You forgot that you're the most mule-headed, stubborn-assed woman on the planet." Crouching at her side, he put his hands on the arms of her chair and turned her to face him. She saw that his frustration was with the situation, not her, that he was indeed looking at her with warmth and affection.

"I can help," he said. "By extending a second loan, or helping you apply to another bank."

His offer tightened her throat so that she could barely breathe. "I don't want to think about that right now."

"What do you want to think about?"

"Maybe about inhaling some chips."

He nodded, letting her lighten the mood. "Except that might clash with all the whipped cream."

"True," she said. "I could work on another crooked scarf."

Holding tight to her chair, the very sexy, gorgeous man shook his head, and she worried that he was going to force this conversation that she didn't want to have.

But she shouldn't have. "I have something better," he said very quietly, his eyes heated.

Everything within her quivered at that. He was close enough to block out the sharp fluorescent light with his shoulders, shoulders that were broad enough to weather whatever burdens came his way.

And hers.

And he could make everything go away for a while, help her let go of all that was wrong, and embrace the one thing that was right.

Him. *He* was right, she thought, staring at his hard chest. It would be warm to the touch and strong enough to offer comfort and safety while making her feel desire.

He slid his hands up her legs and settled them on her waist, just beneath her sweater. His hands were big and callused and felt so damn good on her bare skin.

"You're tense again."

"Yes." She bit her lower lip, but the words escaped anyway. "You fixed me last time. You're good at fixing things."

"Yes. Anything you need, Maddie."

That. That right there was another thing that made him different from the men in her past. He was willing to put her first. They'd known each other two and a half weeks, and he'd do anything for her, and at the knowledge, a powerful emotion surged through her. Desperately afraid to trust it, she shoved it aside, forgetting it entirely when he slid his hands up, taking her sweater up, too, up and over her head.

This left her in just a plain white bra, but when she'd dressed this morning, she hadn't exactly planned on being seduced.

Jax's eyes dipped downward, darkening as he took in
the soft curve of her breasts, not appearing at all bothered
by the plainness of the bra. This was good. She sucked in
her stomach, but he didn't take his gaze any farther south.

In fact, he lifted his head and looked straight into
her eyes. "You're so beautiful, Maddie." And then he
kissed her.

Yes. Oh, yes, this was definitely going to go a long
way toward making her feel better, and when he deepened the kiss, stroking her tongue with his, she slid her
hands beneath his shirt to touch his warm skin. "Here?"
she whispered.

"No." He lifted her from the chair and set her on the
desk. "Here." Eyes hot, he spread her legs with a big
hand on the inside of each of her thighs, then pressed
close. When he slowly ground his erection against her,
she nearly lost it. She tore at the button on his jeans and
was going for his zipper when he captured her hands.
His mouth skimmed her jaw, heading toward her ear, his
hands dropping to her hips to hold her still so that she
couldn't climb him like a tree. "Slow this time," he murmured against her skin, letting go of her hands to stroke
her body, his fingers teasing her nipples. "We have as
long as we want—"

Yes, but she didn't want to think. She needed the
oblivion. *Now.* Maybe she wouldn't have thought of getting it in quite this way, but he'd started it, and she was
on board. So completely on board. Again she reached
out, this time getting his jeans opened and…oh, yes,
her hands inside to wrap around him, so big and hot and
hard—

"Maddie."

She tipped up her head to say he'd better not be thinking of stopping just as he raised his hand toward her face.

In a completely involuntary motion, she flinched back.

He went still. For a single, horrified beat, she did the same. Then she closed her eyes and thunked her head back to the desk, swamped by embarrassment, unease, and frustration. "I'm sorry, I have no idea where that came from. None."

Calm, silent, he leaned over her and slid a hand to the nape of her neck, cupping the back of her aching head, probably checking to make sure she hadn't cracked it.

She could have told him the only thing that was cracked was her damn, worthless heart. Horrified, she kept her eyes closed. She trusted him, maybe more than any man she'd ever been with, so she really couldn't explain why she'd—

"Maddie, look at me."

When she talked herself into opening her eyes, he shook his head. "Don't be sorry. Don't ever be sorry."

How could she not be? Because a minute ago she'd been half an inch from getting her hands on him, and now...now he was moving away from her, easing out from between her legs.

"We're not doing this." His voice was quiet. Terrifyingly gentle. "Not like this, not again."

"Jax—I know you wouldn't hurt me."

"No, you don't. Not yet. But you're getting there. That's not why we're not—"

"Then why?"

A muscle in his jaw bunched, as if it was costing him to back off. It sure as hell was costing her; her entire body was humming, throbbing.

"Because I just realized I don't want to be your escape. I want more. Yeah," he said when she gaped at him. "I don't know when or how exactly that happened, but there it is." He looked at her for a long beat, clearly waiting for her to say something, like maybe she felt the same, but she couldn't say a word with her gut lodged in her throat. He nodded and handed over her sweater before zipping up his jeans and turning to the door, where he paused.

She held her breath. Surely he wasn't really going to walk away. He was going to come back to her, and they'd laugh this off and agree they were just playing...

Any second now...

"Take care of yourself, Maddie."

She blinked at the sound of the door shutting. It sounded pretty damn final.

Apparently, they were not playing. Not even close.

And how had he done that so calmly, when everything within her still trembled and quivered? Whipping around, she grabbed the first thing she could—a file—and chucked it at the door where he'd vanished. It made it only about two feet before it opened and fluttered uselessly to the floor. Dammit. And damn him.

"Fine," she said out loud. But it wasn't fine, and she had the shakes to prove it, not to mention the churning in her stomach. She took in the desk, the organized mess she'd been working so hard on. She needed something to do *now*. Something big. Something new.

Her gaze fell on the key hooks lining the wall behind the desk. Specifically onto the fishing-boat keys. Snatching them in her fingers, she flew out of the building and headed down the dock. It was time for a solo expedition of a different kind.

With Ford's patient, calm voice in her mind, she sailed out of the marina. The wind was low, and the swells even lower. Because the skies were overcast, and also because she wasn't stupid, she stayed very close to the shore. It was a smooth ride, and it felt incredible to do it by herself, for herself.

When she got cold, she turned back to the marina. She did have a bad moment trying to dock. But she managed, and if she accidentally hit the side of the boat hard enough to jar her teeth, that was okay. That's what rental boats were for.

She tied up the boat, hung up the keys, and nodded. She'd done it. She'd actually done it. And if she could do that, she could do anything. Maybe even have a relationship without self-destructing it.

Chapter 18

> *"Always get the facts first.*
> *You can distort them later."*
> Phoebe Traeger

Today would have been Mom's birthday."

Both Tara and Maddie stopped eating when Chloe said this casually over blueberry pancakes. "It's true. She'd have been fifty-five today. She was looking forward to this one because it meant she could get a senior discount in some places. She always wanted to be able to get that damn discount."

Tara looked at Maddie. "Did you know?"

Maddie shook her head. She hadn't been able to think of anything but how Jax had looked walking away from her. "Whenever I asked her how old she was, she said she was ageless. She celebrated Jerry Garcia's birthday as her own."

Tara let out a reluctant smile. "That's what she always told me, too."

"Grandma showed me Mom's birth certificate," Chloe said. "That's how I know."

Maddie dropped her jaw. "You have her birth certificate? Where was she born?"

"Here." Chloe smiled. "Well, in Seattle, which is close enough, right? She grew up in Lucky Harbor, from what I heard."

Thinking about Phoebe going to school here and having a home made Maddie wistful. She was working hard on not resenting how little she'd known about her mother, or how her father hadn't encouraged her to breach that emotional and physical distance. Instead she was trying to concentrate on the here and now that Phoebe had given her.

She'd told her sisters about yesterday's bank rejection. Surprisingly enough, they'd been disappointed. Or at least they'd been kind enough to pretend. They'd agreed to find another lending institution, though Maddie was fairly certain neither Tara nor Chloe expected that to happen. In the meantime, they were going to stick out the month, finish up the bare-essential renovations, and then put the place on the market. Maddie hoped to open the inn and run it until it sold. Hell, who knew, maybe it'd do so well they would miraculously turn it around.

Worst-case scenario, she'd go back to LA and try to get a job through her dad's connections, but she hoped it didn't come to that. She was doing her damnedest not to think about it, not yet anyway. A picture of Jax flashed in her mind—the other thing she was trying not to think about—and her heart pinged, but she hoisted her glass of orange juice into the air. "To you, Mom."

Tara and Chloe looked at her like she was nuts, but she gestured to their glasses, and they obediently picked them up. "I'd love to celebrate who you were," Maddie said to the ceiling. "But I didn't know you well enough. So instead, I think I'll celebrate who we are because of you."

"I like that," Tara said. "Here's to letting go of regrets and even resentments. Here's to what might have been, and to what we will be."

"Happy birthday, Mom," Chloe said quietly, for once her eyes devoid of the mocking sarcasm.

"Happy birthday," Tara and Maddie echoed.

"Oh, and happy birthday to Jerry, too," Chloe added, and they all laughed. It was a rare moment of peace and solidarity as they clicked their glasses together.

Chloe knocked her orange juice back and set the glass on the table. "So, Tara, Maddie wants to tell you something—you snore."

"Excuse me?" Tara's eyes narrowed. "I do not."

"Yes, you do. Like a buzz saw. Or a grizzly bear with sleep apnea. Tell her, Maddie."

Maddie winced. "Okay, well—"

"You did *not* just compare my breathing to a grizzly bear," Tara said to Chloe.

"And/or a buzz saw."

Maddie sighed and reached for her knitting. Solidarity was officially over.

At dawn, Jax gave up on the pretense of sleep and got out of bed. It was ironic that he'd come back to Lucky Harbor to lead the lazy, kick-back life he'd always wanted, and yet it wasn't in him to be lazy.

Unlike Izzy, who was sleeping like…well, a dog. "Time to get up."

Izzy squeezed her eyes tight.

"We're going for a run."

Jax could have sworn that she shook her head. With a sigh, he got up and ran alone. When he got back, Izzy was waiting for him on the porch. "Did you cook breakfast?" he asked her.

She looked at him balefully, like *Dude, no opposable thumbs, or I totally would have.*

Jax showered and dressed, then headed into his office, where Jeanne handed him coffee and left him to himself. Three hours later, she reappeared.

"I'm all caught up. I'm going shopping for some lingerie."

Jax winced. "And I want to know this why?"

"Because maybe you'd like me to pick up a present for somebody."

"Like who?"

"Like the cute curly-haired Traeger sister. The one you're in a fight with."

"What?" He shook his head and stared at her. "How could you possibly know that?"

She smiled. "I didn't, but you're all broody and mopey-looking. What did ya do? Don't tell me, it was something stupidly male, right? Should I get black and lacy, or white and sheer?"

Jesus. "You should mind your own damn business."

"Well, that's no fun." She came close, gave him a sympathetic look, and kissed his cheek. "You could solve it the way Steve solves all of our fights."

He sighed. "How does he do that?"

"Easy. Just admit you were wrong. His always being wrong really works for us." She gently patted his arm and left him alone.

But it didn't feel wrong to want Maddie to see him as more than an escape. It felt...weak and vulnerable, which he really hated.

But not wrong.

Stop thinking, you idiot. He moved through the office and out the back door. The morning was frosty, the cold biting into his skin, reminding him that winter had arrived. Instead of going into his wood shop, he loaded himself and Izzy into his Jeep and went for a drive.

And found himself at the inn.

It looked deserted. He let himself in, noting that it was colder inside than outside. The heater hadn't been turned on today. He walked the ground floor, the sanded but not-yet-finished floors creaking beneath his boots as he took in the walls that still had to be painted, and the bathrooms waiting for their new vanities. He felt a surge of frustration.

It didn't have to be like this.

When something thudded above him, he took the stairs two at a time but found the second floor empty. He hit pay dirt in the attic. The room ran the entire length of the inn. At the moment, it held most of the furniture from the other floors that had been moved to finish the floors. There were tarps everywhere and also stacks of boxes filled with God knew what, dating back to Maddie's grandparents' era.

It was the approximate temperature of the Arctic Circle up here, thanks to the icy air and the equally icy glance Maddie sent his way. She was sitting on the floor, holding her Blackberry as she went through the box in front of her.

"Hey," he said, risking frostbite by moving farther into the room.

She didn't answer.

"What are you doing?"

"Trying to figure out what pieces of furniture are worth selling to cover this month's bills."

Ah, hell. "Maddie—"

"This is a no-talking zone."

When he didn't leave, she sighed, her expelled air coming out in a puffy mist, testament to just how cold it was. "Fine." She jerked her head toward an unidentifiable pile in the far corner. "Can you peek under that tarp and tell me if you see an antique walnut hall bench? I know we had one. Someone's selling a match to it on eBay for three hundred fifty dollars. If I could get half that, I'd be happy."

He moved toward the pile. "You shouldn't be working up here. It's too cold."

"Turns out financial anxiety is a great way to keep warm."

He hated that she was so stressed about money. "Where are your sisters?"

"Drove into Seattle to check out two antique consignment shops to see if they'd be interested in working with us."

"If you sell all the furniture, what will you use if you reopen?"

She shot him a look that said she was worried about his IQ and went back to working on her Blackberry. There were two spots of color high on her cheeks. Her eyes were shiny, too shiny. And her lush, warm, giving mouth was tight and grim.

That's when it hit him. She wasn't mad at him.

She was hurt. "Maddie."

"Go away. I hate everyone right now, and I'm pretty sure that includes you."

"No, you don't."

"Yes, I do. I really do."

"I could change your mind about me."

"I have no doubt, but try it and you'll be walking funny tomorrow."

He couldn't help it, he laughed, and she swiveled her head toward him. "This isn't funny! I wanted you, and you walked away!"

"I wanted you to want *me,* not just the—"

"You're not just an escape, not to me. I'm just a little slower at this than you are."

He looked into her eyes and saw the truth. Remembering Jeanne's words, he shook his head. "I was wrong to push."

"Wow. A man who can say the W word. What else do you have up your sleeve?"

"I don't know. You'll have to look yourself."

She arched a brow. "Strip."

Not much surprised Jax anymore, but this did, and he laughed again as he willingly pulled off his shirt.

She stared at his chest, then his tattoos. Her eyes went a little glazed, but she lifted a shoulder, feigning indifference.

Indifference his ass.

"I've seen you without your shirt before," she pointed out coolly, then murmured so quietly he would have missed it if he hadn't leaned in, "And maybe I'd rather see you without your pants."

"You've seen me without those, too."

"You'd argue with a woman on the very edge?"

He nearly laughed again but recovered quickly, especially since she was still giving him that eat-shit-and-die look. But at least she *was* looking. And the rosiness of her cheeks was no longer about hurt or embarrassment. Mission half accomplished.

Holding her gaze in his, he tore open the buttons on his Levi's, held his breath to brace for the cold, then shoved them down to his thighs.

Her eyes locked in on his forest green knit boxers. Slowly, she set down her Blackberry and then, just as slowly, rose to her feet. "I'm trying to hate you."

"But you can't."

"I could. With some more time."

"Then I'll change your mind," he said.

"But I'm stubborn, remember?"

"Yes, but I'm *very* persuasive."

She nibbled on her lower lip and stared at him, definitely not hating him if her hardened nipples were any indication.

"You're..." She gestured to his erection. "Um."

"Yeah." He was just as shocked as she. It was fucking freezing in here.

"I thought it was supposed to shrink in the cold," she said eyes on "it."

He opened his mouth, then shut it again. She was the only person on earth who could render him speechless. While he stood there, shirt off, pants at his thighs, she stood up and tore off her own sweatshirt.

She wore a pale blue satin bra that barely contained her full breasts. As he soaked in that mouthwatering sight, she unbuttoned and unzipped her jeans and shoved them down. "Crap," she said and glanced up at him.

"Okay, keep in mind I didn't plan on a striptease today. I've got to learn to plan ahead."

If she was talking about the fact that her underwear was a purple lace thong instead of a match to her bra, he could care less. Combined they were going to give him a brain aneurysm.

She tried to kick her pants off, but they got caught on her boot. "And some practice wouldn't hurt, either."

He laughed, and she grumbled, turning away from him to bend over to untie her bootlaces.

And abruptly his amusement was gone, replaced by a wave of sheer, unadulterated lust. It was her cute little thong's fault, the one bisecting her sweet heart-shaped ass and shooting the temperature in the room straight into the stratosphere. "Maddie—" His voice was gruff and hoarse. Probably from blood loss.

She was still fighting with her shoelaces. "Yeah?"

Before he could answer, her cell rang from the floor about five feet in front of her. Shifting gears, she crawled forward.

Yeah. He was going to have an aneurysm. He could feel it coming on.

"Can't," she said into her cell, still on her hand and knees. "I…" She shot him a look over his shoulder, her gaze again dipping down to the front of his tented boxers. "Gotta go." She disconnected with a tap of her thumb. Still staring at him, she paused. "We're in this freezing attic showing our…parts to each other."

"Yes."

"We need to grow up."

"Maybe. But not today."

She drew a breath, still staring at his erection. "Yesterday you said you wouldn't be my escape."

"That was a stupid statement by a very stupid man who wasn't thinking clearly."

"And you're thinking clearly now?"

"Yes. This isn't just sex between us. So if you want escape, and you want to use my body to do it, then I'm your willing victim."

"Magnanimous of you."

Done playing, he crooked his finger at her in the universal "come here" gesture.

She rose to her feet, took a step, and hit the floor with a heavy thud.

"Jesus." He surged toward her and dropped to his knees, pulling her up to face him. "You okay?"

She grimaced. "Tell me you have a clumsy dork fetish."

"Oh, I have a fetish." Her nipples appeared to be a fraction of an inch from breaking free of her bra. He slid his hands up her ribs, his thumbs rubbing over them. "For you. For everything about you."

She sucked in a breath.

"We have some more clothes to lose." He bent to work on untying her shoes, and then his. They kicked them off and then finally lost their pants.

"Maybe we should lose the underwear, too," she whispered and ran a finger over the front of his boxers, right down the length of him, making him groan and reach for her, just as the doorbell rang downstairs.

"I'm going to shoot somebody," Maddie said.

"Sawyer hates when people do that. It's a whole bunch of paperwork."

The doorbell rang again, and Maddie crawled to the window.

Jax stared at her ass and crawled forward, too, planning on tearing those cute little panties off with his teeth. Then he'd grip her hips and bury himself deep in one thrust. Yeah, and then—

"It's Lucille," she hissed. "I can't shoot Lucille."

"She'll go away." Bending, he put his mouth to her hip, then let his tongue snake beneath the string.

"But she's—" she whispered, slapping a hand to the window when he nipped at her with his teeth. "Oh, God."

"Give me a minute and you'll be saying 'Oh, Jax.'" He slid a hand up the inside of her leg, not stopping until he hit lace. "Spread your legs, Maddie," he said, kissing the back of her thigh.

She did just that, and then her other hand hit the glass, and then suddenly she stiffened, but not in a good way. "She sees me," she hissed. "She thinks I'm waving to her." She dropped to her knees and stared at him. "She knows you're here. Your Jeep's here. And I'm in the window without a shirt."

"She's a hundred and ten. There's no way she could see you clearly." He kissed her neck. "She'll go away."

"No, she won't." She batted at his hands as he went for the hook on her bra. "The last time you and I were seen together, our kiss on the pier was the talk of the town. This can't be the talk of the town. This," she said, giving him a poke with her elbow, "is just for you and me."

He blew out a breath and sat back on his heels as she pulled her jeans back on, covering up that sweet ass, jumping up and down a little to work them over her hips. Her breasts jiggled, and he watched as first one and then the other nipple struggled and then managed breakaway status. *Damn.*

She grabbed her sweatshirt and yanked it on, inside out, covering the best view he'd had all week. "*Crap.*" Yanking the shirt back off, she fumbled to right it, then noticed he was just standing there. "Get dressed!"

"Can you be this bossy when we get to a bed? Cuz it's turning me on."

She threw his shirt at him. "Hurry up! You're coming with me!"

"Yeah, now, see, I'd kind of hoped you'd be the one coming by now."

She groaned. "Stop teasing me!"

Lucille talked for eight minutes. Maddie lost track of what the conversation was about, struggling to nod and act as if she was following along—for *eight* long minutes. And for each and every single one of them, she was overwhelmingly aware of the big, tall, silent man standing behind the door, just out of view from Lucille, radiating heat and a sexual frustration that undoubtedly matched hers.

The old Maddie had gone with the flow. Had allowed others' needs to come before her own. "Lucille," she said suddenly. "I'm sorry. I'm really sorry, but I have to go."

Lucille looked puzzled, but she nodded. "Okay, dear. Just come by when you get a chance, and we can finish talking about the project."

"Sure thing. I will, I promise. The, uh, project sounds really worthwhile. A great project, as far as projects go."

She shut the door and closed her eyes. She felt Jax come up behind her, exuding testosterone and pheromones, the only project she was interested in.

A hand brushed aside her hair, and then she felt his mouth on her neck. Her head dropped back to his shoulder as his arm came around her, his hand running up her belly to cup her breast.

"I'm taking you home," he said in a thrillingly rough voice, his thumb brushing over her nipple before he took her hand firmly in his. "To my place."

She opened her mouth to say "Hell, yes," but he pushed her out the door ahead of him, barely giving her time to grab her purse, his big body giving her the bum's rush.

"Jax—"

"This," he said in a repeat of her own words, "is a no-talking zone."

"Lucille at twelve o'clock!" she hissed, jerking her head toward the yard, where Lucille was making her way to her car. Slowly.

"Shit." Jax yanked Maddie back inside as they watched Lucille *finally* get into her car.

"She's killing me," Jax muttered.

It took Lucille even longer to turn her car around and pull out. And then Jax was tugging Maddie down the steps, his long legs eating up the space, forcing her to run to keep up. Izzy loped alongside, ears perked up at the hope that something fun was about to happen. A laugh escaped Maddie, half nerves, half anticipation, and one hundred percent hunger.

At the Jeep, Jax pressed her up against the door and leaned in to kiss her, possessive and deep, as if he had to convince her that she wanted this as badly as he did.

Wrapping her arms around his neck, she plastered herself even closer. "Drive fast," she said and licked the rim of his ear.

He shuddered, then practically shoved her into the Jeep. They drove in silence across town, the only sound being her own heartbeat drumming in her ears. She was so worked up she nearly hit the roof when he touched her thigh. "That was anticipation," she said. "Not... you know."

"Good." He entwined their fingers and didn't speak again.

That worked for her. She couldn't have kept up her end of a conversation to save her life. Not as revved up as she was. Nope, the only thing going to fix this was a man-made orgasm.

A *Jax*-made orgasm.

Driving faster than the speed limit, he turned into a quiet neighborhood on the bluffs three hundred feet above the ocean. His house was the last on the street and the closest to the cliff.

Jumping out, she glanced at his view and stopped in shock. Deep blue ocean as far as she could see, sparkling from the sun's glow. "It's breathtaking," she whispered, taking a step toward it.

"Later. Much later," he said and dragged her inside, giving her nothing but a quick peekaboo hint of wide-open rooms, high wood-beamed ceilings, and gorgeous wood trim and floors before he had her in his bedroom. "I'm going to toss you onto the bed now and have my merry way with you," he said against her lips.

"*Oh*," she whispered, trembling in anticipation, already wet for him.

"Yes or no, Maddie."

"Yes. God, *yes*."

Before she'd even gotten the words out, he'd done just

as he'd promised. He'd picked her up and tossed her to the bed. Before she bounced, he was on her, the fire he'd ignited in the attic flaming back to life. Mouth on hers, he slid his hands beneath her shirt, his fingers teasing her nipples. She gasped, and he pulled back only long enough to peel her shirt over her head, and then his own.

She couldn't take her eyes off him.

He bent and kissed the curve of her breast that spilled out of her bra, and then suddenly even that barrier was gone. "Love your skin," he whispered against her nipple, flicking the pebbled peak with his hot tongue before sucking it hard into his mouth until she was writhing beneath him. "You're so soft."

"It's Chloe's lotions," she said inanely, and he huffed out a rough laugh against her.

"I'm pretty sure it's all you."

His voice couldn't get any lower or any sexier, and she felt like she could come from the sound of him alone. Then he upped the tension by sliding the tips of his fingers into her hip-hugging jeans. "Oh, my God," she whispered.

"I know."

She laughed breathlessly. "No, you don't understand—" She pushed at his chest until he lifted his head. "You got your hand in my pants!"

"Uh-huh." His expression was a mix of lust and amusement. "I was hoping to get even more than that."

Giddy, she grinned. "No, you did it without unbuttoning them. I think it's all that hauling of debris and chopping wood. I'm toning up!"

His eyes were dark and very, very hot. "And that turns you on?"

"Yes." She cupped his face and smiled. "But you turn me on more."

"Good. You turn me on, too." Taking her hand, he placed it over his erection to show her just how much. "We're done talking now. I have other plans for our mouths." To prove it, he tugged her jeans off and then rose off the bed to do the same with his.

Her breath caught at the sight of him in silhouette. Gorgeous. That went without saying. The air shuddered out of her when he bent and kissed her, low on her stomach as he hooked his thumbs in her panties and slowly tugged them down. "You're beautiful, Maddie."

While she melted, he made himself at home between her thighs, taking so long to look at the view in front of him, she squirmed. "Jax."

"If you could see from my point of view..." His broad shoulders nudging her legs wide, he bent and kissed an inner thigh, and she had one thought; *Please be as good at this as you are at everything else.*

Then he gently stroked her with his thumb and she had no more thoughts. With a groan, he ran his tongue over her wet, throbbing skin. She bit her lip and fisted her hands in his sheets, unable to stop from writhing beneath him.

Newsflash—he was indeed as good at this as he was at everything else.

"I love how you taste," he murmured, and when her hips rocked against him, he slid both hands beneath her bottom, holding her still for his ministrations. Quicker than she could have believed possible, she was quivering, on the very edge of an explosive orgasm, and—

And he paused.

"*What?*" she gasped.

Lifting his head, he met her gaze, his own glittering. "The last two times we even got to this spot, we were interrupted. I'm just waiting for it."

She gaped at him in disbelief, panting for breath as she sat up. "You *want* to be interrupted? Because I have to tell you, if we are, I'm going to scream at someone."

He flashed her a devastatingly wicked grin. "Better idea. *I'm* going to make you scream." With that outrageously confident statement, he leaned over her, using the fact that she'd sat up to his advantage. "Soon as I find all your sweet spots." He laved his tongue over a nipple, pressing her back down to the bed. "What you like..." He dipped his tongue into her belly button, then nipped at her hip, taking his cues from her reactions, which she couldn't seem to help.

"How about this?" he murmured, licking the spot where her leg met her body, lingering, taking his time while she shifted restlessly beneath him, trying to get him where she wanted him to go. "Maddie?"

"Y—yes, I like that."

"Good." He kissed her there, then brushed his lips over her mound. "This?" When she didn't answer, he lifted his head.

"*Yes!*"

Doing it again, he slid first one finger into her, and then another, stroking slowly.

She gasped his name.

"Good?"

"*Ohmigod,*" was all she could manage.

"Good," he decided and gently closed his teeth on her center.

She just about lifted off the bed, would have if he wasn't anchoring her with his body. "Jax. Jax, please..."

"Anything," he promised and sucked her into his mouth.

"Don't stop."

He didn't, not when her hands came up to tangle in his hair, not when she cried out and came, shuddering endlessly beneath him. When she was limp, he kissed his way up her still-quivering body.

She tightened her grip on him and kissed him back, feeling him hard and throbbing at her hip. "I need you inside me."

Reaching over her, he took a condom from his nightstand, groaning when she helped him roll it down his length. Then he entwined their fingers and brought their joined hands up to rest on either side of her face. Already cradled by her open thighs, he slid into her. She gasped, rocked to her very core by how good he felt filling her, and he went still. "No, don't stop," she whispered, barely recognizing her soft and throaty voice.

He dropped his forehead to hers, his eyes closing, clearly trying to give her a minute to adjust to him. Wrapping her legs around his waist, she arched up and felt herself soften for him.

"God, look at you," he whispered hoarsely. Squeezing their entwined fingers, he touched his lips to hers. "I love your smile."

She hadn't even been aware that she was smiling. But when she was with him like this, she felt sexy and wanted and beautiful, and on top of her world. And then he was moving with her, setting a pace that stole her breath and captured her heart. Freeing her hands from his, she threaded her fingers into his hair, holding his gaze, knowing her own was filled with shock and wonder.

This. *This* was what it felt like when it was right.

Jax banded his arms around her, sliding them beneath her, up her back to grip her shoulders. The movement pulled them closer, allowing him even deeper inside her, and she cried out, shuddering in pleasure. Her eyes started to drift closed, but he tangled a hand in her hair, tugging gently until she opened them again, allowing him to see everything, allowing her the same as she quivered and trembled against him.

He seemed to lose himself in her eyes. God knew she'd lost herself in his, and as she came, she took him with her for the freefall.

But in his arms, the landing was safe. She had a feeling that with him she'd always be safe.

Chapter 19

*"Since it's the early worm that gets
eaten by the bird, sleep late."*
PHOEBE TRAEGER

The sun was slanting much lower in the sky out Jax's bedroom window when Maddie opened her eyes and blinked into focus a well-defined, muscular chest. Tipping her head back, she met a pair of warm golden eyes that were looking pretty damn alert for a man who should have nothing left in the tank.

"I fell asleep," she said in surprise.

"Just for a little while." He was playing with a strand of her hair, wrapping the curl around and around his finger. "You okay?"

She knew why he asked. He'd seen her face that exact moment he'd pushed inside of her, the single sole heartbeat when her world had slammed to a halt on its axis.

Fear.

Not that he'd hurt her, never that. No, this fear hadn't been physical. Instead, she was afraid of the emotions he had awakened in her. Of what she could feel for him if she let herself.

Jax was on his side, holding her snugged up against him, one hand propping up his head, the other stroking her under the blanket he must have pulled up over them.

"I'm more than okay," she said.

"Then what was the look?"

Trust him to ask bluntly, to put it all out there. She dropped her gaze from his and stared at his throat. "It was good, so very, very good."

"And this surprises you?"

"No. It scares me." She met his gaze. "You've made sure to touch me, to try to put me at ease, as often as possible, and yet you've never asked me about it. About my past. My relationships."

"I figured you'd tell me when you were ready."

And she finally was. "I dated a guy that...well, he wasn't good for me."

Something flickered in his eyes. Something hard. But when he spoke, his voice was as calm and gentle as his hand still whispering over her. "Figured that."

"Until I met you, I'd talked myself into believing all guys were assholes." She chewed on her lower lip, closing her eyes when he lifted his hand to stroke the hair from her forehead, brushing his fingers across her scar.

"Maddie, look at me."

She opened her eyes and found his eyes warm and waiting. "We can all be assholes. I want five minutes alone with your ex to prove it, and I want that badly, but I'd never hurt you. Never."

"Only five minutes?" she asked, trying to lighten the mood.

He wasn't feeling playful. "Violence should never happen in a relationship."

She listened to the vehemence in his voice and took strength from it. "Alex was quiet. Controlled. And when he got pissed, he got *more* quiet and *more* controlled, until he wasn't either of those things." She drew a deep, shuddery breath, remembering how awful it'd been. "The first time he hit me, he seemed so horrified. I can't even explain to myself how I forgave him. He was so sorry and promised it'd never happen again. Then it did. It was..." She swallowed hard, knowing this all played into her fears, how she had no idea what people were really capable of, and how frightening that was. "It escalated, and I left. But I still hate that it happened more than once." She shut her eyes and admitted her secret shame. "It's humiliating that I didn't see him for what he was. That I'd be with a guy like that—"

"You got out," he said quietly, firmly. "You managed a difficult situation, and you got out. That's all that matters now. You have nothing to be ashamed of." He waited until she met his gaze again and softly repeated it. "*Nothing.*"

She nodded, and he kissed her softly. "You're one of the bravest women I know."

That made her laugh.

"You are."

Looking deep into his eyes, her amusement faded, replaced by awe. He meant it. And suddenly, she didn't have to fake the strength. The bravado. It was real. "Did you build this house?"

"Yes. And time for a subject change, I take it."

She smiled at him. "You're a smart man. And I think the house is beautiful."

"You haven't seen much of it."

"That's because you practically shoved me straight to your bed." She looked around at his large bedroom, sparsely filled with big pieces of dark oak furniture that were both masculine and inviting. His sheets were earth tones and luxurious. There were a couple of towels tossed onto a chair in a corner and running shoes lying beneath it. A forgotten pair of jeans was discarded on the floor.

Izzy was snoozing on top of them.

The room was clean but not necessarily neat. Good to know he wasn't a perfect superhero. "I like your furniture."

"I built that, too."

"So you're multitalented."

He smiled wickedly, making her laugh.

"And full of secrets," she added.

His smile faded some. "Yes."

She felt her heart catch at the way he looked at her as he ran the pad of a finger over her lower lip. "You going to share them?" she asked.

He just rolled her over the top of him and ran his hands down her body. "Yes. Secret number one. I'm not finished with you."

"You're right," she said, feeling him hard beneath her. "One of us definitely isn't finished."

With a grin, he pulled her thigh over his hips so that she straddled him, opening her to his touch. "Only one of us?" he murmured and stroked her with his thumb.

It came away drenched.

"Okay, as it turns out, I might not be finished with you, either."

"Feel free to take your time."

She set her hands on his pecs and stared down at him, feeling shockingly at ease given how naked she was. His hands were everywhere on her body, rough and strong and gentle all at the same time. Then he produced another condom and guided her down on him.

It was a deliciously tight fit, and her hands clung to his biceps as she rocked. This wrenched a hungry groan from him, but he gripped her hips. "Slow this time," he demanded, lazily stroking her where they were joined, making her crazy. "Real slow, Maddie."

And he meant it. For torturously long minutes, he languidly stroked, teased, and drew her nearly out of her mind, until she was panting out his name like a mantra, desperate for release. When he finally moved, it was in fluid, rhythmic motions that had her crying out, arching into him, clinging to him as if he was her own personal life support. He was everything.

Simple and terrifying as that.

Eventually they staggered into the kitchen for provisions. Jax made grilled cheese and soup, and then they somehow ended up naked on his big leather couch in the living room. Maddie was currently lying there, gasping for breath, thinking that at this rate, they'd kill each other by Christmas. Damp with perspiration, she shifted, and the friction of her moist skin on the soft leather made a sound that had her going utterly still in horror. Then she became a flurry of motion trying to recreate the sound so Jax would know it was the couch and that she hadn't—

They both clapped their hands to their noses at the same time as the odor hit them, hard and merciless.

"Christ," Jax said, sitting straight up.

"It wasn't me, it wasn't!" Maddie shook her head wildly. "It was my skin against the leather, and—" She broke off because Jax was doubled over, gasping for breath. God. He was dying, he was—

Laughing his butt off, she realized. "It wasn't me," she repeated, beginning to feel insulted.

Jax managed to regain control of himself and then turned to the dog lying at their feet. "Iz, we've been over this—*not* in front of guests. You have to go out?"

The dog leapt to her feet and barked joyously, and—

Let out an audible fart.

Grinning, Jax got up to open the door for her.

"You knew it wasn't me," Maddie accused when he came back, crossing her arms over her chest.

Still grinning, he sank back down and hauled her into his lap. Pressing his face into her hair, he kissed her behind her ear.

Her sweet spot, and he knew it. "Let me make it up to you," he said with a low, masculine laugh.

She lifted her chin softly. "I can't think of anything good enough."

"I can." His eyes were lit with the challenge. "And it's going to be good, Maddie. *Very* good."

Not going to cave, she told herself, holding her body rigid. *Not going to—*

Taking her earlobe gently between his teeth, he tugged lightly. An answering tug occurred between her legs. Cause and effect...

She caved like a cheap suitcase.

Chapter 20

*"If you're going to walk on thin ice,
you might as well dance."*
PHOEBE TRAEGER

Much later, Maddie put a hand to her heart to keep it in her chest. She was trying to think of something to say, but the only thing that came to her mind was *"WOW."* So she murmured it softly and then again, because frankly, it bore repeating.

Next to her, Jax let out a very male sound of agreement and reached for her hand. Entwining their fingers, he brought her palm up to his mouth and brushed his lips across it. "It's dark out," he noted. "When did that happen?"

She had no idea.

"Thirsty? Hungry?"

In response, her stomach rumbled loud enough to echo off the walls, and she closed her eyes in answer to his laugh. The couch dipped as he rolled over her and placed his forearms on either side of her face, his body lowering to hers. "My plan was to keep you naked until one of us begged for mercy. We'll circle back to that."

They showered, dressed, and made it to the Jeep just as a sleek Mercedes pulled up the driveway. Beside her, Jax stiffened. Glancing into his face, she was surprised to see that his look of satisfaction had vanished. "What is it?"

Before he answered, a man stepped out of the car wearing a well-cut suit and a flash of sophistication. His eyes went straight to Maddie.

Resisting the urge to pat down her crazy hair and squirm, she jumped a little when Jax took her hand in his and ran his thumb over her fingers. Other than that small, comforting gesture, he didn't move a single muscle.

"So I see why you haven't returned my phone calls," the man said to Jax.

Jax didn't respond. Maddie wasn't even sure he was breathing. The other man was as tall as Jax and incredibly fit, and could have been anywhere from late forties to sixty. "As I told you in the emails you didn't answer,' he said to Jax. "We need to talk about Elizabeth."

"And as I told you, don't show up here without an appointment." Jax's eyes were colder and harder than Maddie had ever seen them.

"Christ," the man said. "You're worse than a damn woman. Fine. Can I...*please*..." He paused for sarcasm's sake. "Have an appointment?"

A tight smile curved Jax's mouth, but it wasn't a pleasant one. "Busy."

The man let out a snort, his gaze flicking back to Maddie, who hadn't been born in a barn, so she held out her hand. "Maddie Moore."

"Jackson Cullen. Are you a client, or a friend?"

"None of your business," Jax said and put a hand on Maddie's lower back, nudging her to the Jeep. "Let's go," he said. "Now."

Only a little while ago, she'd been kissing her way down his amazing body, licking and nibbling, coaxing the sexiest sounds from him, including lots of that "now," in a different context of course.

She loved knowing she had the power to make him lose control. She loved his warm body, his scent, the texture of his skin, the taste of him on her tongue, and the strength of his hands, and how she trusted that strength. She loved his generosity of spirit, loved the way he could be gentle and endlessly patient, and yet still vibrate with testosterone. She loved how much he cared about his friends, his dog, everyone in the town. She loved his mischievous smile. The way he looked at her. How he teased her, laughing with her, not at her.

And she was desperately afraid she *loved* him.

Jax opened the Jeep's passenger door for her, and she started to get in. "He'll never love you, you know," Jackson said directly to Maddie.

When she looked up at him, he nodded. "He's cold. It's what made him so successful. Ask his old bosses. Ask Elizabeth. His fiancée." He cocked his head and studied her face. "Did he tell you about her?"

"Dad," Jax said tightly. "Back off."

Jackson sent his son a long look. "Oh, he talks a mean game," he said, still speaking to Maddie. "And he can spin wheels of logic in your head until you think you're getting what you want from him, but it is a game. It's *all* a game." His smile was dark and grim. "You seem like a nice girl, Maddie, but you're out of your league here. I'd get out while you can."

"Maddie, get in," Jax said and stood there as if guarding her until she did. Then he turned to his father. "Get off my property and don't come back."

Violence shimmered in the air, and Maddie stared at them through the windshield, her pulse kicking hard. Jax looked at her. With a flash of something that might have been regret, he moved around to the driver's side.

"You're fucking up your life," his father said, grabbing Jax's arm as he turned away.

Jax spun back, and at whatever Jackson saw in his son's face, he dropped his hands from him.

"You can't push me around anymore, Dad," Jax said. "You can't get to me."

"It's not too late to get your life back on track."

Again, Jax locked eyes with Maddie through the windshield. "I'm on track." With that, he slid into the driver's side and thrust the engine into gear.

Jax was silent as he pulled out.

She was silent, too, though she eyed him very carefully as he drove. Had he inherited his father's temper? It was possible. She of all people knew anything was possible, that people could hide parts of themselves and keep those parts under wraps until they decided to reveal them.

He finally spoke. "You okay?"

"I was thinking of asking you the same. You're... mad."

He shifted his inscrutable gaze to hers, then turned back to the road. "And that worries you."

She squirmed in her seat over that one, and he blew out a low breath. "I was hoping we were past this, Maddie."

Her, too, but unbidden came the images of Alex, how he'd lashed out when he appeared so calm and in control. It pissed her off that her brain could do this to her, betray her now, make her feel so irrational. But that was the thing about fear. She could ignore it all she wanted, but it didn't go away. Nope, it merely hung out, biding its sneaky time.

Jax let out a long breath and didn't speak again. As they got on the highway, with the mountains on their left and the ocean churning on the right, the silence grew.

And grew.

And thickened into something ugly.

"You believed him," he finally said, voice low.

"No. I—"

"You did."

"I'm sorry. I'm…" What? *Overwhelmed by seesaw emotions?* Check. *Unnerved because even not wanting to, I let your father scare me?* Check and check. Both were ridiculous and childish and stupid, and she knew this. "I'm sorry," she repeated lamely.

"Don't," he said, voice tight. "You don't mean it. So don't apologize."

He was right. She hadn't meant to apologize. She'd meant to ask him how he planned on releasing his anger, because he clearly *was* angry. She could read the tension still in his body—she'd become somewhat of an expert on the subject. "For what it's worth, I really do know you wouldn't hurt me. Logically, anyway."

He slid her a searching look but said nothing.

She let out a breath. "So what's your father's problem with what you do for a living?"

He was quiet so long she'd decided he wasn't going

to answer. Then he suddenly spoke. "He sees working with one's hands as beneath him." He turned off onto the asphalt road at the end of town. Lucille was on her front porch and waved.

Maddie automatically waved back.

They drove down the dirt road, and then they were at the inn. Jax parked, and they both sat there.

"What does he do?" Maddie eventually asked.

"He's a lawyer. We used to be one and the same."

She tried to picture Jax in an expensive suit and an uptight expression and couldn't. "No. I don't believe you were ever like him."

"Believe it. Hell, I even thrived on it."

She searched his face for the easygoing, sexy, playful lover she'd been with all afternoon but couldn't find him. This did not help her nerves. "Why did you quit?"

"Lots of reasons, but mostly I hated who I'd become."

"Elizabeth?"

He shrugged. "She was part of the lifestyle."

"You don't talk about her."

"I try not to think about that time in my life."

She stared at him for a full minute, waiting for more. When it didn't come, she felt her own temper stir. "I've learned the hard way that when people aren't forthcoming, there's a good reason."

"I'm not like him, Maddie. Not even close. Don't compare us."

She felt like he'd slapped her. *Not a mouse,* she reminded herself. Hold your ground. "So you didn't keep parts of yourself purposely hidden from me? You're not still keeping parts hidden?"

A muscle ticked in Jax's jaw. "You're going to let him

win." His words were short and clipped. He was pissed. "You're going to let him drive that wedge he wanted between us."

"This isn't a court case to win or lose, Jax. It's my life." She stared at him while he stared straight out the windshield. "Is there anything else about your past I should know?"

He was quiet for a beat too long, and she let out a breath. "Jax. Is there?"

"There's always something."

"That's no answer, and we both know it."

But given his silence, it was the only answer she was going to get. Honestly, she couldn't quite believe it, that they'd found themselves here, in this place. She'd had little hints from him that he hadn't been the open book she'd thought, but she'd ignored them.

Logically she knew that, given how hard it'd been for *her* to open up about her past, she needed to cut him some slack for not being completely forthcoming himself. But she couldn't find it in her at the moment. "I have work to do."

He shoved his fingers through his hair. "Maddie—"

"Lots of work." She hopped out and shut the door hard. Her exit wasn't exactly graceful, since she had to yank it open again to pull out the hem of her shirt, which had gotten caught.

Without looking at him, she walked into the inn and shut that door hard, too, then put her forehead to the wood. When she couldn't stand the suspense and peeked out the window, he was gone.

Chapter 21

♥

*"Men are like roses.
You have to watch out for the pricks."*
PHOEBE TRAEGER

The three sisters sat in the back booth at Eat Me Café having a late night dinner. Tara had just gotten off shift, and at this hour, there were more Christmas decorations than customers.

Chloe was eating the night's chicken special. Tara was carefully stirring her hot tea and adding honey with the precision of a drill sergeant moving troops.

Maddie was knitting, and *not* with the precision of a drill sergeant. She was also thinking too hard: about Jax's father, about Jax's ex-fiancée, about Jax. About their fight. At the moment, she wasn't sure where they stood, or even where she wanted them to stand, but with a few hours of distance, she could definitely admit one thing.

She'd overreacted.

Fear did that to a person, made them completely...
stupid. She hated that. She thought about going over to

his house to talk to him. Or better yet, *not* talking. She could let her fingers do the talking for her.

Chloe glanced at her and rolled her eyes. "You and your orgasmic glow need to shut it."

"Don't mind Chloe," Tara said. "She's just jealous, bless her heart."

"I'm going to bless your dead body," Chloe said. "And are you saying you're *not* jealous? The Mouse is clearly getting some, and we're getting the big fat zip."

"Sugar, you can't miss what you can't even remember."

Maddie sighed. "There's really nothing to be jealous of."

"Uh-oh." Chloe cocked her head. "Trouble in paradise? What happened? Don't even try to tell me he didn't fill out a condom. I've seen how he fills out his jeans."

Tara choked on her tea.

"Oh, like you haven't noticed." Chloe turned back to Maddie. "Before we get to why you're pouting, can we at least hear the juicy details? Does he talk dirty in bed? He's good with his tongue, right? Please tell me he is."

So good, Maddie thought and wriggled as she felt her body respond at just the memory.

"This isn't fair." Chloe slouched in her chair, pouting. "I'm good with my tongue, and I can't even do it without getting an asthma attack."

"I know I'm going to regret asking," Tara said. "But how do you know you're good?"

"I practiced with zucchinis. What?" she asked when both sisters laughed. "You asked."

Tara rubbed her temples as if trying to remove the image burned into her brain. "So what happened?" she asked Maddie, clearly desperate to move on. "What happened with you and Jax?"

"I happened," she said miserably. "I let my past dictate my present and possibly ruin the future."

"Huh?" Chloe asked.

"I met his father. Who's not a nice guy, by the way. And I found out that Jax gets really quiet when he's mad. Like the calm-before-the-storm quiet."

"Ah, sugar." Tara pushed aside Maddie's knitting to squeeze her hand. "That doesn't mean he's going to blow up."

"I know that." Sort of.

"And we all have pasts," Chloe pointed out, surprisingly void of sarcasm. "*And* exes."

"I know that, too. I just realized that, for as open and laid-back as he is, there's more to him, a lot more than he's shown me. I'm tired of playing the game when I don't get a copy of the rules. He can go play with himself." She paused. "Okay, that came out wrong."

"But it sure is a great visual," Chloe said.

"I say back off," Tara said. "You've had your fun with him, and that's all you need for now."

"But—"

"Trust me," Tara said. "Backing off *before* you fall is the safest." She got up and came back with an apple pie and a quart of vanilla ice cream. "This is my Can't Get It Together apple pie. It's got a million calories, but it cures everything. Broken budget, broken heart, you name it."

They each took a huge piece and added ice cream.

"Uh-oh," Chloe said to Maddie. "Your foods are touching."

"Shut up." The warm, buttery crust melted in Maddie's

mouth and made her moan. Not as good as being naked with Jax, but a close second.

"So one week left until Christmas," Chloe said, mouth full.

Maddie set down her fork, her stomach clenching.

"Honey." Tara shook her head, looking surprisingly upset. "It all comes down to money. Our cards are maxed out now. We have no buffer. We're finishing up the bare necessities and getting it on the market. It's for the best."

"Plus you two want out of here," Maddie said softly.

"And that," Tara said honestly.

Chloe took Maddie's hand. "Come on. Let's go back to the cottage, turn on our Charlie Brown Christmas tree lights, and sing bad Christmas songs. I have a brand-spanking-new facial mask to try out on you guys that takes away fine wrinkles."

"I don't have wrinkles."

Chloe patted her hand. "And remind me to remind you to get your eyes checked."

The next morning, Maddie opened her eyes and had to laugh. Once again she'd fallen asleep knitting and was wrapped in her yarn. And also once again, she was entangled with her sisters beneath their tree like a pack of kittens. She crawled over a snoring Tara and pulled herself free from her latest knitting project. She'd finished it last night, and beautiful as she thought it was, she had to admit—it was her most crooked scarf yet. "Okay, one of these days, I'm going to get the hang of this."

Chloe sat up, and Maddie gaped at her. And then at Tara. "Why is your hair green?"

"What?" Chloe touched her hair. "*What?*"

"And your face is white."

"Omigod. So's yours! And yours!" Chloe said, pointing at Tara, too.

It was like a bad game of blind man's bluff. They all ran to the tiny bathroom and fought for space in front of the mirror.

Each of them had green-tipped hair and a face mask that had hardened like clay, cracking across their skin.

"Oh, God," Tara groaned, then whirled on Chloe. "This is your fault."

Chloe tossed up her hands. "Why is it always the baby who has to take the blame?"

"Because you are to blame? You said the mask would soak in overnight."

She'd talked them into some new conditioner she'd made out of seaweed and avocado. "It must have stained. Okay, no one panic."

"Why, because I'm sporting a hair dye that makes me look like I should be starring in a Dr. Seuss book?" Tara yelled.

Maddie bent to the sink and scrubbed off the face mask and brushed her teeth. Chloe and Tara followed suit, then they all stared at themselves until the doorbell rang.

Maddie went to the door.

Jax stood on the porch holding a container of four steaming hot coffees. Something tumbled inside her at the sight of him, but the warm fuzzy was immediately chased by a cold dose of reality. She had no idea where they stood.

He was wearing his usual sexy-as-hell work

uniform—jeans, boots, and a big, warm-looking hoodie sweatshirt. Minus his usual easy smile. He handed her a coffee. "About my father and my ex," he said, characteristically going right to the meat. "I don't talk about them because neither are involved in my day-to-day life anymore. I spend long chunks of time not thinking about them at all. We don't keep in touch; we don't have fond memories. Both of those relationships ended badly, so believe me, there isn't anything you'd want to hear."

Fair enough. She and her father had a very decent relationship, but her time with Alex certainly wasn't anything anyone would want to hear, either. "I'm sorry. I overreacted." She offered a small smile. "I guess I'm still working on those trust issues. But you can't deny that I really don't know very much about you."

His warm caramel eyes met hers. "We could work on that."

Out of everything he'd given her—his time, a sense of renewed confidence, his friendship and more—this was perhaps the most meaningful of all. "That'd be nice," she said. "Getting to know each other even better."

"Maybe we could start with why you have green hair."

"Basically, it's because Chloe's evil. Notice my scarf matches."

"There's a lot of green going on," he agreed.

She pulled off the scarf and wrapped it around his neck, holding the ends. Playfully, she went up on tiptoe and brushed his lips with hers. "It's a little crooked, but I prefer to think of it as unique. And it's warm."

"Reminds me of you," he said softly, hands going to her hips to hold her against him. "Unique and warm."

She kissed him again. "Thanks for the coffee, and especially thanks for being so patient with me."

He tightened his grip when she moved to pull away. "Have we negotiated a truce, then?"

"I think so. We're..." What? What were they? She realized she had no idea what he wanted from her.

He looked at her for a long moment. "I'd like to keep going with us, Maddie. Adding in more talking, minus a few misunderstandings. You?"

She stared at him, feeling her emotions swing like a pendulum. Not only had he said what he'd wanted without a sign of panic or fear, he'd asked her what she wanted. "I'm on board with that. Though I'd add in more of what we did yesterday at your house before your dad showed up."

With his first real smile and a soft laugh, he pulled her in and pressed his mouth to her temple. He ran a hand down her hair, tugging very lightly on the green tips, the small smile still curving his mouth, the one that tended to melt her bones with alarming alacrity.

Her sisters appeared on either side of her, green hair and all. Jax offered them coffees, which were gratefully received.

"You need a clone," Chloe told him and sipped. "To share with the rest of the female population. What are we doing today?"

Maddie knew what she wanted to do. *Jax.*

But clearly his superhero powers of ESP were broken. "Painting," he said to Chloe. "An entire day of painting."

Damn.

They painted.
And painted.

Well, Tara and Maddie painted. Chloe worked on her skin care line.

Jax worked outside and away from them on the wood trim. By the time Tara and Maddie quit at sunset, Maddie's arms felt like overcooked noodles.

Chloe, restless as usual, rode off into the sunset on her Vespa.

"Stay out of trouble," Tara called after her. Shaking her head, she sighed. "She's not going to stay out of trouble." She turned to Maddie. "I'm going in for my dinner shift. Come over when you're hungry, and I'll feed you."

"Will do." Maddie stood in the middle of the living room of the inn and took stock as if she were looking at the place for the first time. The floors were looking good, and without the rooster and cow wallpaper, the rooms looked bigger and more airy. Even so, there was still something almost antiquated about the place, which was okay, because it fit like an old glove. It had character. And charm. It felt like a place that she could get comfortable in and stay a while.

Too bad that wasn't going to be the case. For her entire life, "home" had been transient, a place to hang her coat, to rest her head, but not a place to stop for any length of time. Now she'd finally found a true home, one that embraced her, comforted her, and gave her peace.

But just like everything else in her life, it hadn't worked out. She'd been trying to keep that thought at bay, but the Denial Train was leaving the station.

And soon, all too soon, Maddie was going to have to leave, too.

Chapter 22

*"Catch and release when you're fishing,
and catch and release when you're dating."*
PHOEBE TRAEGER

Jax spent the next few days installing the bathroom vanities and finishing the floors. The painting was done, as well. Tara had wielded a paintbrush with predictable meticulousness. Maddie had painted as she did everything else in her life. She'd started out tentative but had ended up giving her entire heart over to the process.

She made him smile.

And ache. He had no idea what would happen—if and when she'd be leaving, if she'd ever let herself fully trust him—but he knew what he wanted to happen.

He wanted her to stay.

As darkness fell on Christmas Eve, he stood outside the inn in the blustery, frigid air, cleaning up his tools, watching as first Tara sped off in Maddie's car, and then Chloe on her Vespa.

He turned to take in the single light shining into the

dull, foggy dusk from the marina building. Setting down his tool belt, he headed that way and found Maddie at her desk. She was lit by the soft glow of the lamp, the rest of the marina in shadow. She had her back to him in her chair, feet braced up on the wall, computer in her lap, fingers clicking away.

Helpless against the pull of her, he stepped in a little closer. She'd showered and changed from the day's work and wore a pair of bright red sweats, snug enough to show her curves, yet covering her from head to toe. The hood was edged in white and had two white tassels hanging down, dangling to her breasts like two arrows. Along one leg were white letters spelling out "Mrs. Claus."

Her hair was piled messily on top of her head, held there with her knitting needles, and she was frowning, looking tousled and annoyed and beautiful. "Hey," he said.

She didn't budge, and he realized she wore earphones, the cord trailing to her pocket, a tinny sound giving away her iPod. Smiling, he pulled out his phone and IM'd her.

(JCBuilder):   Busy?

(ILoveKnitting): Trying to relax.

(JCBuilder):   I could help with that.

(ILoveKnitting): Yes, you could. By telling me something about you. Your favorite childhood memory, your most embarrassing moment, what makes you tick—*something*.

(JCBuilder):   Eating ice cream on the Ferris wheel, plowing my first truck into Lucille's mailbox, and living for the here and now. Now you.

(ILoveKnitting): Making s'mores on a movie camp-
fire set with my dad, every single second of that
first time we met, and knowing that there's always
tomorrow to get it right.

(JCBuilder):   It?

(ILoveKnitting): Life. You got a recipe for life that I
can follow?

(JCBuilder):   Feeling brave?

She laughed when she read that one, and Jax felt a
weight fall off his shoulders.

Tugging out her earphones, she leaned back even
deeper in her chair. "If you only knew..." she murmured.

"What?" he asked her, stepping closer. "If I only knew
what?"

She gasped and whipped her head around, losing her
balance in the process and crashing to the floor.

"Christ." He came around the desk and crouched
down at her side. "You okay?"

"I've *got* to stop doing that." Still in her chair, she
was flat on her back on the ground, clutching her laptop,
appearing annoyed until she got a good look at him and
the crooked green scarf around his neck. "*Aw.* You're
wearing it."

"Yeah." He'd been taking shit about it from Ford and
Sawyer, too. He took her computer and set it on the desk,
then reached for her, holding her down when she tried to
scramble to her feet. "Wait. Just lie there a minute. What
hurts?"

"Besides my stupid pride? My butt."

Still on his knees, he lifted her out of the chair and pulled her over to him so that she was straddling his thighs in those Mrs. Santa sweats. "Cute," he said, sliding his hands to said butt. "Better?"

"Mmm. The sweats are Chloe's. It's laundry day. All my clothes are in the washer."

"Don't tease me with the washer, Maddie."

She bit her lower lip between her teeth, and he laughed softly. "You know, I've never been jealous of a spin cycle before."

She grimaced in embarrassment. "Stop."

"You have no idea what the thought of you on that thing does to me." He was hard already. And since his hands were on her ass, cupping her, he realized something else.

She wasn't wearing any underwear.

With a groan, he slid his hands up to her breasts. No bra, either.

Oh, Christ, he was a goner. "Maddie, where's your underwear?"

She lowered her voice to a whisper, as if imparting a state secret. "In the washer."

"You realize that puts you on the naughty list." He slid a finger into her drawstring resting just below her belly button and very slowly began to tug.

"What are you doing?"

Unwrapping you… "Checking for injuries."

"Jax—"

"That's Dr. Jax to you."

Her eyes lit with humor, but she put her hands over his, stopping their progress. "I feel different with you. Good different. I just wanted you to know." She removed her hands from his. "You can carry on now. Doctor."

He kissed her, then pulled back to look into her eyes. "I feel different, too."

"You do?" she breathed, her entire body softening for him. "What else are you feeling?"

Hot. Hungry. Devastatingly seduced by the look in her eyes, the one that said she was falling for him. "Like I want you. All of you. Wrapped around me. Lost in me." Having untied her bottoms, he reached for the zipper of her sweatshirt.

She held her breath as he slid it down, revealing a strip of her creamy skin from chin to belly button, and more than a hint of the curves of her breasts.

"I'm going to be cold," she whispered.

"I'll keep you warm." Leaning forward, he pressed his mouth between her warm, full breasts. Gently scraping his lips over one plumped curve, he worked his way to her nipple, which had already tightened for him.

"I don't think I got hurt there." But her fingers slid into his hair to hold him in place.

"You can never be too sure." Slowly, he drew her nipple into his mouth and sucked.

Her head fell back, and she let out an aroused murmur that went straight through him. "But I fell on my butt."

"You're right. You need some serious TLC." He slid his hands into her loosened sweatpants, tracing his fingers down the center of her sweet bare ass. Lingering... "Here?"

She gasped and shifted away. "No!"

With a smile, he slid his fingers lower. Wet. God, so wet.

Her arms clenched around his neck, and her breath was nothing more than little pants of hot air against his skin as he stroked her. "How about here?" he asked, slowly rubbing the pad of his callused finger over her, groaning when she spread her legs a little farther apart for him, giving him room to work. "Are you injured here?"

"N—no." She clutched at him, panting for breath in his ear. "Jax—Jax, please—"

He loved the sweet begging, but it wasn't necessary. Because he was going to "please." He was going to please the both of them.

She rocked into him, her hands running over his chest, his abs, trying to get inside his clothes, trying to get inside him. He felt the same. He couldn't get close enough. She was warm and curvy and whispering his name, and that worked for him, big-time. He reached down to tug off her shoes so he could get her out of the Santa sweats when red and blue lights flashed from outside, slashing into the office window.

Chapter 23

*"Sisters are the true friends who ask how
you are, and then wait to hear the answer."*
PHOEBE TRAEGER

Maddie straightened and stared at Jax, before zipping
herself back up. She got to the window just as Sawyer
opened the back door of his sheriff's car.

Chloe huffed out and stormed toward the cottage.

"Oh, boy," Maddie said, feeling Jax at her back.

"Sawyer's pissed," he said.

"How can you tell? He's wearing a blank expression."

"*That's* how you tell. He gives nothing away when
he's in that kind of mood."

Maddie's gut tightened. "What do you think she did
this time?"

"This time?"

Maddie hurried outside. "Chloe?" she called out.

Both Sawyer and Chloe turned around.

"It wasn't my fault," Chloe said.

Sawyer snorted.

Chloe tossed up her hands, whirled, and started walking again.

"You're welcome for the ride," Sawyer said to her back.

Chloe flipped him the bird and slammed the cottage door.

"What happened?" Maddie asked Sawyer.

"She talked Lance into taking her hang gliding by moonlight. The two of them climbed Horn Crest and flung themselves off the cliff, landing on Beaut Point with about six inches to spare before they would have plunged to their deaths."

At 6,700 feet, Horn Crest was the highest peak in the area. Beaut Point was the plateau overlooking Lucky Harbor, and it was about the size of a football field, sitting three hundred feet above where the Pacific Ocean smashed into a valley of rocks below. Picturing what Chloe had done, Maddie felt sick. "Is she all right?"

"Are you kidding me? She's like a cat with nine lives. I don't know how many she has left, though." Sawyer shook his head in disgust. "Lance was under the influence. I'm hauling his ass in until he sobers up. Chloe wasn't drinking, so technically, I can't hold her. And they didn't actually break any law since it's actually not illegal to be stupid, but they were trespassing, and I should have ticketed her." He blew out a breath. "At this point, it's a waste of paper."

He rubbed his hands over his face and turned to Maddie. "She was lucky tonight, damn lucky. I'd ask you to try to talk some sense into her, but I'm not sure that's even possible."

•   •   •

A few minutes later, after having said good night to
Jax and Sawyer, Maddie walked through the cottage to
the small bedroom, where she found Chloe sprawled
facedown and spread-eagle across the bed, already out
cold.

The Wild One...

Maddie had always secretly yearned to be the Wild
One. Anything would have been better than the Mouse.
Except that no longer really applied, did it? A mouse
wouldn't have given this place a shot. A mouse wouldn't
be having spectacular sex with a man who had a singular
ability to obliterate her heart. A mouse wouldn't be fighting to get to know her sisters, and herself.

Maybe what was happening with the inn was inevi-
table, and maybe she couldn't save it. And maybe what
she had with Jax was truly just a little snapshot in time
and couldn't be saved either.

But she *could* save her relationship with her sisters.
And she could save herself from going back to the way
she'd been before.

She could be whoever she wanted. Knowing it, she
felt herself smiling and pulled out her phone. "Still close
by?" she asked when Jax picked up.

Jax watched Maddie peer out the Jeep's windshield at
the unlit, unmoving Ferris wheel. "It's closed," she said
with disappointment.

"It's Christmas Eve." He had the Jeep running, the
heater on full blast. The interior of the vehicle was dark
except for the glowing light from the instrument panel,
but he had no trouble seeing the life in her eyes or the
smile on her face.

He knew if asked, she'd say he put that smile there. She'd been coming to life a little more every day, but the truth was that he'd had nothing to do with it. She'd taken on her world, and it was sexy as hell to watch.

"I guess I'll have to find another adventure tonight," she said and turned to him. Her hair fell around her face in soft curls, just past her shoulders. He knew what it smelled like, knew how it felt brushing over his bare skin. He knew how she tasted and how to make her moan his name. He knew she was slow to open her heart, but that once she did, she was fiercely loyal to those she cared about. He knew what foods she craved, that she had a low tolerance for alcohol and a penchant for drinking it anyway. He knew that she pretended to be annoyed by Tara's steely resolve but really admired it, just as he knew she also admired Chloe's spirit. He knew that after a life in Los Angeles, she thought Lucky Harbor would be heaven. He knew she was looking for more...

And that she hoped she'd found it.

She knew things about him, too, more than he'd revealed to a woman in a long time. Unable to help himself, he ran a finger along her temple, tucking a strand of hair behind her ear. "Name it," he said. "Tell me what you want."

"But we don't have a condom."

He couldn't help it, he laughed.

She grinned. "I'm sorry. I think it's the fresh air here. And the pounding surf. And maybe also, it's you."

"No," he told her quietly. "It's all you. Come on." He turned off the Jeep, pulled two heavy coats from the back seat, and handed her one. When she was bundled up, they walked the pier.

They passed Eat Me, and Maddie's stomach growled. "I could use some of Tara's Badass Brownies right about now."

"Badass?" he asked.

"As in they're so badass that you turn badass just by smelling them."

He laughed and pulled her in close for the sheer pleasure of touching her. "Do you want to go in? I'll buy you a Badass Brownie."

"No, Tara's in there. She'll be annoying."

They hadn't gotten five steps past the café when they heard a loud voice.

"Maddie Moore, I see you."

Maddie jerked around. "What—"

Jax pointed to the loudspeaker on the corner of the building, just above the large picture window on the café, where several faces were pressed up against the glass, watching them.

"Step away from the good-looking man," came the disembodied voice.

Tara.

Maddie groaned but surprised him by tightening her grip on his hand instead of dropping it. "What does she think she's doing?"

"Amusing her customers." Jax's gaze locked in on their audience in the window, some shoving for better position, a few others waving.

"Madeline Annie Traeger, this is your conscience speaking," the loudspeaker said. "We're watching you. And—Hey, are those my Gucci boots?"

Maddie tipped her face up to the stars as if looking for divine intervention. "Some people have normal families," she said. "They get together once a month or so and have dinner. My family? We have pancake batter food fights, steal each other's footwear, dye our hair green, and yell at each other over loudspeakers in public."

"Keep it moving, sugar. No loitering on the pier."

"Everyone loiters on the pier!" Maddie yelled at the speaker.

"And especially no standing beneath the mistletoe for any reason at all."

Both Maddie and Jax looked up at the mistletoe someone had hung on the building's eaves. "What does it say about me that now I want to stand beneath it?" Maddie asked him.

"That we think alike?" Jax stepped closer, bent his head, and—

"Hold it!" the voice of Maddie's "conscience" called out.

Maddie sighed. "Jax?"

"Yeah?"

"I need a chocolate shake."

He didn't point out the fact that it was thirty degrees or that her breath was crystallizing in front of her face. They headed toward the ice cream shop.

It wasn't Lance serving tonight, mostly because he was still sitting in the single holding cell at the sheriff's station. Instead, it was Tucker, Lance's twin brother.

"Sawyer's keeping an eye on him," Jax said to Tucker's unasked question. "He'll be out in time to celebrate Christmas. He's okay."

"He's an idiot. We'll have the rent to you next week. We're a little behind."

"It's okay," Jax said. "It's a slow time for everybody."

Tucker nodded his thanks, handed over a chocolate shake, and Jax and Maddie walked on.

"You're their landlord?" Maddie asked.

"Yes."

She thought about that a minute. "Do you own the whole pier?"

"No. But I own some of the businesses on it."

She walked to the end of the pier. Leaning over the railing, she stared at the churning sea beneath her, clearly thinking and thinking hard.

She needed answers, deserved answers, but the truth was he wasn't sure where to start. For a man who'd made a living spinning words his way, it was pretty fucking pathetic. He came up beside her. "I own some businesses in town, too."

"Interesting that you've never mentioned this, Mr. Mayor."

He winced. "You really do know a lot about me." *Lame.*

"Hmm," she said, distinctly unimpressed.

He drew a deep breath. "You once told me some of your faults."

"I told you *all* my faults."

He smiled and played with one of her curls. "Want to hear mine?"

"I know yours. You don't like to share yourself. You think dog farts are funny."

"Everyone thinks dog farts are funny."

"You make me talk during sex."

He grinned. "You like that."

She blushed. "That's not the point."

When she didn't come up with anything else, he

raised a brow. "Is that it? Because I have more faults, Maddie. Plenty of them. Like...I ate only cereal until I was five."

"I like cereal."

"I jumped off Mooner Cliff into the water when I was ten. I thought I could fly, but I broke both legs."

"So you were all boy. Big deal."

"I got laid in the USC law school library when I was nineteen and nearly got arrested for indecent exposure. I failed the bar exam the first time because I had a hangover." He paused and let the big pink elephant free. "Then I took a case where an innocent woman got trapped between both sides. I tried to warn her, breaking my oath as a lawyer to do so, and instead of using the info to get herself out of a bad situation, she took her own life."

He paused when she inhaled sharply. He couldn't read the sound and had no idea if it was horror or disgust. But he'd gone this far—he had to finish. "I stopped practicing law after that. It'd sucked the soul right out of me." He paused. "I haven't gotten it back yet."

She stared at him then, and he held the eye contact. He figured she was going to walk away from him in three, two, one—

She moved, but not away. Instead she came close, her hand on his chest, gently stroking right over his heart. "You have a soul," she whispered, her voice shaking with emotion. "And a huge heart. Don't ever doubt it. You have a *superhero* heart," she said fiercely.

He shook his head. "I'm not a superhero, Maddie, not even close. I'm just a guy, with flaws. Lots of them. I do the restoration and the furniture making because I love it, but neither is all that profitable."

"But you have that big, beautiful house. How could you..." She paused. "Your father," she breathed.

"No. *No,*" he said firmly. "Not my father. I'm good with investments."

She searched his face. "This bothers you," she said.

He shook his head, unable to put it into words. He'd tried to give back some of what he felt he'd taken by his years at the firm, but instead he'd profited.

"You know, you're standing right here," she said softly. "And yet I feel like you're far away. You hold back so much. Do you do it on purpose?"

"Yes. I've done it on purpose for so long I'm not sure how to do it any differently. You know me, Maddie. You know what I do, where I like to go—"

"I know that about a lot of people, Jax. I know that about Lucille, about Lance. Hell, I know that much about Anderson." She poked him in the chest. "I want to know more about *you.* I want—" She was toe to toe with him, getting mad, standing up to him.

She wasn't afraid of him. She was in his face, holding her ground, and he'd never been more proud of her. "You know more," he said quietly. "You know my friends, and that I have a screwed-up relationship with my father. You know I drive a beat-up old Jeep so that my big lazy dog can ride with me wherever I go. You know that I don't pick up my clothes and that I like to run on the beach."

She made a soft noise, and he stepped closer and brushed his hand over her throat, where, to his chagrin, she had whisker burn. "You know how much I like to touch you."

Her eyes drifted shut. "And I like all those things about you," she admitted. "Especially the last..." A soft sigh escaped her, and she met his gaze. "But you're still hiding—I can feel it. What are you hiding, Jax?"

With a long breath, he took her hand. "Telling you would involve breaking a promise. I can't do that."

"Because of what happened to you when you were a lawyer?"

"Nothing happened to *me*," he corrected, voice rough with the memory.

She slid a hand up his stomach to his chest, holding it over his heart. "You were trying to help her, Jax. You didn't know what she'd do. You couldn't have known."

"I failed her." He closed his eyes, then opened them again. "And now here I am, back between the rock and a hard place."

"I don't understand."

"I know you don't." He looked into her face, so focused on him, so intent, and drew a deep breath. "Your loan on the inn. I know who holds the note. I know that if you'd make contact, your refinancing would be approved."

Her brow furrowed. "You can't know that for a fact."

"I do. I know it *for a fact*. I've tried to get you to look into it, but—"

"Oh, my God." Her mouth dropped open, and she stepped back from him. "It's you. *You* hold the note."

He reached for her, but she slapped his hands away. "No. No," she repeated, her chest rising and falling quickly. "Is it you?"

"Yes."

She stared at him. "Why didn't you tell me? All those times we talked about it—"

"And every single time, I tried to steer you—"

"You *tried* to steer me. You tried to *steer* me." Her eyes were filled with disbelief. "I'm not a sheep, Jax. I was lost and stressed and overwhelmed and freaked out, and you...you had the answer all along."

"I was trying to protect the here and now, and also you. I wanted you to refinance. With me. But your stubborn-ass pride would have reached up and choked you if you thought you were accepting anything from me that you didn't earn. I knew that unless it was your idea, you'd go running hard and fast."

She shook her head. "So you kept it from me to be noble?"

He grimaced, swiping a hand down his face. "Yes, but in hindsight, it sounded a lot better in my head."

Rolling her eyes, she turned away from him, then whipped back. "And the trust outlined in Phoebe's will. You know all about the trust, too?"

He wished she would just kill him dead and be done with it. "Yes."

"Is it you? Did she leave the trust to you?"

"No."

"Then—"

"I can't tell you."

"You mean you won't."

"That, too."

She jerked at his answer as if he'd slapped her, and she pretty much sliced open his heart at the same time.

"I remember distinctly asking you if there was anything else I should know about you," she said very quietly.

"This isn't about me. It wasn't my place. It still isn't my place—"

"You're my friend. You're my—" She broke off,

staring at him from eyes gone glossy with unspeakable emotion. "Well," she finally said quietly with a painful pause. "I've never been exactly sure what we are, but I'd hoped it was more."

"It was. It is. God, Maddie. I *couldn't* tell you. I made a promise—"

"Yes. I'm getting that. And since you certainly never made me any promises, I have no right to be mad." She ran a shaky hand over her eyes. "I'm tired. I want to go back to the inn."

"Not until we finish this."

"Finish this?" She let out a mirthless laugh and started walking to the Jeep, her steps measured and even, her fury and hurt echoing in each one. "I think we just did."

Maddie tiptoed into the dark cottage. The only lights came from their Charlie Brown Christmas tree. Pressing a hand to her aching heart, she went straight to the kitchen, to the cupboard where Tara kept the wine.

It was empty. "Dammit."

"Looking for this?"

She whirled at Tara's voice, squinting through the dark to find her sister sitting on the kitchen counter in a pristine, sexy white nightie, holding a half-empty bottle of wine in her hand.

"I'm going to need the rest of that," Maddie said.

"No. The sister getting regular orgasms doesn't get to have any pity parties."

"Yeah, I'm pretty sure the orgasms are a thing of the past."

"What? Why?"

"Because he hid things from me. From us." Moving

into the kitchen, Maddie hopped up on the counter next to Tara. "You're probably too drunk to retain any of this, but it's Jax. *He's* the note holder."

Tara had gone very still. "Did he...tell you that?"

"Yes, because suddenly he's a veritable pot of information. He knows about the trust, but he remained mum on that, the rat bastard."

Tara stared at her for a long moment. "He probably had his reasons. Good reasons. Maybe even *very* good reasons."

Maddie sighed and thunked her head back on the cabinet. "Why are you drinking alone?"

"I do everything alone."

"Tara..." Was there no end to the heartaches tonight? "It doesn't have to be that way."

"Oh, sugar." Tara tipped the bottle to her mouth. "Are you always so sweet and kind and...sweet and kind?"

"I'm not either of those things right now."

Tara closed her eyes. "I look at you, and I feel such guilt. I'm so full of goddamn guilt, I'm going to explode."

"Guilt? Why?"

"You maxed out your card for me. You were willing to stay here, even alone if you had to, to take care of things. And all I wanted was to leave. You have so much to give, Maddie. You're a giver, and I'm a..." She scrunched up her face to think. "Sucker. I'm a life sucker. I suck at life."

"Okay, no more wine for you." Maddie took the bottle. "And we *all* maxed out our cards. Well, except Chloe, cuz she turned out not to have any credit, but you and I both—"

"For different reasons," Tara whispered and put a finger over her own lips. "Shh," she said. "Don't tell."

"Okay, you need to go to bed," Maddie decided.

"See that." Tara pointed at her and nearly took out an eye. "You love me."

"Every single, snooty, bitchy, all-knowing inch," Maddie agreed. "Come on." She managed to get Tara down the hall and into the bedroom, where Chloe was still sleeping. Tara plopped down next to her and was out before her head hit the pillow.

Kicking off her shoes, Maddie changed into pj's and crawled over one sister and snuggled up with another, both making unhappy noises as she let her icy feet rest on theirs beneath the covers.

"Maddie?" It was Tara, whispering loud enough for the people in China to hear. "I'm sorry."

"For drinking all the wine?"

"No. For making Jax hurt you."

"What?"

Tara didn't answer.

"Tara, what do you mean?"

Her only answer was a soft snore.

Maddie bolted awake sometime later, fighting for breath. Gasping, she sat straight up as horror and smoke filled her lungs. "Oh, my God!" she cried, fear clenching hard in her gut. Fingers of smoke clouding her vision, she shook her sisters. "Get up, there's a fire!"

"Wha—" Tara rolled and fell off the bed.

Chloe lay on her back, eyes wide, wheezing, hands around her throat, desperately trying to drag air into her already taxed lungs.

Maddie leapt off the bed and dragged a suffocating Chloe with her. God, oh, God. "Who's got their phone?"

"Mine's in the kitchen," Tara rasped through an already smoke-damaged voice.

So was Maddie's.

Nearly paralyzed with terror, they turned to the door and staggered to a halt. There were flames flicking in the doorway, eating up the doorjamb, beginning to devour their way into the room.

No one was getting to the kitchen.

Tara ran to the window and shoved at it. "It's jammed!"

Chloe dropped to her knees, so white she looked see-through, and her lips were blue. Maddie grabbed a T-shirt off the floor, dumped water from the glass by the bed onto the material, which she then held over Chloe's mouth. "Inhaler. Where's your inhaler?"

Chloe shook her head. It was clenched in her fist and clearly hadn't given her any relief. By the way she was fighting for air, she was deep in the throes of the worst attack Maddie had ever seen.

"Maddie, help me get this open!" Tara cried, straining at the window.

Maddie already knew that window was a bitch. The sill and window frame had been heavily painted over several times, the last being a decade ago at least. They hadn't worried about that before because it'd been too cold to open it.

"Air," Chloe mouthed, no sound coming out of her, just the wheezing, her eyes wide with panic.

Her panic became Maddie's. The window wouldn't budge, and they didn't have time to fight it. Chloe was going to pass out. Hell, Maddie was going to pass out. The smoke had thickened in the past sixty seconds, the heat pulsing around them and the fire crackling at their backs.

Maddie grabbed the small chair in the corner, dumped the clothes off of it, and swung it at the window. She used the chair legs to smash out the last of the sharp shards and grabbed the blanket from the bed, tossing it on the ledge so they wouldn't get cut on the way out.

They shoved Chloe out first, and she fell to the ground, gasping for fresh air. Tara went next, holding on to Maddie's hand to make sure she was right behind her.

Maddie hit hard and took a minute to lie there gasping like a fish on land. From flat on her back in the dirt, time seemed to slow down. She could see the stars sparkling like diamonds far above, streaked with lines of clouds.

And the smoke closed in on the view, clogging it and blocking out the night.

Sounds echoed around her, the whipping wind, the crackle of flames, and, oh, thank God, sirens in the distance.

"Good," she said to no one and closed her eyes.

Chapter 24

*"If you're always saving for a rainy day,
you're never going to get out of the house."*
PHOEBE TRAEGER

At two o'clock in the morning, Jax was lying in bed attempting to find sleep when his cell rang. Hoping it was Maddie saying that she'd changed her mind, that she wasn't dumping his sorry ass, he grabbing the phone.

It was Sawyer, and Jax took a long breath of disappointment. "Been a while since you've called me in the middle of the night. Ford need to be bailed out again? Or are you just that excited for Santa?"

"You need to get out to the inn, now. There's been a nine-one-one fire call."

Jax rolled out of bed, grabbed his jeans off the floor and a shirt from the dresser. He jammed his feet into boots, snatched up his keys, and was out the door before Sawyer got his next sentence out.

"—Fire and rescue units have been dispatched. Do you have Maddie?"

"No." Christ. He sped down the highway, heart in his throat. "I dropped her off an hour and a half ago."

"I'll be there in five," Sawyer said.

"I'll be right behind you."

It took him an agonizing seven minutes to get into town, and when he passed an ambulance racing in the direction of the hospital, his heart nearly stopped.

He flew down the dirt road, his heart taking another hard hit at the sight of the inn with flames pouring out of the windows and leaping high into the night.

The lot was a mess of vehicles and smoke and equipment, making it nearly impossible to see. He peeled into the area, pulled over, and barely came to a stop before he tore out of his Jeep. His pulse was pounding, and his legendary calm was nowhere to be found.

The cottage was gone. Completely gone. The second floor of the inn was on fire. It was a living nightmare. The lights from the rescue rigs slashed through the night as he passed police and fire crew and leaped over lines of hoses and equipment to come to a halt before the blackened shell of the cottage.

No Maddie.

A hand settled on his shoulder. Sawyer. Through the thick, choking smoke, his friend's face was tight and drawn, but he pointed to the low stone wall between the inn and the marina.

Huddled there, wrapped in a blanket, face dark with soot, sat Maddie.

He took his first breath since Sawyer had called. An EMT was talking to her. Her head was tilted up, facing the still-blazing inn, devastation etched across her face.

Jax crouched in front of her, his hands on her legs. She was shaking like a leaf. Or maybe that was him. "Maddie, Jesus. Are you okay?"

She met his gaze, her own glassy. "It's gone. The cottage is gone. And the inn—"

"I know, sweetheart." Just looking at the charred remains made him feel like throwing up. Very carefully, he pulled her against him, absorbing the soft, sorrowful sound she made as she burrowed against him. She wrapped her arms around his neck so tight he couldn't breathe, but he didn't need air. He needed her. "I saw the ambulance, and then the remains of the cottage, and I thought—" He closed his eyes and held her in that crushing hug, pressing his face into her neck. "How did you get out?"

"Through a window. The flames were blocking the door, and the window was painted shut. I broke out the glass with a chair."

He was probably holding her too tight, but he couldn't let go. She smelled like smoke and ash, was filthy from head to toe, and she'd never looked better to him. "Chloe and Tara?"

"Chloe had an asthma attack. That's who is in the ambulance. Tara rode with her."

Weak with relief, Jax sat on the rock wall and held her in his lap, opening the blanket she had around her so he could get a good look at her. She wore only a T-shirt and panties. Her arms and legs were streaked with dirt and soot. Her knees were scraped and bleeding. Gently he took her hands in his and turned them over. She had a few cuts on her palms.

The thought of that stuck window had his blood

running cold. A couple more minutes and it would have been too late. With as much care as he could, he wrapped her back up in the blanket and looked at the EMT. Jax had gone to school with Ty Roberts, and they sometimes played flag football together on the Rec league.

"She's refusing to be taken in," Ty said.

"It's just a few cuts," Maddie murmured. "That's all." She was back to watching the inn. The firefighters had a good handle on it now. The flames were nearly gone.

Ty looked meaningfully at Jax and then to the ambulance. He wanted to take Maddie in.

"Maddie." Jax made her look at him. "Let me take you to the hospital. We can check on your sisters and get you cleaned up."

"Not until it's over."

So they sat there and watched the blaze. When the flames were completely out, Sawyer spoke to the fire chief, then came over. "When the cottage caught fire, the wind carried sparks to the inn's roof. That's how the second floor ignited. They were able to contain it there." He squatted beside Maddie and ducked his head until he could see into her eyes. "They're not going to let you go in there until tomorrow. It's okay to leave. I want you to get into the second ambulance and go get checked out."

"No, I'm fine, I—"

"You're going," Jax said, willing to out-stubborn her. "I'll take you."

Maddie opened her eyes when the Jeep came to a stop. It wasn't quite dawn, and the sky was still inky black.

Christmas morning.

For a minute she sat still, remembering the panic of

waking up choking on smoke, the flames licking at the bedroom door, and watching Chloe fight for air...

God. Chloe was okay, or she would be. At the hospital, they'd learned she was being held overnight for smoke inhalation. Tara was staying with her, and Maddie could have, as well, but Jax had stepped in. "She's coming with me."

Four simple words that had filled Maddie's head while the nurse had cleaned and dressed her wounds—no stitches required, thankfully—and then given her a pair of scrubs to wear.

She'd been too numb and tired to argue with Jax.

No, that wasn't true. She was tired, to-the-bone exhausted, but she could have still argued. After all, she had no reason to go home with him.

Except she didn't want to be alone in a hospital chair.

She wanted to be held.

She wanted to feel safe.

The Jeep's heater had been on her full blast as they left the hospital, but she was still shivering. She felt like her teeth were going to rattle right out of her head. Jax had driven with his left hand, keeping his right hand on her, rubbing up and down her thigh, squeezing her icy fingers with his warm ones.

The passenger door opened, and she jerked.

"Just me," Jax murmured, having exited the Jeep and come around for her. Crouching at her side, he unhooked her seat belt and held her for a moment, fiercely, before lifting her into his arms.

"I can walk," she said, even though she made no attempt to do just that.

"Pretend you still believe I'm that superhero."

With a sigh, she looped her arms around his neck and pressed her face to his throat, breathing him in. The scent of him filled her, and her burning throat tightened.

She already missed him. Letting out a shuddery breath, she kept her eyes closed as she heard him open his front door and make a low comment to a sleepy Izzy. A few moments later, he let her feet slide to the floor.

Because she was still barefoot, she could tell she was on tile. But this tile was deliciously warm thanks to his heated floors.

Keeping one arm around her, he leaned away for a beat, and she heard the shower go on. "You're shaking," he said.

"I think that's you."

"Maybe."

She opened her eyes and found his, dark and shadowed with concern.

"Do you know how fast that fire moved?" he asked. "How much of a miracle it is you all got out?" He ran a hand over his eyes. "Christ, Maddie. If you hadn't woken up when you did..."

Her heart caught at his raw voice. "But I did," she whispered, reaching for him. "I'm okay, Jax. Look at me. I'm indestructible, apparently."

"*Resilient,*" he said and tilted her face up, looking at her from fathomless eyes. "Strong and giving and resilient."

She thought about the things that meant so much to her and could count them with the fingers on one hand. Her sisters. The inn.

Jax.

And all of it was in jeopardy. "I'm still mad at you," she whispered.

"I know."

She pressed a hand to her heart, which ached more than her cuts and bruises, and then to his. "I don't want to be alone tonight. Today. Whatever it is." Words failed her past that. She wanted comfort, and she wanted to feel alive, and she knew he could provide both.

"You need to get in the shower and warm up."

"With you."

Pressing his forehead to hers, he let out a slow breath. His hands, when he lifted them to her, were careful on her body as he stripped her out of the scrub top, taking in each and every one of her cuts and bruises. Then he slid the bottoms down her legs and paused at the sight of her Supergirl bikini panties. "Did I ever tell you," he murmured, dropping to his knees to press a kiss to her bruised hip, "that I'm pretty convinced you have your own superpowers?"

Bending her head to take in the top of his, she gave him a shaky smile that she knew didn't make it to her eyes. "What are they?"

"The power to get past all my walls…"

"Jax." She closed her eyes as he hooked his thumbs in the sides of the undies to slowly drag them down. She gasped when her world tilted as he picked her up and deposited her into the shower. He stepped in behind her and, without a word, washed her hair and then her body, quickly and efficiently.

She could feel him behind her, hard and aroused, but his touch remained gentle and soothing. It was just as well. With exhaustion sneaking up on her again, she could do little more than lean against him.

The next thing she knew, the water was shut off, and he wrapped her in a big, soft towel. He redressed her cuts, drew one of his own big, soft T-shirts over her head, and placed her on his bed.

She heard him move to the door. "Jax—"

"Sleep."

"'Kay." She listened to him moving around the house for a while. His phone rang, and she heard him quietly telling someone he had her.

He had her.

It was true, she realized. He had her heart and soul...

No. That wasn't right. He'd held back from her. Was still holding back...

Or was that her?

God, she was so confused, and tired...

"Sleep," he said again, back in the room now, running a hand down her arm.

She caught his fingers in hers. "Stay," she said, tightening her fingers on his.

"Always." The mattress dipped beneath his weight, and then she was carefully scooped up against his big, warm body. Their legs were entangled like it was the most natural thing in the world, as if they'd been sleeping together for years. His touch slid over her like a soothing balm, making her ache from deep inside, making her shiver for more. "Just for tonight," she whispered, snuggling in, feeling the steady beat of his heart beneath her ear.

Just for tonight.

Another lie, of course. She'd fallen for him, just as she'd fallen for her sisters, for the inn. And she was losing them all, one by one. She felt the sting of tears against her closed eyelids and, to hide them, buried her face into his throat.

His hands slowly stroked over her body, tender but sure. She knew he was offering comfort, but she took more, pressing in closer, anticipation humming through her. They were on their sides facing each other, and she drew a leg over his. Rocking her hips, she let the very tip of him, velvet over steel, slide into her.

He groaned roughly and tightened his grip on her, holding her still. "Maddie. You're hurt—"

She impaled herself, and, with another groan, he rolled her beneath him, filling her so entirely she saw stars. Bending low, his lips rested on the strong pulse in her throat, and she both felt and heard her name on a whispered breath.

Restless, she ran her hands down his back, digging her fingers into him, urging him on. Lifting his head, he held her gaze prisoner as he began to move within her, long, slow, delicious thrusts, a mind-blowing grinding of his hips. On the edge, her eyes began to drift shut in sheer, numbing pleasure.

"No, look at me. Feel me. Feel *us*."

Opening her eyes, she looked right at him. She saw her life, her heart echoed in his eyes, and she burst in a kaleidoscope of colors and emotion, unlike anything she'd ever felt.

When she could breathe again, he was waiting for her, still hard inside her. His forearms were alongside her face, his hands cupping her head. "I love you," he said, honest and sure, more a vow than a confession as he thrust into her and came, sending her spiraling again.

It was the last thing she remembered before sleep claimed her.

Twice she woke them both up with nightmares, hyperventilating and caught up in the sense of being trapped. In between the dreams, she tossed and turned.

Jax would have fought her demons for her if he could, she knew that by the way he spent the hours holding her close. It was close to noon before she woke up fully, and she opened her eyes to find Jax watching her.

"It's gone," she said, voice still a little hoarse. She knew her eyes were puffy and red, and that her hair had to be as wild as ever. "It's Christmas, and it's all gone."

Propping his head up on his hand, he used his other to tug her in close. "Yes."

Closing her eyes, she swallowed hard and pressed her face into his chest, her scratched-up arm gliding up to hook around his neck. She felt her tears wet both of their skin, and he made a low sound of regret. "You'll rebuild," he said.

She shook her head.

"There's fire insurance on the property."

It wasn't the words that set her off. It was the reality that he'd always known more about all of this than she did, even though it was her life. Not his fault, not her fault, she got that. It was no one's fault, but it didn't make it any easier.

Worse, even if they rebuilt, they'd still sell, because that's what her sisters wanted. Majority rules.

It devastated her.

As did knowing that walking away meant walking from Jax, too. She rolled out of the bed and began jerking on clothes. *His* clothes.

"Let me guess," he said. "You just remembered you're mad at me."

Mad? More like confused as hell. She turned to the door, wearing his sweatpants, a Henley, and her heart in tatters on the sleeve.

"Maddie." He snagged her hand in his, halting her progress.

"I'm going to call a cab to go to the hospital."

A muscle in his jaw ticked. "I'll take you."

He drove her in silence, not saying a word until she went to get out of the Jeep. Taking her hand in his, he brought it up to his mouth and kissed her bandaged palm. "You used to be afraid of me, and I understood that. But now it feels like you're afraid of what you feel for me. Of what I feel for you. And that I *don't* understand. Not one bit, Maddie."

Her eyes misted, and she shook her head in denial, causing him to pull her over the console and into his lap, nose to nose. Though he was careful not to hurt her, he wasn't gentle. "You think you're losing everything," he said, running his hands up her arms. "But it's not true. You have the power to stop this, Maddie. To not give up. Make a stand. Make a stand and take what you want."

Chapter 25

*"Remember, it's always better to be the
smartass rather than the dumbass."*
PHOEBE TRAEGER

Maddie sat on the dock at the marina, each exhalation
a little white cloud in front of her face as she watched the
sun make its route across a quiet sky. Behind her was the
burned-out shell of her dream. In front of her, the Pacific
Ocean was rough and churning this morning, matching
the pitch in her stomach.

She dropped her head to her bent knees and squeezed her
eyes shut. She'd just left the hospital. She was supposedly
grabbing breakfast for her sisters and then going back to
pick them up. But she needed a moment to herself, so she'd
come here first. She felt empty and exhausted and defeated.

And sad.

So damn sad. It wasn't the loss of the cottage or her
things. She'd survived far worse.

Jax loved her. Her. He wanted her to make a stand.
Take what she wanted.

But it wasn't that easy, not for her.

It could be, said a little voice. Angrily, she swiped at a tear, then went still when she heard footsteps. Someone steady on their feet, but not trying to sneak up on her.

Jax.

She felt the weight of his jacket as he wrapped it around her, surrounding her with warm leather and his scent.

Lethal combination.

He crouched at her side, eyes dark and full of so many things she couldn't put her finger on a single one of them. His familiar easy smile was nowhere in sight. The lines etched around his eyes and mouth spoke of exhaustion and worry.

"What are you doing here?" she whispered.

"There are some things that need to be said."

"Jax—"

"Not by me." He looked over his shoulder at someone and nodded.

More footsteps sounded. Tara. She walked past Jax, and the two of them exchanged a long look. Jax's was warm and encouraging, but Tara's was guarded and tense, and dread filled Maddie. "What's going on?"

Tara sat next to Maddie. She was wearing scrubs and smelled like some odd combination of hospital disinfectant and smoke, but other than that, she appeared no worse for wear from the fire. "We need chairs out here, sugar. This is beyond undignified."

Maddie looked at Jax, who gave her a tight smile that didn't come close to reaching his eyes. Then he turned and walked away. She opened her mouth, but Tara reached for her hand. "He brought me here. Said it was time. He's been telling me that for weeks now, but I think he's about done with subtleties." She sighed. "So am I."

"Oh, God." Maddie stared at her, afraid to breathe. "This isn't the part where you tell me you're sleeping with him, right?"

"Oh, Lord love a duck. No, I'm not sleeping with him—not that he isn't one fine man. One really fine *hot* man, but honey, he's yours. He's been yours from day one."

Maddie started to shake her head, but Tara squeezed her hand. "I know you're upset with him. He was holding back information you feel he should have shared, and you're right. You're one hundred percent right to believe that when you're in love with a man, he should definitely tell you he's holding the note on the property that you consider your home, except—"

"Wait a minute." Maddie could have used some oxygen from that cute EMT about now. "No one said anything about love."

Tara rolled her eyes. "…Exceeeeept," she said. "It wasn't his place to tell you. He'd made a promise."

"But—"

"I know. In a relationship, you share things, but as it turns out, he was protecting someone." She paused, and when she spoke again, her voice was very quiet and halting. "He was protecting someone you know."

"Who?"

"Phoebe. And…" Tara shook her head and slumped as if the weight of the world was heavy on her back. She covered her face with her hands. "Me. I lied to you, Maddie. From the very beginning, I lied right to your face, and then I pulled a double punch by going to Jax and

begging him to keep his promise, to keep this from you
and Chloe." Shame laced every word that tumbled from
her mouth.

Maddie stared at her, floored. "But... why?"

"Because I couldn't handle the truth coming out, not
if I had to be here again. God, it hurt to be here again,
still does."

"You couldn't handle *what* coming out? And what do
you mean 'again'? You told me you've never been here
before."

"No. You assumed that." Tara rubbed at her chest
absently, as though to soothe an unrelenting ache, and
cleared her throat. "I should start at the beginning."

"Okay." Maddie nodded, heart pounding. "That's a
good idea."

Tara stared out at the water. The air was heavy with
sea salt and the acrid scent of burnt wood. It was chilly,
but Maddie wasn't feeling a thing past the icy ball of hurt
in her chest.

"A few years back," Tara said. "Someone near and dear
to Phoebe needed money. Phoebe didn't have any, but she
wanted to help. She mortgaged the resort property." Her
voice seemed distant, as though she was trying to remove
herself somehow from the words she was saying.

"To Jax," Maddie said. "He lent her the money."

"Yes. He'd grown up here and had always been kind
to her, and he'd recently come back to town and had been
known for helping out financially when anyone needed
it. She needed it."

"Why?"

Tara drew a deep breath. "I spent a summer here in
Lucky Harbor when I was seventeen. My grandparents

were going on a world cruise, and my daddy was working all the time. I was a lot like Chloe back then. Wild, spoiled, unrepentant." She shook her head. "No one could tell me what to do, but no one was listening to me, either. I was shipped here without ceremony. I arrived with a chip on my shoulder and a bad attitude, neither of which endeared me to any of the girls my age that were around. There was only one person who'd talk to me, and he…" She closed her eyes. "I got pregnant that summer."

"Oh, Tara," Maddie whispered. "I had no idea."

"No one did. No one knew but me and him, and Phoebe. God, it was awful. I felt…well, there's no way to explain how I felt, really. There's not many missteps you can take in life that can change you the way that can." She looked off onto the water as if there was something only she could see, and whatever it was made her ache. "And it did change me. It never left me," she whispered. She shook her head as if disgusted with herself for going down that road. "We were young and stupid and immature, and not in any position to be parents. I knew that even then." Her eyes were haunted. Hollow.

"I went to Seattle for the pregnancy, then gave the baby up for adoption—" Her voice broke, and she shook her head again, unable to go on.

Heart squeezing, Maddie hugged her even though they mostly showed their affection in other ways—like dying their hair green together. "I'm so sorry. You must have been so scared."

"Yes." Tara sniffed and searched her pockets for a tissue, which of course, she found. "I was terrified. But I knew enough to understand that I was just a kid. I…I did the right thing."

"Well, of course you did."

"I left Lucky Harbor and never looked back. I planned to never come back."

"What about the father?"

"We never spoke again. I went on with my life," Tara said. "Spending the next years *purposely* not thinking about it. But then..." She paused, her eyes solemn. "The baby grew up and got sick. Her heart had a faulty valve and required surgery. There were lots of medical bills, and Phoebe—" A shaky smile crossed her lips. "While I'd been doing my best *not* to think of what had happened, Phoebe had never *stopped* thinking about it. She found out that money was needed for medical care."

"So she mortgaged the place to help." Maddie shook her head. "I'd never have guessed that one. I never thought much of her mothering skills, but no one can deny she was a genuinely good person."

"Yeah." Tara dabbed at her eyes. "She made the donation to the baby's adopted family anonymously. She didn't want the child or her family to feel indebted."

Maddie squeezed Tara's hand again and smiled. "You had a girl."

Tara's smile was weak but proud. "A beautiful girl, and healthy now, thank God. By all accounts, she's happy and settled, and..." Her smile faded. "And I'm not a part of her life."

"Are you okay with that?"

"I have to be. I chose it," she said simply. "I chose it a long time ago, and I live with it. But Mom never really accepted it. I think maybe she felt her own guilt, you know, because maybe she didn't give her daughters up, but she sure didn't raise us. Anyway, she arranged a trust." She held Maddie's gaze. "She left the resort to us, but everything liquid went to her only grandchild. She hid the details from everyone but me in order to protect all parties, but mostly to protect me." Tara's eyes filled again. "I'm sorry, Maddie. I've been holding this in for so long, and truthfully, I would have held it forever, except..."

"Except?"

"You," she whispered. "You came here ready to accept what Mom wanted from us, what she hoped for. You came ready to accept us as a family. You maxed out your credit card to improve the inn that had been mortgaged to save my daughter." She shook her head in marvel. "You gave this place your all, when the only thing I could think about was running like hell." She swallowed hard and repeated, "I'm so sorry, Maddie. I'm so very sorry."

"No." She wrapped her arms around Tara. "You did what you had to. I'm proud of you, Tara. So proud."

Tara dropped her head to Maddie's shoulder, her body shuddering as she tried to keep her pain inside. Maddie held Tara tight and stroked her sister's hair as she lost more than a few tears of her own.

Tara finally pulled back, carefully swiping the mascara out from beneath her eyes as she let out a shuddery breath. "Well. That's never pretty."

"Feel better?"

"No, but I will. It's Christmas, sugar. We have to get Chloe sprung from the hospital, and you have a man to forgive."

"There's nothing to forgive," Maddie said, realizing it was true. It wasn't about what Jax hadn't told her. It wasn't that simple. "There's nothing to forgive, but—"

"Nothing good ever comes out of a *but*. Listen, I realize I did my part in keeping you from falling for him, but I was wrong. I was acting out of my own fears and past."

"Yes. And now I'm acting out of mine," Maddie admitted.

"You're afraid of him?"

"No." She hesitated. "Maybe. Yes. But not how you think. Dammit," she muttered, rubbing her temples.

Opening herself up and making herself vulnerable to a man didn't always end well, but even she knew that Jax was unlike any man she'd ever known. He was worth it. He was worth the potential heartache, because without him she was pretty sure her heart would cease to work anyway. "I'm not afraid of him. I'm afraid of what I feel for him—which means he was right. God, I really hate that. I mean, how do you deal with a guy who's always right?"

Tara laughed ruefully. "Sugar, if I knew that, I'd still be married."

The three sisters sat at Eat Me Café, which was open for a big brunch special for Christmas. Tara was mainlining caffeine in the form of a lethally strong coffee, and Chloe and Maddie were stuffing their faces.

Tara had made Bottom-of-the-Barrel Waffles, made with pumpkin and cinnamon and topped with lots of whipped cream. Heaven on earth. Maddie was shoveling them in, momentarily letting her mind go blank. It might have been the sugar high. She was keeping an eye on Chloe, as was Tara, but Chloe's color was good and she wasn't wheezing at all. Maddie knew Tara planned to tell Chloe about her past. She also knew that she wasn't eager to do so.

"We look like hell," Chloe said, eyeing herself in the reflection of her spoon, turning her head left and right.

"At least we're breathing," Tara said.

And breathing was good, Maddie thought, looking at her sisters, the two women who'd been like strangers to her only a month ago. "Last night in the terror and chaos, something became crystal clear to me," Maddie said softly. "I love it here. And I love you guys, too."

Chloe slid her a long look. "I'm not sharing my waffles."

Tara rolled her eyes and sent a small but warm smile to Maddie. "I love you, too, sugar. Both of you."

She and Maddie both turned to Chloe, who sighed. "Well, way to make me feel like a bitch." She kept eating, until she realized they were still staring at her. "What, I feel it. I just can't say it."

"Ever?" Maddie asked.

Chloe shrugged. "Maybe I'll work on it."

Everyone in the café came by their table. Hell, it felt like everyone in Lucky Harbor came by, wanting to commiserate and express their sympathies and condolences. Word spread quickly, because people were bringing them stuff—clothes, bathroom essentials—things to get them through the next few days since everything they had was destroyed.

Afterward, Tara cleared her throat and told Chloe everything, every painful detail. It was no easier for Maddie to hear the second time, but there were cleansing tears and a group hug.

"Wow," Chloe kept saying. "Wow."

"Okay, we're going to need a new adjective," Tara said. "That one's getting old."

"Well something finally makes sense to me," Chloe said. "Mom asking me when I was going to give her *more* grandkids. I never understood that."

"You were in regular touch with Mom?" Maddie asked.

"Well, yeah. I was her soft spot, I think. You know, because I'm so sweet and adorable." Her mouth quirked, but she looked a little shy about it. "I called her. I did it every week or so, just to check in from wherever I was. It seemed to mean something to her."

"And it meant something to you," Tara said softly.

"It did." Chloe nudged Tara. "And from what she told me, you were a lot like me before you grew up and got old and snooty—you were reckless and wild."

"Hey, I'm only eight years older than you. *Not* old." She sighed. "But yeah, I was. Your point?"

"Well, that there's hope for me, of course." Chloe shrugged. "It tells me that someday I can get myself together as well as you have."

"You think I have it together?" Tara asked in disbelief. "I had a baby when I was little more than a baby myself and gave her up. I have a failed marriage and a job I hate, and I'm in debt up to my eyeballs."

Chloe laughed. "Well, when you put it like that..." She turned to Maddie. "Maybe I should covet your life instead."

"You might want to wait until I get it together first."

"Oh, jeez, you still holding back on the sexiest mayor in Whoville?"

"You don't understand."

"Let's see...He only saved the resort when Phoebe needed a loan, then as much as promised us a refinance even though at least one of the three of us is incredibly financially unstable. He did the morally right thing and protected Tara's secret and proved himself trustworthy over and over again. What a self-serving bastard. Do you think we can drag him to the middle of the town square and stone him?"

Maddie sighed, then went still as a shiver of awareness shot up her spine. When she looked up, Jax was coming toward them in his usual long-legged, easy stride.

"Now's probably not a good time," Chloe said to him when he got within hearing distance. "I haven't quite finished talking you up."

Maddie shot Chloe a dirty look and, in doing so, realized the entire café had gone silent.

Everyone was listening.

"I was just listing all of your positive attributes," Chloe told him. "Leaving out the parts where you didn't tell her shit and kept yourself from her, of course. That was your bad."

Jax never took his eyes off Maddie. "Okay, first, I never kept myself from you. Maybe I didn't tell you enough about who I used to be, but Christ, Maddie, I hated that guy. And I guess I was hoping the man I am now would be enough for you."

"*Aw.*" Chloe's head whipped back to Maddie. "Did you hear that?"

Maddie's heart swelled painfully, pressing against her ribs. "I'm right here, Chloe."

"Sounds like a reasonable request to me," a guy from two tables over said. Maddie recognized him because he worked at the gas station. "And I can vouch for Jax being a good person. He gave my sister a loan when the bank wouldn't. She'd have lost her business and her house otherwise."

"And he did our house addition," a woman called out. "And when my husband lost his job, Jax accepted small, irregular payments. He didn't have to do that."

"Jesus," Jax muttered, hands on hips, eyes closed.

"And he donated new flak vests for the entire PD," Sawyer said, having just come inside.

"That was supposed to be an anonymous donation, you jackass."

"It looked to me like you were sinking fast. Thought I'd toss that in."

Shaking his head, Jax grabbed Maddie's hand and pulled her out of the booth and toward the door, moving so fast she had to run to keep up.

"Where are we going?"

"To talk without the entire fucking town throwing in their two cents."

He opened the café door, and they ran smack into a man wearing a rain slicker and carrying a clipboard with the name of a national insurance company on the front. "Excuse me," he said. "I'm looking for the owners of the Lucky Harbor Resort."

"That's me," Maddie said, very aware of Jax at her back, protective. Steady. "Give me a minute?" she asked the insurance guy, and at his nod, she pulled Jax aside. "I'm sorry," she whispered. "We have to have this meeting before any of us can leave town."

"Leave?"

"Yeah." She met his gaze, her chest so tight she could

scarcely get the words out. "I'm pretty sure that's what Tara and Chloe are planning on doing now. We have no place to live, and they've been wanting to get back to their lives for weeks now."

"And you?"

"It's majority rules."

"Bullshit." He shook his head and said it again. "You came here a fighter, Maddie. Maybe you'd lost a round or two, but you were on your feet. You want to stay in Lucky Harbor? Fight for it. You want a relationship with your sisters? Fight for it."

"What about you? What about a relationship with you?"

He pulled back to look into her face as if memorizing her features. His voice, when he spoke, was low and gravelly with emotion. "I'm already yours. Always have been. All you have to do is step into the ring."

Chapter 26

"My motto was always: never chase after person, place, or thing, because something better will come along. Turns out I was wrong."
PHOEBE TRAEGER

The insurance adjuster slipped out of his rain slicker and introduced himself as Benny Ramos. He was tall and lanky lean, wearing cowboy boots, a matching hat, and Wranglers that threatened to slide right off his skinny hips. It was impossible to tell if he was barely twenty-one or just really good with a razor.

Jax had led both Maddie and Benny back to their table. Jax gave Maddie a quiet, assessing look that she had no idea how to read and then left.

Her head was spinning. He'd given everything he had, and he wanted the same from her. He wanted her to fight for what she wanted.

Made sense. Made a lot of sense. It's what any good, strong leading lady would do.

"So," Benny said. "The cottage is a total loss."

"No duh," Chloe said. "Now tell us something we don't know."

"The fire department believes the fire originated with a set of old faulty Christmas lights that were strung…" He consulted his clipboard. "On a dead plant of some sort in the living room."

Tara snorted.

Maddie closed her eyes. *Poor Charlie Brown Christmas tree, may you rest in peace…*

"Anyway," the adjuster went on. "The inn isn't as bad as it looks. The bedrooms upstairs need a complete renovation, new carpeting, walls and bathroom replacement. New roof. But the downstairs is all cosmetic and can be cleaned. You're in decent shape there."

They were in decent shape. Good to know.

Step into the ring.

Jax thought she was a fighter. That hadn't always been anywhere close to true. She'd let life happen to her. She'd gone with the flow.

She hated the flow. The flow was working like a dog at a go-nowhere job, trying to please too many people who didn't care. She was done with going with the flow. She wanted to be a fighter. "Excuse me," she said to Benny. "But the downstairs *is* water damaged, so we're not in 'decent' shape there. We expect proper compensation."

Tara raised a brow, like *Go, kitten. Show him those claws.*

Chloe out-and-out grinned and gave her a thumbs up. "You heard my sister," she said to Benny. "We expect proper compensation. You go back and tell your people that."

"Actually, we're on the same side," Benny said and

made some more notes on his computerized clipboard. Maddie was dizzy. She was heartsick. She was out of control, but she was having some serious clipboard envy. She needed a clipboard like that. She also needed to fight for her new life. "We'll need rental compensation, as well."

"Of course," Benny said.

She blinked. Was it really that easy? Say what you want, get what you want? Jax had suggested it was, and it'd always seemed to work for Tara.

Benny looked over his clipboard. "I figure we can get all the paperwork taken care of by next week and get you a check to get started."

"And I figure today or tomorrow would be better," Maddie said smoothly. "Bless your heart."

Tara grinned. *Grinned.* Maddie took in the rare sight and returned it.

Benny went back to his clipboard, his ears red. "Tomorrow. How's tomorrow?"

"Fan-fucking-tastic," Chloe said. "Thank you." She beamed at him.

Benny looked a little stunned. "Uh…You're welcome."

Chloe walked him to his truck, then came back with a piece of paper in her hand.

"Are you kidding me—you got his phone number?" Tara asked. "He's barely twelve. I bet they haven't even dropped yet."

"Hey," Chloe said. "Don't talk about my future boyfriend's balls. He was cute, and Maddie scared the hell out of him."

"I thought you thought Lance was cute," Tara said. "And his brother."

"Uh-huh. And your point?"

"And Officer Hottie. Sawyer, right? You were looking at him the other night like you wanted to eat him up alive."

"If I was looking at him at all, I was planning his slow, painful death. Did you hear what we were just told? We're getting a big fat check tomorrow." Chloe looked at each of them. "Our plan?"

"Big fat checks divide into three nicely," Tara noted.

"True." Chloe nodded. "I guess that means by this time tomorrow, we're cut loose." She smiled. "You guys will miss me. Say it."

Maddie tried to sit there calm and in control, but suddenly it was all too much. The fire. The terrifying escape. Tara's revelation, making her realize that she'd misdirected her emotions. Her sisters all gung ho to take the check and run. Jax saying those three little words that she'd never heard before, three words that meant so much more than she'd imagined they could. Her heart clenched hard. "I'm the middle sister," she said softly, then repeated it more strongly.

"Very good," Chloe said. "Can you say the alphabet, too?"

"As the middle, I'm the logical choice for mediator. We have decisions to make, and they get made right now. Majority rules." She looked at each of them. "We walk away or rebuild. We're voting, now. Youngest first."

Chloe pulled out an iTouch, which Lance had lent her in the hospital, and brought up a Magic 8-Ball application. "Magic 8-Ball," she intoned with great ceremony. "Should I stay here in Lucky Harbor?"

Maddie was boggled. "What? You can't leave your vote up to a Magic 8-Ball!"

"I can't?"

"No!" But Maddie bit her lip, trying to see the iTouch screen. "What did it say?"

Chloe looked down and sighed. "*Outlook not so good.* Just as well. I'm ready to blow this popsicle stand anyway."

Disappointment practically choking her, Maddie turned to Tara.

Tara held her hand out for Chloe's iTouch. "Let me see that thing."

"You aren't serious." Maddie's throat felt like she'd swallowed shards of glass. "Please say you're not serious."

"Okay. I'm not serious." Tara reached for Maddie's hand, her smile a little watery. "I vote we stay here."

"Me, too," Chloe said. "I was only kidding before. We can't leave now. Things are just getting good."

"Two yeses," Tara said. "Maddie?"

She was dizzy, overwhelmed, and confused as hell.

"Aw, look at her," Tara murmured. "Like a long-tailed cat in a room full of rocking chairs."

"She's got fear written all over her," Chloe agreed. "Definitely a high flight risk. Makes me wonder if she wanted us to vote the other way."

"Huh," Tara said, nodding. "Interesting. You mean she wanted us to make the decision for her so she didn't have to be accountable?"

"Exactly."

"I'm right here," Maddie said. "I can hear you."

"You know what you need?" Chloe asked. "You need to get over yourself."

"Hey," Maddie said. "When you first showed up here with your bad 'tude, did I tell you to get over it?"

"Yes, actually. Several times."

Okay, true. Maddie turned on a smug Tara and narrowed her eyes. "And you."

"Me? What did I do?"

"I gave you sympathy. *I* want sympathy!"

"Are you kidding me? You have the sexiest man on the planet wanting you. You're getting laid regularly. No sympathy for you!"

Maddie stood up. "I need some fresh air."

"Last time you said that, you went to the bar, got toasted, and kissed a hottie."

Halfway to the door, Maddie came back and snatched Chloe's iTouch out of her hands. "And I need this."

Just outside, she closed her eyes and whispered, "Am I going to get it right this time?"

The iTouch clouded and then cleared with her answer:

Ask again later

Dammit! She shoved the thing in her pocket and got into her car. She drove along the beach, which was dense with fog. The water was gray and choppy today, an endless cycle of unrestrained violence.

Sort of how her gut felt.

Somehow she ended up at the pier, ticket in hand, staring up at the Ferris wheel. *Do it,* the brave little voice in her head said.

Live.

Which is how she found herself in the swinging seat, clinging to the bar in front of her, her legs like jelly as she rose in the air.

And—oh, shit—rose some more.

And more...

And then, when she was as high as she could go—and not breathing—the Ferris wheel stuttered to a stop.

Her heart did the same.

Around her, the few others on the wheel with her gasped and woo-hoo'd their delight.

She wasn't feeling delight. She was feeling stark terror. Whose idea had this been? What the hell had she been thinking? Life was just as good on the ground!

She tried to look at that ground, but her forward motion had the bucket tilting forward, and she felt her head spin. "Oh, God, oh, God—" She had a death grip on the bar now. She couldn't feel her legs at all. And her stomach was sitting in her throat, blocking all air from coming through.

Stop looking down. Forcing her head up, she stared out at the view. It was incredible. If she discounted the vertigo, that is. From this high, she had a three-hundred-sixty-degree vista of the sparkling Pacific Ocean and the rocky shores for as far as she could see.

And the town. She could see all of Lucky Harbor from here, and it was as pretty as a postcard. It was a perspective she never would have appreciated had she not faced her fear and come up here.

Okay, so she hadn't quite overcome the fear, and she was a minute from hyperventilating, but she'd get there.

Thing was, she had a lot of fears to overcome. She had a lot of "roads not taken," or "rides not taken." There'd been things she'd convinced herself she couldn't do.

For instance, she'd convinced herself her mother hadn't been interested in more of a relationship. It was too late for what-ifs on that one, but what about her sisters? It didn't seem too late for them, even though she'd told herself that they hadn't wanted her in their lives. The truth was, she hadn't reached out, either, and she could have. She should have.

She'd done the same to Jax. He might not have been forthright, not completely, but he'd shown her from the beginning how he felt, without words. He'd pushed her to want more—more of the truth from him, more of everything. Why hadn't she wanted to hear it?

Fear. She'd let it rule her.

That had to change. If she lived through this stupid ride.

Just as she thought it, the Ferris wheel jerked and her bucket swung as the ride started moving again. And ten minutes later, after she'd gone around three times and finally had her feet firmly back on the ground, she grinned.

She'd made it. She got back into her car feeling better and more determined and drove without a destination in mind.

No, that was a lie. She knew *exactly* where she was going. She pulled into Jax's driveway and parked. It was forty-five degrees out, and she was sweating.

You know what to do, he'd said.

And he'd been right. She wanted to stay in Lucky Harbor, and she wanted to be a family with her sisters.

Both of those things were within her reach.

She also wanted Jax.

Hopefully he was still within her reach, as well. She knocked on his door, and when he didn't answer, she twisted around and eyed his Jeep. He was home…

Then she heard it, the steady, rhythmic banging,

and she followed the sound around to the back of the house. He was there in battered boots, a gray Henley, and beloved old Levi's faded to threads in spots. He was chopping wood, the ax rising and falling with easy grace. His shirt was soaked through with sweat and clinging to his every hard inch.

He had a lot of hard inches. Just watching him gave her a hot flash.

He had to have seen her come around the side of the house. He had instincts like a cat, and she was making no move to be secretive, but he kept chopping.

Saying nothing.

Finally, she risked life and limb and stepped close enough that he was forced to stop or put her in danger from the flying shards of wood.

Lowering the ax, he leaned on it, his breath coming steady but hard.

Still saying nothing.

"Hey," she said softly.

"Hey. What are you doing here?"

Fair enough question, since she'd asked him the same only this morning. It figured that he'd get right to the point. He was good at that.

She wasn't. "I was…confused. And I guess a little mad at everyone, and then I went for a drive and my car came here."

His mouth quirked very slightly. "Did your car forget that you're mad at me, as well?"

"Well," she said, "out of all the people I'm mad at, I think I'm the least mad at you."

"Why's that?"

Maddie fought the urge to pull out Chloe's iTouch and

ask the Magic 8-Ball how she was doing with Jax, but she had a feeling she knew.

"Why, Maddie?"

Dammit, he wasn't going to let her off the hook. She went with flippant. After all, it was her number-one defense mechanism. "You did recently put a damn good smile on my face. Maybe you get partial immunity. I don't know."

He eyed her for a long moment, clearly seeing right through her. "I gave you more than a smile," he said, setting down his ax and walking into the house.

Jax headed into his kitchen and straight for the refrigerator, pulling out a bottle of water for his suddenly parched throat.

Do-or-die moment. Either she'd come to say thanks for the memories and vanish off into the sunset, or she was here to...Hell, he was afraid to hope.

When he'd been a lawyer, he'd walked into court every day knowing he was going to win. Always.

It'd be nice to know the verdict on this.

Distance. He needed some. He downed the water, tossed the bottle aside, and moved through the house. Not a total ass, he'd left the slider open in case she wanted to come in and destroy him some more, but without looking back, he went into his bathroom. Stripping out of his sweaty clothes, he cranked the shower up to scalding and stepped in. Bowing his head beneath the spray, he let the water bead down his back and tried to clear his mind.

Not happening.

Instead, images came to him: Maddie standing beneath the hot water with him, glistening and soapy, her eyes soft and warm on his; him gliding his hands over that body until those eyes glazed with passion, listening to her pant his name over and over as she came—

When the door opened behind him, he didn't move, didn't lift his head, didn't open his eyes. Her arms came around him, and he felt her naked body press up against his.

And here was the thing. All his good intentions went out the window as those hands drifted down his chest and over his abs, because it was hard to remain distant with the hard-on of his life.

"Why are you here?" he asked again.

Maddie swallowed hard and tried to channel... which actress? Damn, she couldn't think of an actress to save her life! She was on her own. "Well, you seemed pretty sweaty," she said in her best come-hither voice. "Thought maybe I could help wash your back." She leaned in and licked a droplet of water off his neck.

She felt him draw a deep breath. "Maddie."

Okay, so he wasn't in the mood for flippant. She could understand that. She paused, her eyes on the smooth muscles of his back. "You bared yourself to me."

He turned to face her. "Yes, as it happens, I'm as bare-ass naked as it gets."

They both looked down. Yeah, he was naked. Gloriously so. "I meant more than your body," she whispered. "You bared yourself to me, and... and it took me longer than it should have to notice."

God, he was perfect. Hard and ripped and heart-stoppingly perfect. She ran her finger over the drops of water on one pec, and, whoops, grazed his nipple.

"Maddie?"

"Yeah?"

"Up here."

She tore her gaze off him and met his eyes. They were slightly warmer, and maybe, possibly, amused. Relief hit her so hard she nearly slid to the tile floor. "Oh, Jax. I'm sorry that it took me so long to get with the program. That I doubted you, that I pushed you away. I wasn't looking for this. And I know you weren't, either, even less than me, but you...you handled it better."

His hand slid over her stomach and settled on her hip, which made it all but impossible to think, but she struggled to try. "I know I said some things...about where we're at."

"Actually, you made yourself pretty clear about where we *weren't* at." Reaching for the soap, he turned away and began to scrub up.

"About that. I was wrong." She was a little breathless just from watching his hands run over his body, leaving soapy trails in their midst, and lost her train of thought.

He didn't say anything, just finished what he was doing. Finally he put the soap back, rinsed off, and then moved unexpectedly, pulling her in close, wrapping his arms around her and just holding on. Tight. She didn't mind. She could have stayed like that forever, feeling safe and warm and stupidly happy. But she had more to say. "Jax, I—"

"Whatever you want," he said, his voice low and raw. "Except for letting go. I'm not going to let go."

"I hope you mean that. Because you were right about something else, too. I *was* scared, scared to the bone." She grimaced. "I might have panicked even."

"You did do a lot of knitting," he said with an utterly straight face and then moved his lips down her neck.

Shivering at the feel of his mouth brushing over her wet skin, she clutched at him. When he lifted his head, he was smiling. The sight threatened to short out her brain. Or maybe that was his touch. She wasn't sure, except she was breathing hard and was dangerously close to leaping into his arms and impaling herself on him. "You said to fight for what I want. You said to get into the ring." She looked down. "Um, not to change the subject, but you want me."

"Hard to hide it."

"I want you back," she whispered, which isn't what she'd meant to say. Exactly.

"For how long?"

"As long as you'll have me."

He drew a shuddery breath. "So this is you, fighting for what you want?"

"Yes." It was hard to concentrate. His hand was on her hip, slowly making its way north until it cupped her breast. His thumb glided over her already pebbled nipple, his expression a mixture of heat, affection, need, and so much more that it took her breath. She slid her arms around his waist and laid her head on his chest, shivering when he cupped the back of her neck. "I came to Lucky Harbor out of obligation, but really, I was looking for something."

"Did you find it?"

She loved the way his voice rumbled through his chest, his body radiating into hers. "Yeah, I found it. I'm staying in Lucky Harbor, Jax. We're going to rebuild. For the first time in my life, I fit. I have my sisters, a place that's mine—well, it's only one-third mine, and we still owe you a ton of money, not to mention it's half charred—but you know what I mean."

His lips twitched.

"And!" She drew a breath, because this was the big one. "I let myself love and, in return, be loved."

He went utterly still, his eyes twin dark pools. His fingers brushed up her spine, sinking into her hair. "Did you?"

"Yes." Her heart clenched that he'd doubted it, even for a minute. "I love you, Jax. And you love me back."

"I do," he said, warm emotion thickening his voice, and all her worries began to fade completely away. He pressed his mouth to the beat of the pulse at the base of her neck. When he lifted his head and met her gaze, his eyes were shining fiercely. "I love you more than you'll ever know."

Looking at him, she saw her future and felt all the ragged tears in her heart heal themselves. "I fit," she whispered in marvel, stepping into him. "I fit with you."

He nodded and wrapped his arms around her. "Perfectly."

Maddie's Boyfriend Scarf

Materials:
One skein super-bulky yarn, at least 100 yards
1 pair size 13 needles (straight)
1 size G (4 mm) crochet hook

Instructions:
1. Cast on 15 stitches (or enough stitches to make the scarf 6 to 8 inches wide).
2. Knit every row—this is called a garter stitch—until your scarf is 60" long. (If you have more yarn left and a very tall boyfriend, you may choose to make the scarf a bit longer.)
3. Bind off.
4. Use your crochet hook to weave in the ends at the top and bottom. See how easy that was!

Personalize your gift:
1. Feel free to use a different weight of yarn but check on the label to see what size needles are recommended and use them instead.
2. Knit with two different strands held together throughout. This creates a unique yarn only your beloved will have.
3. Create stripes by buying several colors of yarn, starting a new color at the end of a row, and leaving a tail for each color (which will be woven in with the crochet hook during step #4 above).
4. Add fringe: Cut 64 lengths of yarn approximately 10" each. Take four lengths of yarn and fold them in half. Insert the crochet hook into one of the corners of the scarf. Pull the loop through the scarf with the crochet hook. Then bring the ends of the yarn through the loop and tighten. On the narrow edges of the scarf, make 8 tassels spaced evenly.

Tara promised herself
she'd never return to
Lucky Harbor—until now . . .

♥

Please turn this page
for a preview of

The Sweetest Thing

Available now.

Chapter 1

*"Remember, no one is listening until
you make a mistake."*
TARA DANIELS

Muffin?" Tara asked with a smile that was beginning to feel a little forced as she walked the long line of people waiting to enter the pier's summer festival. "Have a fresh Life's-a-Peach Muffin." The large basket she held was heavier than she'd planned on, and the late-afternoon sun beat down on her head. A little trickle of sweat dripped between her breasts.

She hated to sweat.

At least her dress was lightweight and halter-cut. She'd bought it because it screamed sophistication and elegance, and because it would hopefully make her legs look long and give her some badly needed confidence.

It was a tall order for a dress.

"Muffin?" Each had been painstakingly wrapped in cellophane and ribbon. Tara had slipped a flier advertising the inn under each ribbon.

The method to her madness.

"I'll take one of your muffins anytime," a man said with a smile and leaned in close. Clearly feeling brave, as he was surrounded by his friends, he added, "In fact, I'll take two."

Tara recognized him from the mechanic shop. His name was Dan. Stan. *Tim!* Tim had changed her tires last month. He'd offered to change her life—from in his bed—but she'd politely declined.

It might have been two years since she'd had sex, but she had high standards. Truth was, she was waiting to feel that sense of... *wow* before she got naked for a man again.

Unfortunately, there'd been a sad shortage of *wow* in her life lately. "Sugar," she said with her classic southern belle smile that she knew damn well could render a man deaf and dumb, "you don't have what it takes for more than one of my muffins at a time."

At this, several of his so-called buddies burst out laughing and shoved him good-naturedly.

Tim grinned at her sheepishly but still took two muffins.

No harm, no foul. She kept her smile in place as she moved along the line, but it was proving difficult.

She wasn't exactly chipper by nature.

"Muffin?" she asked the others in line. She was on a mission, and that mission was different than it had been last year. Last year she'd wanted peace on earth and her manicure to last a full two weeks.

This year things were more basic. She wanted to be able to pay her bills on the thirtieth of the month. That was all. Just a single month in which her means met her ends. Thirty days during which she wasn't constantly angsting and fretting over the arrival of a paycheck.

Or lack thereof.

"Muffins," she said again, determined to land some customers for her family inn. *Family* being a loose term for her and her sisters. The three of them were still somewhat warily circling each other after six tumultuous months of rebuilding the Lucky Harbor Beach Resort together. And they weren't done yet—they still had decorating to do, which was going to be interesting with three very different personalities and tastes.

The sun continued to beat down on her as she walked. It seemed as if the entire town had shown up at the pier for the Summer Music Fest, but that wasn't a surprise to Tara. The only thing the people of Lucky Harbor liked more than their gossip was a good social gathering, and there would be plenty of both tonight. A warm night, good music, dancing, drinking...even she herself began to feel a tiny bit looser as she approached the end of the line.

And for someone known as the Steel Magnolia, that was saying something. "Here you go, sugar," she said to Lucille. Lucille ran the art gallery and was somewhere between seventy and a hundred years old. "Enjoy."

"I will, dear, thank you." Lucille was wearing her favorite pink track suit. Eye-popping hot pink that said Juicy across her saggy tush. "There's supposedly going to be a lot of honeys here tonight playing bingo." She gave a saucy wink from an eye lined thickly with blue eyeshadow.

Tara didn't want to think about Lucille having "honeys."

"You ought to join us," Lucille said. Like Tim, the older woman snatched a second muffin from right beneath Tara's nose and shoved it into her purse, which was the size of a suitcase. "You're wound a little tight these days." Leaning in, the older woman said in a conspirator's whisper, "I bet a man could unwind you, real nice."

Tara sighed. No use arguing the truth. "I don't need a man."

"Darling, every woman needs a man. Why, even your momma—bless her soul—used to say, 'You can't buy sex on eBay.'"

Tara blinked, but she had no comeback for that one. Hoping her smile was still in place, she moved on.

The sun sank low on the water as if it was just dipping in its toes to cool off. There were only about five people left in line and then, Tara thought, then she'd be free. "Here you go," she said to the next person in line, looking up as warm, long fingers brushed hers.

And up.

And just like that, her smile congealed.

"Nice of you to offer me a muffin," he said, his voice low and almost unbearably familiar.

Ford Walker.

He was six foot three with a linebacker build that should have seemed bull-in-a-china-shop, but he had a way of moving all those he-man muscles with easy, male, fluid grace.

Stupid muscles.

He had sun-kissed brown hair, stark green eyes, skin bronzed from long days spent out on his sailing boat, and a ready smile. Half the people in Lucky Harbor were in love with him.

The other half were men and didn't count.

She was the odd person out. Not only was she *NOT* in love with him, he tended to step on her last nerve. There was a very good reason for that.

Several, in fact.

But she'd long ago given herself permission to pretend the Thing That Happened *hadn't* happened. Silently she offered him her basket and he perused the muffins as if he was contemplating his life's path.

"Just take one!" she finally snapped, making him flash a grin.

Sweet baby Jesus, he was gorgeous, and it irritated the hell out of her. "What are you doing in line?" she asked him. "Why aren't you running the bar?"

He owned the town's most popular bar, the Love Shack, mostly because, near as she could tell, he'd majored in shooting the breeze. During the months he wasn't off sailing with the world's best, he spent his time behind the bar mixing drinks. He cocked his head and ran his gaze over her like a caress. "Maybe I got in line hoping you'd offer me a morsel, a crumb."

She smacked him on the broad chest. Not that she could hurt him if she tried, the big, sexy lout. "Like you'd settle for a crumb."

"Once I settled for whatever crumbs you'd give me. Remember?"

Again she tipped her head back to meet his gaze. He was still smiling, but his eyes were serious, and something pinged low in her belly.

Memories. Unwelcome ones. "Ford—"

"Ah," he said very softly. "You *do* remember my name."

She felt herself tighten again, all the tension back in a flash. Damn him. She remembered everything, and if he thought she didn't, he was an even bigger ass than she'd given him credit for. She opened her mouth to tell him so, but he reached in and stole a second muffin and was gone before she could blink.

"Irritating man," she muttered beneath her breath.

"They're all irritating." Chloe popped up at her side and double-fisted the last two muffins.

Tara opened her mouth to complain but ended up just shaking her head as Chloe ogled Ford's backside.

"I'd still take him for a spin," Chloe said.

Tara just slid her a look.

"What," her sister said guilelessly, biting into a muffin and moaning. "Goddamn, you can bake." She chewed and thoughtfully watched Ford as he walked through the crowd. He moved sure and easy, his long-legged stride in no hurry as he was stopped to greet nearly everyone that he passed.

Chloe let out a low hum of pure enjoyment and shook her head. "You telling me that you don't want to grab a handfulla his muffins?"

Tara closed her eyes. "I absolutely do not."

Chloe's low laugh ran in her ears, calling her out for the liar she was.

Hello Readers,

Thanks for coming to Lucky Harbor. I'm sure your presence has already been noted by Lucille and the rest of her blue-haired posse and will shortly be posted on their Facebook page. Hope you don't have toilet paper stuck to your shoe.

Or any secrets...

I thought you might enjoy some fantastic recipes from my very own kitchen, and in the cooking of these recipes, I can guarantee you a culinary experience that will make you forget your troubles.

Happy reading, happy cooking, and happy eating!

Tara Daniels

You're My Honey Bun Muffins
(Honey Banana)

Makes 12 muffins

Things You'll Need

½ cup (1 stick) butter
½ cup brown sugar
¼ cup honey
1 egg
3 to 4 ripe bananas
1 teaspoon vanilla
½ teaspoon almond extract or black walnut extract
1½ cups self-rising flour

Directions

Preheat oven to 400°F. Prepare a 12-cup muffin pan by spraying with nonstick cooking spray or lining with cupcake holders.

Heat butter in microwave until softened. In a mixing bowl, combine butter, brown sugar, honey, and egg. Peel bananas and mash them on a plate with a fork. Add mashed bananas to the mixing bowl and stir until smooth. Mix in the vanilla and almond or walnut extract. Add flour and stir until it forms a thick, smooth batter.

Spoon batter into muffin pan. Bake for 15 minutes. Remove muffins from pan immediately to cool on wire rack.

Serve warm with milk and try not to eat them all in one sitting.

Egg White Omelet

Makes 1 omelet

Things You'll Need

2 teaspoons butter
2 egg whites, whisked
Veggies of your choice (mushrooms, peppers, etc.)
    chopped into bite-size pieces and sautéed

Directions

Melt butter in a 10-inch skillet over medium heat; add egg whites and swirl to coat the bottom of the pan. When the bottom of the egg is set, lift the cooked edges using spatula to let uncooked portion flow underneath. When bottom is browned, add veggies of choice, fold omelet in half and slide onto serving dish.

Add whole wheat toast with strawberry jelly for a guaranteed great start to your day!

Good Morning Sunshine Casserole

Serves 10 to 12

Things You'll Need

- 1 layer of tater tots (enough to cover the bottom of a 9-by-13-inch pan)
- 1 layer of ham cubes or sautéed, crumbled sausage or cooked, crumbled bacon (whatever makes your skirt blow up)
- 1 layer of grated cheddar cheese (there's no such thing as too much cheese for breakfast)
- 6 eggs
- ½ teaspoon salt (or more, if no one's looking)
- ½ teaspoon pepper
- 1 teaspoon ground mustard
- ½ cup chopped onion
- 3 cups milk
- 2 teaspoons Worcestershire sauce
- ½ cup butter, melted

Directions

Preheat oven to 350°F. In a 9-by-13-inch pan make a base layer with the tater tots, followed by the meat, and then the cheese.

In a medium mixing bowl whisk together the eggs, salt, pepper, ground mustard, onion, milk, and Worcestershire. Pour the egg mixture over the layers in the pan. Drizzle with the melted butter. Bake uncovered for 45 minutes or until the eggs are set.

Tara's Kickin' Chili

Serves 6 to 8 hungry people

Things You'll Need

1 pound ground beef
2 to 4 teaspoons chili powder
1 teaspoon garlic powder
1 (15-ounce) can stewed tomatoes
1 (15-ounce) can kidney beans, drained
1 (15-ounce) can white beans, drained
1 (15-ounce) can garbanzo beans, drained
1 (15-ounce) can pinto beans, drained
1 (8-ounce) can tomato sauce
¼ cup fresh salsa

Directions

In a large pot, brown meat over medium-high heat, then drain the fat. Add chili powder and garlic powder and stir to coat the meat. Add tomatoes, beans, tomato sauce, and salsa. Bring to a boil, then reduce heat and simmer for 15 minutes.

Chloe's Chicken Salad
(which she stole from Phoebe)

Serves 4 to 6

Things You'll Need

For the Salad
>   2 packages shredded cabbage or coleslaw mix
>   3 to 4 green onions, sliced
>   3 packages Top Ramen Oriental Flavor noodles, broken
>   into small pieces
>   ½ cup sliced almonds
>   2 to 4 tablespoons sesame seeds

For the Dressing
>   3 tablespoons sugar
>   ½ cup oil
>   3 tablespoons rice vinegar (do not substitute)
>   1 package Top Ramen seasoning

To Assemble
>   4 cooked chicken breasts, cut into bite-size pieces

Directions

Make the salad: In a large bowl, mix together all the ingredients.

Make the dressing: In a small bowl, whisk together all the ingredients.

Assemble the salad: Pour the dressing over the salad and toss. Add the chicken and serve.

Pigs in a Wheel Delectables
(Pinwheel Sandwiches)

Things You'll Need

   1 (8-ounce) package of brie, rind removed
   16 ounces sour cream
   1 (1-ounce) packet Hidden Valley Ranch Dips Mix
   1 pound deli ham, sliced thin but not shaved (not
      honey ham!)
   1 (14-ounce) package flour tortillas

Directions

In a large bowl, mix together cheese, sour cream, and ranch dip seasoning mix. Beat it until you feel nice and relaxed.

Put a thin layer of the cheese mixture on a tortilla—don't go all the way to the edge. Place slices of ham on top—again don't go all the way to the edge. Tightly roll up the tortilla, keeping everything inside. Then roll it up tightly in plastic wrap and place in the fridge or freezer. Repeat steps until you run out of ingredients.

When you're ready to serve, unwrap the plastic, and cut the long tortilla rolls into small, round pinwheels. You should get 8 good pinwheels per long roll. If you freeze the rolls for a little while rather than refrigerate, cutting is easier and presentation is perfect.

Tara's Gourmet Burgers

Makes 5 burgers

Things You'll Need

4 tablespoons butter
1 large onion, chopped
4 to 6 ounces mushrooms, chopped
1 pound ground sirloin
½ teaspoon salt
1 teaspoon freshly ground pepper
1 tablespoon steak sauce
Flour for dredging
2 tablespoons extra-virgin olive oil
5 large rolls of your choice, toasted
Cheese of your choice (optional but encouraged)

Directions

In a large, heavy skillet, melt butter over medium heat. Add onion to pan and cook over medium heat until golden brown. Add mushrooms and cook until they're tender. Set aside the mixture until cool.

In large bowl mix the ground sirloin, salt, pepper, steak sauce, and onion-mushroom mixture. Divide the mix and form into 4 to 5 burger patties. Dredge the patties in flour.

In same skillet, heat the oil over medium heat, and cook the burgers until done, turning only once. Top with cheese (if using) after flipping to second side.

Put on roll and moan.

Ford's Fried Chicken

Serves 4 to 6

Things You'll Need

1 whole chicken, cut into pieces
Salt
Ground black pepper
Garlic powder
1 teaspoon paprika
1½ cups all-purpose flour
Oil of your choice for frying

Directions

Season chicken pieces with salt, pepper, garlic powder, and paprika. Roll the pieces in the flour.

In a large, heavy skillet, heat ½ to ¾ inch of oil to about 365°F. Place chicken pieces in hot oil. Cover and fry, turning once, until brown and crisp, about 15 to 20 minutes. (Dark meat takes a little longer than white meat.) Drain on paper towels.

Mia's Fantastic Applesauce
Brownies

Makes 3 to 4 dozen brownies

Things You'll Need

1½ cups plus 2 tablespoons (for topping) white sugar
½ cup margarine
2 eggs
2 tablespoons unsweetened cocoa powder
1½ teaspoons salt
1 teaspoon baking soda
1 teaspoon ground cinnamon
2 cups all-purpose flour
2 cups unsweetened applesauce
1 cup semisweet chocolate chips
1 cup chopped walnuts (optional but preferred)

Directions

Preheat oven to 350°F.

Combine 1½ cups sugar and margarine. Whisk in eggs. Sift together cocoa powder, salt, baking soda, cinnamon, and flour, and add to sugar-margarine mixture. Mix until just combined. Stir in applesauce.

Pour batter into a 10½-by-15½ jelly roll pan.

Combine the remaining sugar, chocolate chips, and nuts. Sprinkle over batter.

Bake for 30 minutes.

Serve and bask in the love that comes your way . . .

Tara's Kick Ass Strawberry Pie

Makes 1 pie

Things You'll Need

8 cups fresh, whole strawberries, washed, hulled, and
   halved
1 cup sugar
3 tablespoons cornstarch
¾ cup water
Few drops red food coloring, optional
1 (9-inch) pastry shell, prebaked
Whipped cream

Directions

Mash 1 cup of the strawberries and set aside.

Make the glaze: In a medium saucepan over medium
heat, combine sugar, cornstarch, water, and mashed berries. Bring to a boil, stirring constantly. Stir in food coloring if desired. Cook and stir 3 minutes more. Cool for 10
minutes.

Spread about ⅓ cup of the glaze over the bottom and
sides of the pastry shell. Arrange remaining strawberries
in the pastry shell. Then spoon remaining glaze over the
top of the berries.

Chill the pie for 1 to 2 hours (if you can handle waiting
that long without eating it!).

Just before serving, garnish with whipped cream.

The pie is best served the day it's made.

Bone-Melting Hot Chocolate

Serves 10 to 12

What You'll Need

  2 cups whipping cream
  6 cups milk
  1 teaspoon vanilla
  1 (12-ounce) package semisweet chocolate chips
  Whiskey, optional
  Whipped cream, for garnish
  Candy canes, for garnish

Directions

In a large pot, over medium heat, stir together whipping cream, milk, vanilla, and chocolate chips.

Cook until chips melt, then reduce heat to low until you're ready to serve. Ladle into mugs, add a dash of whiskey (if desired), and garnish with whipped cream and candy canes.